THE ECHOES

JESS MONTGOMERY
THE ECHOES

MINOTAUR BOOKS · NEW YORK

First published in the United States by Minotaur Books, an imprint of St. Martin's Publishing Group

THE ECHOES. Copyright © 2022 by Sharon Short. All rights reserved. Printed in the United States of America. For information, address St. Martin's Publishing Group, 120 Broadway, New York, NY 10271.

www.minotaurbooks.com

Library of Congress Cataloging-in-Publication Data

Names: Montgomery, Jess, author.
Title: The echoes / Jess Montgomery.
Description: First edition. | New York : Minotaur Books, 2022. | Series: The kinship series ; 4
Identifiers: LCCN 2021047609 | ISBN 9781250623423 (hardcover) | ISBN 9781250623430 (ebook)
Subjects: LCGFT: Novels.
Classification: LCC PS3613.O54858 E27 2022 | DDC 813/.6—dc23
LC record available at https://lccn.loc.gov/2021047609

Our books may be purchased in bulk for promotional, educational, or business use. Please contact your local bookseller or the Macmillan Corporate and Premium Sales Department at 1-800-221-7945, extension 5442, or by email at MacmillanSpecialMarkets@macmillan.com.

First Edition: 2022

10 9 8 7 6 5 4 3 2 1

To my bright and beautiful daughters, Katherine and Gwen.
You inspire me every day.

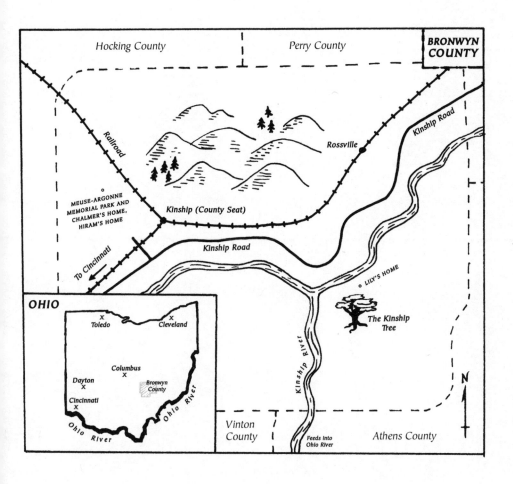

Hocking County   Perry County   **BRONWYN COUNTY**

Railroad

Rossville

Kinship Road

MEUSE-ARGONNE
MEMORIAL PARK AND
CHALMER'S HOME,
HIRAM'S HOME

Kinship (County Seat)

Kinship Road

To Cincinnati

LILY'S HOME

The Kinship
Tree

OHIO

Toledo   Cleveland
x   x

Columbus
x

Dayton
x   Bronwyn
             County

Cincinnati
x

Ohio River

Ohio River

Kinship River

Vinton
County

Feeds into
Ohio River

Athens County

N

THE ECHOES

PROLOGUE

ESMÉ

Monday, July 2, 1928
4:32 p.m.

Esmé nearly escapes.

She's just shoved her tweed-covered suitcase under the thick chain link and is about to duck under, grab the suitcase, and dash up the metal stairs. But the ship official—the man Esmé thinks of as a gendarme—appears three steps up. He glares down at Esmé, crosses his arms over the straining buttons of his blue uniform. Then he pulls out his baton, gripping it so hard in one hand that his knuckles go white and whacking it ever so slightly into the palm of the other.

Esmé quickly halts, with one foot under the chain, and her boots almost slide out from under her on the slick floor. Oh, why did she have to be spotted by *this* gendarme—the one who'd nearly caught her two days before, sneaking around outside of steerage?

She tries to turn around, but suddenly she's shoved forward. The chain, waist-high for most adults, strikes petite nine-year-old Esmé Chambeau across her neck. She gasps, tries to push away from the chain. Her eyes water.

Even as her vision blurs, Esmé makes out that the gendarme is grinning at her predicament: either get trampled or escape the crowd by ducking under the chain, only for him to catch her. And then will she ever be let off the ship? Will he throw her in the ship's jail—as he'd screamed at her when he'd tried to chase her down? Or will she be sent back to France?

The crowd shouts questions at the smugly silent gendarme about when they will be able to disembark. Esmé is overwhelmed by their strident voices, by festering human smells churned over four days of choppy ocean crossing. Sparkles dance before her eyes. A sudden lurch of the SS *Île de France* sends the crowd tumbling forward. The chain cuts into Esmé's neck.

For a horrible moment, her eyes bulge and her breath squeezes out of her windpipe.

The great ship shifts again, opening enough space for Esmé to move back from the chain, gasp for breath. But then her feet skid, and she falls backward. A man behind her curses, and the mucky bottom of the man's boot descends toward her face. Esmé throws her arms over her face, squeezes her eyes shut. Hands grab her ankles. The gendarme, pulling her toward him. She kicks as hard as she can. He yelps but doesn't let go.

And then, suddenly, someone grabs Esmé under her armpits, swoops her up.

Esmé opens her eyes. She's in the arms of Monsieur Durand, who yells at the crowd to make space. She inhales deeply—such sweet relief, even this stale, sour air—but then cries out and points at the gendarme. He's holstered his baton but holds up her suitcase, as if he means to bash it to the floor. His taunting look suggests that her suitcase is trash. That she is trash.

She must retrieve the suitcase! She doesn't care so much about the clothes, even the new ones that Mémère carefully made, though she could ill afford the new fancy silk and cotton and her hands are twisted with arthritis. But Esmé cannot lose her few relics of Papa: letters, and a cap he'd left behind from the U.S. Army.

Esmé again struggles to free herself, but Monsieur Durand is strong, large, and she barely moves at all. He glares at the gendarme with such bold fierceness that the crowd falls silent around them. And the gendarme hands over her suitcase to him.

As Monsieur Durand carries Esmé back through the crowd, she lets her head sink to his shoulder. For the first time since she left her home in Sainte-Menehould with Mémère and Father Bernard and Madame Blanchett to travel to Marseille to board this big boat, Esmé cries.

Back in the hold, now half-empty with the crowd by the stairs, Monsieur Durand carefully lowers her to the floor. He hands Esmé's suitcase back to her. Then he pulls a handkerchief from his pocket and offers it to her with a gentle smile.

Esmé wipes her nose. The handkerchief is surprisingly fresh, lavender scented. Soothing.

She holds the handkerchief up to him. "You can keep it," Monsieur Durand says, amusement tingeing his voice. "It's the least I can do."

Monsieur Durand and his three children—he is a widower, he'd explained—had been in the cots by Esmé and her chaperone. The youngest child, a baby girl, had been fussy the whole passage, but Esmé had taken over feeding the baby tinned milk and changing her diapers. Esmé had helped Mémère, after all, tend to babies in the village when their mamas were sick. His older children were still too little to be of any help.

Now Monsieur Durand regards Esmé with concern. "Why did you run?"

Minutes before, when the SS *Île de France* shuddered and shook, Monsieur had reassured his children, as well as Esmé and her chaperone, that the ship was slowing to come into port. Esmé had grabbed her suitcase, run from the hold, and wormed her way through the crowd already gathering before the stairs.

"I must see her," Esmé says. "Lady Liberty."

She'd been dreaming of *le statue de la Liberté* ever since Mémère had told her she must make this trip, had shown her a picture of the statue from an old war bond her American *grandmère* had sent to them. Mémère had told her that the berobed lady with the strong arms, the uplifted flame, was a gift from France to America and would be waiting to welcome her.

Often during the crossing, Esmé had conjured an image of Lady Liberty whenever sadness heaved in her chest. And on the night she had briefly escaped from steerage to explore the rest of the ship—oh, the resplendent ballrooms and dining halls on the first cabin level, with their marble floors and velvet-and-mahogany furnishings and silver lighting fixtures—she found herself out on a deck. Even more grand than the elegant rooms, Esmé discovered, was the vast, blue-black ocean. She'd stared over the railing at the moonlight speckling and shimmering on the ocean surface and imagined Lady Liberty waiting for her on the dark horizon.

"Will you be all right?" Monsieur Durand asks. He casts a wary glance at the woman approaching them. She is tall, thin, with a long, hard face. Her dress is filthy and stained and, Esmé knows all too well from having to share a cot with her, smells of sickness. Her hair, which had embarked as an elegant swirled updo, will soon disembark as a messy crow's nest. It had not been an easy crossing for Madame Blanchett, Esmé's chaperone.

Even so, her expression now is fearsome, and she bears down upon Esmé and Monsieur Durand with thunderous purpose.

For a moment, Esmé is tempted to beg Monsieur to take her wherever he is going, to plea that she could work as a caregiver for his children.

But she had promised Mémère that she would telegraph her when she was safely with her American *grandmère*.

"Oui," Esmé finally answers. Then she realizes she has said nothing of what awaits her. She blurts, "I am going to a place called Kinship. In Ohio." What odd place-names, so different from those of the villages and provinces of her home. A pang of homesickness flashes over her. Would it be so bad, to be sent back to France? "To be with my *grandmère*. And her daughter."

Mémère had told her that her aunt—Papa's sister—is a sort of gendarme. A sheriff. This struck Esmé as odd—there are no lady gendarmes, at least not in her village of Sainte-Menehould. As she thinks of the rough gendarme, doubt creeps into Esmé's heart. What if this aunt of hers is mean like this gendarme? She frowns. "My papa's family."

Monsieur Durand tilts his head to the side, regarding Esmé with kindness and a little sadness. He gently pats her cheek. "Oh, *cher enfant.* If they are your papa's family, then they are your family, too, *non?* You will be fine."

He hurries to the back of the hold, barely nodding at Madame as they pass, eager to get back to his own children.

Suddenly Madame Blanchett is by her side. She puts down her suitcases, grabs Esmé's arm, digs in her fingertips. Madame, a woman from the village who often bragged that her rich cousin in Saint Louis longed for her to visit, had been paid handsomely to accompany Esmé for the whole of the trip. Esmé pulls away, weary of being grabbed by adults.

Madame narrows her eyes on Esmé. "What were you thinking, *idiote?*" Her voice is like the odd hissing noises Esmé has heard on the ship from time to time. "I had to send Monsieur Durand after you, and watch after his snotty children!"

Well, she hadn't done a good job watching after them, had she? She'd abandoned them.

Esmé's mind churns with doubts about Madame. Will she abandon her, too? Mémère had said they'd cross in second cabin. But after they got on the ship, Esmé had seen Madame confer with someone— another passenger—and an exchange of tickets and money took place. She suspects Madame sold their comfortable berth to a passenger who was unhappy at the ship being full except for steerage and pocketed the gain. While cleaning up after Madame on the trip or bringing her broth, Esmé had what Mémère and Father Bernard would call an uncharitable thought—that it served Madame right, for trying to profit off the tickets both of her *grandmères* had surely paid dearly for.

"Pick those up." Madame points to her two suitcases.

Esmé stares at the three cases and looks around for Monsieur. Perhaps he could help?

But he is nowhere in sight, and people are shoving past them—it's finally time to exit steerage. Sorrow rises in Esmé's heart. Instinctively, she knows she will never see Monsieur or his children again. She has heard the mutterings, how America is a vast place, easy to get lost in.

Esmé forces a bright smile. "Madame, I am sorry to cause any trouble. I could make the rest of my way to . . ."—she hesitates, wanting to get the name of the place that will be her new home just right—"to Kinship, and you could go straight on to your cousin's in Saint Louis."

Madame's face draws long with shock, eyebrows up and chin dropping into her stringy neck. Esmé waits for her expression to clear, for her to halfheartedly ask, *Are you sure?* and then to agree, and try to disguise her relief at being rid of Esmé and free to go on about her own way.

Instead, Madame's eyes suddenly glint. "Oh no, *ma chère.*"

Esmé startles at her tone. For the first time on this trip, Esmé's stomach nervously roils.

"I will make sure," Madame says—then pauses to smile, another first for this trip—"to get you to your appointed destination."

Esmé tucks her suitcase under one arm. Then she picks up both of Madame's suitcases.

A half hour later, Madame and Esmé emerge onto the deck. It's a bright, hot day, and the sunlight blanks Esmé's vision.

But once it clears, Esmé gazes around, desperate to see *her.*

And then she does—afar in the distance, on her own island. Lady Liberty.

CHAPTER 1

LILY

Tuesday, July 3, 1928
7:30 a.m.

Mist rises and hangs in the morning's still-cool air over the summer-warmed pond, making it near on impossible for Sheriff Lily Ross to see more than a few inches below the barely rippling surface over the edge of the canoe. But she puts on a show for Chalmer Fitzpatrick and his grandmother, MayBelle, watching from the dock on the pond's edge. Lily pokes her paddle into the water, as if she might stir something more sinister than stocked fish in a man-made pond.

MayBelle Fitzpatrick isn't so easily fooled—or mollified.

"You ain't looked t'the middle yet." The elderly woman's wobbly voice carries with surprising vigor over the water. She doesn't bother disguising her annoyance with Lily. "Done told you that's where I saw her."

True, MayBelle had said as much after Lily came across her just a half hour earlier, sitting folded up on the top of the Bronwyn County, Ohio, courthouse steps in the posture of a little girl sent to sit in a corner, though the large liver spots and loose skin of her scrawny arms belie her age—as much as ninety-seven years, by some accounts, though

7

MayBelle claims ninety-two. There are no records for her birth, and she's outlived her husband.

This was the third time this week that the old woman had come to the courthouse with the same complaint, though never quite so early. Lily had gently shaken her by the arm, afraid of sending her tumbling down the steps, but MayBelle had jolted awake and stood up with surprising swiftness and litheness, then poked her face right up to Lily's and intoned: *There's a girl floating facedown in Chalmer's pond.*

Lily, who had checked the pond on the previous two complaints, had carefully guided MayBelle back down the steps and to Lily's automobile, parked near the courthouse. On the drive back to Chalmer Fitzpatrick's property—mostly cattle farm, except for the hilliest part—MayBelle had been quiet, staring out at the lush, leafy woods flashing by.

The stuffy automobile intensified MayBelle's scents of sweat from her long walk mixed with talcum powder and lilac perfume. The latter reminded Lily of her mamaw—Mama's mother, who had passed away when Lily was fifteen. The reminder of her own mamaw stirred Lily's heart to tenderness, and she'd glanced over at MayBelle, tried to engage her by pointing out her own farmhouse as they drove past, other people's farms, the surprising sight of a large owl out in the daytime. MayBelle had suddenly turned to her, fixing her opaque gray eyes on Lily with a sharp stare, then intoned: *Stop your jabbering! I seen her, I did. Floating in the middle of the pond. Blue dress.* Alice in Wonderland *blue. From the storybook. The puffy short sleeves. Big white bow in her hair. Dark hair. The hair fanning out in the water. Long, thin arms.*

Lily had driven on in silence, considering these new details. In her first two reports, MayBelle had simply reported a girl in the water.

Now MayBelle frantically hollers, "I done told you—the *middle* of the pond!"

"Mamaw!" Chalmer's chastisement is gentle enough, though frustration edges his tone. "The sheriff hasn't found anyone because there's no one to find—"

Lily paddles to the middle of the pond.

The fishing pond is just one part of Chalmer's huge project: an amusement park, set to open on July 4. The *Kinship Daily Courier* has been covering it frequently and enthusiastically, and not just because Chalmer owns The Mill—the lumberyard on the north end of Kinship, the county seat of Bronwyn County. Chalmer's Meuse-Argonne Memorial Park will be free to all veterans and their families, and a nominal charge to all others with the proceeds going to the local veteran's fund. It will have, in addition to the fishing pond, shooting and archery ranges, a stage and dance floor for bands, singers, and other entertainers—even a gasoline-powered generator for lights for evening dances—a games area including bowling, pony rides, and more to come. It's the biggest development in the county—well, truth be told, in the region—in years. Not like the magnificent Coney Island in Cincinnati, but yet—an amusement park, right here. Lily's children—as well as Mama's change-of-life baby, Lily's little brother who is about the same age as her son—are certainly talking about it with great excitement.

Slowly, Lily stands up in the middle of the canoe, careful not to tip to one side or the other. Here, where the sun more directly hits the water, the mist is nearly gone. Lily notes writhing dark shapes of fish darting about just below the pond's surface. She guesses: carp, trout, catfish. Probably some crappies.

Plenty of fish. But, as before, no body.

The last of the mist dissolves, and sunlight glints on the water.

It's impossible even to imagine a body floating here.

Lily slowly sits back down on the canoe bench and paddles to the dock. Chalmer rushes over to grab the front of the canoe. Unnecessary—and irritating. But she doesn't shoo him away.

She's deferential because her brother Roger and Chalmer had been close. Before the Great War, Chalmer, though only a few years older than Roger, had been the baseball coach for Roger's high school team. And in the war, Lily's now deceased husband, Daniel, had been a gunner, Roger his assistant gunner, and Chalmer their ammo man. Roger had pulled a soldier who had panicked in the trenches back to safety. Chalmer, in turn, spotting a sniper, had tried to save Roger—but Roger had died from sniper fire, in Daniel's arms. Chalmer had sustained an injury as well, a bullet in his thigh that also nearly took his own life.

Now Chalmer offers a hand to help her out of the boat, and as she rises and steps to the dock he lifts his eyebrows in a semi-amused look as he tethers the canoe to the dock. Now *that* irritates Lily. MayBelle's worries may be unrealistic, but they're not entertaining.

So Lily steps toward MayBelle, as carefully as if approaching a skittish deer, and gently takes the elderly woman's hands into her own. Thin, loose-skinned, and liver-spotted though her hands may be, there's a corded strength in MayBelle's grasp.

"Mrs. Fitzpatrick, I did look carefully," Lily explains, her tone somber and respectful, "but all I saw were fish. Is it—is it possible you might be thinking of a nightmare?"

MayBelle jerks her hands away and gives a surprisingly strong stomp, wobbling the dock. "Not a nightmare." MayBelle rolls out her lower lip, like a pouting child. "No one believes me. I'm no fool, or crazy—"

"Mamaw," Chalmer says, his voice soothing, "no one thinks that—"

"*She* does."

At first, Lily thinks MayBelle means her, but the older woman points up the hill to the house. *Oh.* She must mean Chalmer's wife, Sophia. Lily knows her from the Presbyterian church and the Woman's Club. Well, Lily is aware of Sophia. Lily doesn't really *know* her. Neither of them attends either organization regularly; Lily only goes when Mama insists it's been too long and she'd better put in an appearance. Lily's general impression of Sophia, however, is that she's a quiet, somewhat mousy woman. Not someone who would sass her husband's beloved mamaw.

"Now, Mamaw, you know Sophia has been gone for a few months. She's not been here to think about any of us." He looks over MayBelle's head at Lily, lowers his voice. "Sophia's spent most of the summer so far in Virginia tending to her aunt. She got back a month ago, when a cousin took over the care, and then returned to Virginia after receiving word that her aunt had passed away. Sophia got back from the trip to the funeral last night."

Ah, that's right. Chalmer had met Sophia in Virginia. After the war, he had gone off to college—one of very few people in the area who had done so. For that matter, only a lucky few—like Lily and her brother—had the opportunity to go to high school. When Chalmer returned to Bronwyn County, he'd brought a wife with him and had quickly settled down to take over the lumber mill from his father, who had just passed away, only months after his mother. Chalmer's only sibling, a much older brother, had long settled up in Columbus—and had no interest in returning to either the county or the lumber mill.

MayBelle gives Chalmer a hard look and a sharp poke with her elbow. "I can hear you. And it ain't like I'm too delicate for the topic of death."

Lily puts her hand to her mouth, shielding an impulsive smile. MayBelle may be ninety-two—or ninety-seven—frail-looking, and skinnier than a switch from a willow tree, but she is just as tough.

"Now, since neither of you believe me, I'm going home," MayBelle declares.

Home, Lily learned on her previous two visits, is a log-and-mortar cabin at the top of the highest rise on the property where MayBelle still lives alone in the simple home her husband's grandfather—the first known white settler in Bronwyn County—had built on his land grant.

Lily casts a worried look at Chalmer. Should MayBelle really be left to her own devices for the day? Or at all, for that matter?

Chalmer sighs. "How about we go to my house, for now, and you take a nap on the sleeping porch?" His large farmhouse tops a nob, just high enough to overlook pasture cleared for beef cattle in one direction and woods set aside for hunting and, now, for the Meuse-Argonne Memorial Park in another. This pond is the park's closest feature to the house, a corner of which is visible from the dock.

MayBelle gazes across the pond, as if to a far-off time and place. Regret flashes across her face. The old woman's shoulders slump, and for the first time this morning her expression softens. But not, Lily notes, in peace. More like in defeat.

MayBelle lets Chalmer gently guide her off the dock and up the path back to the house. As Lily follows, something nags at the back of Lily's mind—old talk of a feud between MayBelle's husband and his brother that yet continued among the descendants. Maybe what MayBelle imagines she sees in the pond is a manifestation of lost relationships or regrets over what should have been repaired long ago but has been allowed to fester into a sorrowful heirloom, passed down father to son.

Mama would know the story; she could ask her at lunch—*oh*. Another nagging thought: Lily and her mama had had their own tiff this morning. And Lily had said a few things that she's already regretting.

As they finish the climb up a gentle slope and come around a bend, the Fitzpatrick house pops into full view: a grand two-story, wrapped in clapboard freshly painted white, with a wraparound porch. Bright red geraniums grace neat beds around the porch. A gray-blue porch swing—just like the one at Lily's house, and many other houses, made by a local craftsman—hangs stiffly from the porch roof.

It should be, Lily reflects, an inviting tableau. But she eyes her Model T, parked just a few yards behind her on the main gravel drive up to the house, and suddenly longs to get away. Out here, in the clearing around the house, the heat is more intense than in the woods. Sweat trickles down Lily's neck, under her dress's collar.

Lily inches back toward her Model T as Chalmer nudges MayBelle toward the house. "Let's get you inside. Sophia will be glad to see you, make you a nice cool glass of lemonade before you take a nap—"

MayBelle's fight returns, spurred, it seems, by Chalmer's patronizing tone. She pulls away from his grasp of her elbow. "Sophia ain't never glad to see me. And I don't need a nap this early in the day. But the lemonade—yes—"

Lily's by her automobile, one hand on the door handle, impatiently waiting for MayBelle to go into the house, so Lily can wish Chalmer good luck and get on about her day.

But MayBelle turns, her gaze twisting back to Lily. Dark foreboding in the elderly woman's eyes makes Lily want to look away, but she dare not.

"Mayhap I was seeing what's yet to *be*," MayBelle hollers, punctuating that last word—"be"—so hard that it seems to take shape and strike Lily. "But a fancy modern woman like you—reckon you don't believe in the sight, do you?"

Here in the now bright, hot July morning, goose bumps run over Lily's arms.

"Mamaw!" Chalmer starts. "Don't—"

Lily gives him an admonishing look and he snaps his mouth shut. She lets go of her automobile's door handle and comes a little closer to MayBelle, offering a reassuring smile. "I believe there is more to this world than we can ever know."

MayBelle's gaze softens a bit. "Tragedy's a-comin'."

Tragedy is always a-comin', sooner or later, Lily thinks.

Loss and pain—even on a glorious bright blue summer morning, sun beaming down on woods and cattle pasture and fishing ponds—is always tucked away, waiting just out of sight.

And so Lily can, with great sincerity, reply to MayBelle, "I know it is. And when it does, I'll do my best to if not stop it, then help afterward."

A moment passes as Lily and MayBelle face each other, gazes connected. A silence shrouds them, even with the buzz and bang of men from Chalmer's lumber mill working in the surrounding woods to put the final touches on the park. The sound is discordant with morning birdsong, with cicadas already starting up their own buzz.

Perhaps the creation of the park itself has stirred MayBelle's sight—though why of a drowned young girl Lily can't imagine. But she can, at least, acknowledge the general truth of MayBelle's fearsome vision.

And that seems, finally, enough for MayBelle, who sighs deeply, then turns and walks slowly to the house, and up the porch steps. Each step appears to be painful. The five-mile trek into town is finally taking its toll on her.

After MayBelle enters the house and the front door slams to, Lily looks at Chalmer. "Part of my job is checking in on people, and their concerns, before there's real trouble. Have you and Sophia discussed seeing if your mamaw could move in with you?"

Chalmer looks away from Lily, back toward the woods. "Sophia—well. She and Mamaw have never gotten on. When Mamaw took a turn for the worse last year, Sophia hired in help—a spinster she knows from the Woman's Club."

Chalmer's comment tickles a memory. "Oh—I heard something about that. Pearl Riley?" Lily asks. Another quiet woman, who lives alone in her deceased parents' house, no siblings or husband or children. Now that Chalmer mentions it, Lily does remember Sophia and Pearl always sticking together at meetings, not quite fitting in—Sophia clinging to her role as an outsider to Kinship, which admittedly some of the women do nothing to alleviate, Pearl always socially awkward—

Lily's ruminations stop abruptly as she notes that Chalmer has turned red. "Yes, but Miss Riley didn't work out. Mamaw didn't like her, so I had to dismiss her earlier this year."

Too bad, Lily thinks. "Have you thought about the Widows' Home, then?" The home, in the northwest corner of the county, was established to take in widows of men who'd fought in the Civil War. But it's remained in operation for other widows, usually the elderly who can't live independently or with relatives. It's not free, but Chalmer could certainly afford it.

"No," Chalmer snaps, and Lily nearly jumps at his vehemence. "Sophia already brought that up, but Mamaw would never agree to the Widows' Home."

She wants to ask if anyone had talked to MayBelle about that. To point out that denying every possible solution to a problem doesn't make the problem go away. But while he's preoccupied with his park is probably not the best time to ask or say such things.

He turns to her with a sudden grin. "Lily, since you're up here anyway, can I show you around a bit? We're almost done with the park. And I know you'll be directing traffic tomorrow—"

"I have deputies helping me tomorrow," Lily says. "Deputies" meaning her regulars, including one of her best friends, Marvena. She'd thought about engaging temporary extras but thinks her regulars will suffice.

"Well, I'm expecting quite a crowd for the grand opening and dedication of the park. I hope you have plenty of help," Chalmer says.

Lily gives a quick reassuring flash of a smile but holds back a sarcastic reply—*yes, yes, I really do know what I'm doing.*

"And you and your family will be at the dedication, right?" Suddenly Chalmer seems anxious. "Eleven thirty or so, at the stage by the dance floor."

"Yes, of course. And after that, we're going to have a picnic on the grounds here. Mama's already busy baking and cooking. I'll have plenty of time tomorrow to enjoy the park, Chalmer. Don't want to spoil any surprises the park might hold."

Chalmer looks taken aback and seems to search her face—for what, she's not sure. But then he seems reassured and grins. "Tell your mama not to overprepare. We'll have a pig roast and plenty of beverages—all legal, don't you worry, Sheriff Lily."

Lily smiles wanly, trying not to show her irritation. Chalmer had been good to her brother Roger. She can smile at the same old tired joke she's heard plenty of times, especially since solving a big Prohibition case in the county at the end of the previous year.

"You've no doubt read about the bowling lane and the games area," Chalmer says, "but I also decided we need a baseball diamond—with bleachers. That's a lot of the work you heard on the way up. A baseball diamond—right there in the middle of the woods, can you imagine? Remember how Roger loved to play baseball—and was terrible at it?"

Suddenly tears prick Lily's eyes, and she looks toward the pasture, trying to escape an old memory, but it finds her.

The day before the men shipped out, Mama had cooked up most everything she could think of for Lily's new husband, Daniel, and Roger and several of Roger's buddies for a large dinner at the house they'd lived in, at the time, in Kinship, just down the street from her daddy's grocery. Daniel had laughed—so calm, so easy—and said, *We'll get rations, Mama McArthur.* She'd look so crestfallen at the comment that he'd eaten enough for two meals. Meanwhile, Roger was so nervous he could barely eat.

Maybe that was why Lily felt sure Daniel wouldn't come back—he was so calm—whereas Roger was so nervous she figured he'd be put at the back of the line and stay out of harm's way. Or have a fainting spell on the ship and get sent back home.

Clearly, she doesn't have the gift of sight like MayBelle Fitzpatrick. Daniel had come back, thank God. But dear, sweet, tenderhearted Roger had not.

Now Lily blinks to clear her stinging eyes. She looks back at Chalmer. "I remember," she says. "He always swung too soon. I told him as much."

"He did get better at the end. Told me he'd been training." Chalmer gives Lily an appraising look. "Asked him who he'd been training with—and he'd never say. 'It's a secret,' he said. Never thought him one for secrets."

Lily gives a casual shrug. She'd made him practice, out at their grand-parents' farm, using a tree limb that was about the right size for a base-ball bat, and a heap of mayapples in lieu of baseballs. Roger had called her first successful hit lucky, but after she'd smashed five mayapples he allowed as how she might know a thing or two about timing a swing just right, and he'd taken her advice.

"Do you think he'd like this place?" Chalmer's voice tightens as he peers into the woods.

Lily is taken aback by the question, by the urgent prodding of it, the sudden switch of tone. Well, she can't ask Daniel or Daddy or Roger what they think. She hasn't even asked the living. Mama. Or Benjamin Russo, one of Daniel's army buddies who had, through his work in the Bureau of Mines, ended up in this area and has been courting Lily for the past half year.

"Yes—I'm sure he would. You've done a wonderful job with this park. He'd be proud."

Chalmer looks relieved. "Good. This park, and helping your mama—"

Lily frowns. "Helping her do what?"

"Oh—I meant, I hope it helps your mama."

Uneasiness stirs in Lily's heart and she's about to press for a clearer explanation, but suddenly Chalmer's wife, Sophia, emerges from the woods. She's sweaty and dressed not unlike MayBelle, in a too-big floppy hat, and an oversize dress, and boots. Lily is surprised to see her in such a state. At Woman's Club gatherings, she's always neat and prim.

But now she looks amused. "Oh please, reassure him," Sophia says. A sneer puckers the bottom half of her petite face, and she swipes away a blond strand of hair. "He *needs* reassurance." She rolls her eyes.

The unkind twist of words, wielded to poke at her husband, is even more surprising than her state of dress. When Sophia did speak at Woman's Club, it was so meekly and quietly that more often than not she was asked to repeat herself.

Chalmer speaks to Lily, even as he coldly glares at his wife. "Sophia does not approve of the park. Thinks the woods should just remain unspoiled—as she likes to put it."

Sophia regards Lily. "He started it while I was gone, tending to an aunt who never married or had children, so she had no one to watch over her in her later years."

"Chalmer mentioned she'd passed on. May I offer my condolences—"

Sophia waves a hand to stop Lily. "My aunt was quite elderly." She gives Chalmer a sharp look. "At least she didn't have a husband who started projects while she was away—"

Chalmer's face wrenches in a hard twist that's supposed to be a smile. "The project is a memorial that will bring joy to many people—"

"People trampling all around our house, day and night—"

"A good distance from the house, and only on summer weekends. God, have you no heart for the men who sacrificed their lives—" Chalmer stops, gives Lily an apologetic look.

But Lily is more alarmed by the discord between the couple than by Sophia's resistance to a project she hadn't approved. Is there a domestic issue she should be concerned about? Is Sophia's bitterness solely over Chalmer turning part of his property into a park?

A slamming door breaks the tension and draws their attention to the house, where a woman is coming out of the side door right behind a man.

"Hiram, we need to talk about this," the woman cries.

"I told you—leave me alone," he shouts back at her. He picks up a tool box from beside the wood bin next to the side door.

Lily stares in shock at the pair, siblings Hiram and Dorit Fitzpatrick. Lily quickly calculates: they're Chalmer's first cousins once removed, children of MayBelle's husband's brother. On the other side of the family rift. It's surprising to see them here. The pair stare back in their own shock at seeing Lily, Chalmer, and Sophia.

Lily studies them—Dorit and Hiram are the same size and height, which makes Dorit appear stocky while Hiram is small for a man, both so different from their tall, scrawny cousin Chalmer. And yet Hiram and Chalmer each have large ears and a similar square set to their shoulders, their sandy hair thinning in similar patterns at their temples.

This is the first time that Lily has seen Hiram since their high school years.

As for Dorit, Lily vaguely recollects that she is about ten years older than her. Had Dorit gone to high school? Unlikely. Even Hiram had dropped out after the second year. Now Dorit, at nearly forty, looks a good ten years older than her age, not so much from crow's-feet or other wrinkles, but from an angry expression baked into her face. Sorrow resides in her eyes.

And Dorit wears, Lily notes, a blue dress with puffy sleeves. Her hair is tied back in a white work scarf. Not quite a young Alice in Wonderland, but could Dorit's outfit have been the source of MayBelle's specificity this morning?

Chalmer says to Lily, "Hiram's been working at my lumberyard for over a year now. He came, asking for work, and why wouldn't I hire him? I don't care about old family feuds. Mamaw MayBelle and Hiram's mother Ida have clung to bitterness over choices their husbands, who were brothers, made, but I see no need to keep that going. Besides, Hiram is a good worker. And he's got good ideas, too—suggested bringing in railcars beyond repair for use on the rail lines, and fixing them up as camping units. I told him sure—gave him money to buy one, put it at the far end of the property." He waves his hand to indicate the general direction. "It's not ready yet, but maybe in a month or so. We'll see. And after I—we—had to let Miss Riley go, Hiram mentioned Dorit cleans houses and tends to some elderly folks in Kinship, so I brought her on to help around the house and with Mamaw while Sophia was first away—"

"Because what he missed about me most was my housekeeping services," Sophia says.

"You were more than eager to go tend to your aunt in Virginia, though you won't lift a finger with Mamaw, and I needed help. Besides, Hiram and Dorit are family—" Chalmer starts, his voice rising in anger.

"And you thought hiring these two as help would somehow patch up MayBelle's ancient family rift with their mother?" Sophia gives Lily a pensive smile. "Family loyalty." Another roll of the eyes.

She starts back toward the house. "Come on, Dorit. You can help me tend to MayBelle."

But Dorit remains stock-still, staring at Hiram, who in turn gazes at the ground.

"Dorit," Sophia snaps.

She moves slowly, as if her feet are stuck in a swamp of sorghum. But at last she follows Sophia.

Chalmer sighs as the two women head back into the house. "I'm sorry, Lily, that you had to witness so much family drama this morning." He gives a nervous laugh. "Tension before the big day." He looks at Hiram. "We have work to finish up on the stage."

"I know, but I want-wanted to show you what I've done with the rail-car. It's j-just about ready. I could have it ready for people to at least look at tomorrow, a prototype for what I think could be—" Hiram starts.

"Hiram, it's like I always told you on the baseball team—and overseas. You have to focus." Chalmer turns and heads down a path in the woods, toward the sounds of the workmen.

For a moment, it's just Lily and Hiram.

Lily tries to recollect—had Hiram been one of Roger's chums at that last dinner before shipping out? They'd briefly been on the baseball team together, hadn't they? Yes. So surely Roger, who always included everyone in any activity, had invited him. Tenderhearted, always kind Roger. It's been ten years. Lily doesn't remember—though, suddenly, inexplicably, it seems important that she should.

She reckons she'd just assumed Hiram had returned from the war, gone back to living on a hardscrabble farm on the other side of this hill, with his mother and sister, Dorit. The family, which had always kept to itself with snarling sourness, was easy enough to forget since those high school days.

Though there'd been that run-in she'd had with Hiram's now-deceased father, right in the middle of Kinship, in front of her father's grocery, during the war. . . .

Lily shudders, shunts that memory aside for now.

Hiram stares at Lily, his gray eyes wide. Dark circles make him look weary. No, not just weary, Lily thinks. Haunted.

Suddenly shame rises within her. That look in his eyes brings the memory back at last. Yes, he'd been at that dinner. Quiet. Even then, before going to fight in the war, he'd had those dark, haunted eyes. After returning from the front, he had retreated to life on the farm with his widowed mother and his older sister. Lily longs, somehow, to reassure him the way Roger would have. But about what? That she hadn't really forgotten him—though he'd know that wasn't true. That whatever is tormenting him will be fine—though she can't know that's true. Lily can't find any words. Roger was the one who knew how to comfort others or gently tease them into feeling at ease with themselves. Lily had been the one who knew how to whack mayapples as if they were baseballs, and outrun her older brother in footraces, and catch fish while he preferred to read a book of poetry under a tree.

"Your brother Roger, he, his—"

The door slams again. Hiram jumps as if he's heard a gunshot and stutters to a stop.

Lily looks toward the house; Dorit stands outside the side door, arms crossed.

When Lily looks back toward Hiram, he's gone. It's again as if he's never been there.

Another door slam. Dorit is back in the house.

Lily is alone by her automobile, free at last to leave. But she gazes down the path that leads to the pond, where there is no dead girl floating, only writhing fish.

CHAPTER 2

⁂

BEULAH

Tuesday, July 3, 1928
11:30 a.m.

Sunlight flashes through the thick windowpane into Beulah McArthur's eyes. Beulah squints out at the endlessly blazing blue sky, pauses to swipe a bit of perspiration from her brow. But then she presses on with her work at her treadle sewing machine: stitching together two hexagon pieces of cloth. Normally, she'd hand piece the quilt top, but she's trying to speed up her work, just a little. She needs to have this particular quilt done by July 6.

The slow up-and-down of the needle, triggered by the bare pressure she puts on the treadle, eases Beulah's thoughts into a trance. The scene from this morning replays in her mind.

She'd been pressing out a shirt, one last source for the quilt pieces, with the sadiron, heated in the coal-fired stove, on the worktable in the kitchen in the cool of the morning, when Lily came into the kitchen.

Mama, why're you quilting in the heat of summer? It's already hot this morning—

A wise, quiet voice whispered from the back of Beulah's mind: *Now, now, tell her now.*

But the actual words that popped out of Beulah's mouth were anything but wise or quiet: *Child, you might be able to push Jolene around, but not me. I have my reasons!*

Lily recoiled, and Beulah immediately regretted her sharpness. But Lord, her daughter—though she'll be thirty in just under a month—can still try her patience.

Especially when it comes to how Lily treats her own children—specially nine-year-old Jolene, always harder on her, expecting too much, and seeming to favor seven-year-old Micah.

Well, Lily said, grabbing a biscuit straight from the pan, *Benjamin will be by for the boys.*

Still think you oughta let Jolene go fishing, too, Beulah muttered. *Especially with all your talk about girls being just as capable as boys.*

The minute the words fell from her lips, Beulah wished she could snag them back. The success of Beulah and Lily living together in the same farmhouse—with Beulah's change-of-life baby and Lily's little brother, seven-year-old Caleb Jr., and Lily's two children—rests in part on an agreement that neither woman interferes with how the other disciplines her children. It's worked just fine—until now. The children are getting old enough to have stubborn notions and conflicts of their own.

Anyway, Beulah would not usually argue for her granddaughter to go fishing with the boys—she still believes that her husband had catered too readily to Lily's tomboyish desires to hunt and fish and hike around the woods when she was a girl—but she'd heard Jolene cry herself to sleep the night before in her bedroom next to Beulah's, sincerely bereft, and not just dramatic sobs for effect. The girl had dug up enough night crawlers for all the children and Benjamin Russo—Lily's beloved, though Lily refers to him as "a good friend"—and half the county, too.

It's not just talk. Lily's voice turned ice-cold, stifling. *But she needs to behave better.*

Then Lily had left with just a dry biscuit for her breakfast—not even any coffee.

Now, several hours later, Beulah scoots back from her treadle machine on the sewing stool—a wedding gift from her parents, her own dear mama having cross-stitched the stool cover, pink rose and green leaves against a black background. She stands and slowly stretches, working out the kinks in her neck and between her shoulders and lower back. Goodness, this is harder and harder, especially at her age—she's just turned forty-eight.

Her gaze shifts to her side notions table, to the jar of ointment prescribed to her by the new doctor—they'd lost the last one in a shocking case last year that had gained Lily some fame beyond these hills. Dr. Walter Twomey. He's only been in Kinship a few months. Beulah's home remedies, and even her friend Nana's tinctures and teas, had stopped being effective for her arthritis, so she'd finally visited him. Ended up inviting him to church, turning bright red in the process, as she babbled on about how *a widower of his age, new to town, must be right lonely and he could make some friends. . . .* He'd barely tamped down the smile twitching behind his thick white mustache. But he had come to church after all. He'd been a hit with most everyone—except Lily, who found him stuck up. *Hmph,* Beulah'd thought. Lily barely graces church, and only at Beulah's nudging reminders.

Now Beulah shakes her head at herself, then stares for a long moment at the pieces she'd just finished cutting this morning, then laid out on her bed on top of another quilt, one she'd made from some of her old clothes shortly after she and Caleb were married.

The pieces are from Roger's old clothes, items he'd left behind when he went off to the Great War that she never could bring herself to give away or do anything with—until now.

She homes in on the shirt and pants he'd worn his first day working at his father's grocery—a grocery that Caleb had hoped his son Roger and his son-in-law, Daniel, would help him run and eventually be stakeholders in. But Roger had died in the Great War. Daniel had come back and decided that instead of working in the grocery, he'd run for sheriff—a decision that Caleb took well but that left Beulah quietly seething for months, until one day Caleb said, *Be grateful Daniel came back, Beulah; be grateful Lily lives just down the road from us; be grateful for our granddaughter.* And later, *Be grateful for our son*—meaning

Caleb Jr., whose arrival had surprised and delighted them both—*and our grandson.*

Family had meant everything to Caleb, just as it does to Beulah, but Caleb had always been quicker to accept foibles and upturned expectations. Caleb's mother died in childbirth with him, and his father a few years later in a mining cave-in. Caleb was adopted by the previous owners of the grocery, an older, childless couple who passed away when Caleb was in his early twenties. But he'd known their full love and grace and shared it bountifully with his own family and others. Then four years ago, Caleb, too, had died, trying to save men in a mining cave-in similar to the one that took his father.

A few months later, at the beginning of March 1925, Beulah had gotten the first letter—the most shocking news of her life.

She wished she could ask Caleb what to do.

She left Caleb Jr. with Lily, telling her she needed to do some shopping in Kinship. But she'd walked all the way to the Kinship Cemetery, knelt before the markers of her husband and oldest son, hoping for a sense of guidance. When that hadn't come, she'd prayed to the Good Lord for insight.

And when even that eluded her, she wept until she could weep no more, and trekked back to Kinship, leaning into the stiff, sharp wind, remnants of tears freezing to her lashes and cheeks. By the time she got home, she had decided that she would seek Lily's counsel.

But Caleb Jr. had developed a fever. And when he recovered, laundry needed catching up on. The garden plot needed hoeing. Each time the right moment to talk to Lily seemed just in grasp, it would slide away in the needful wake of tedious everyday life.

Then, on March 25, 1925, they got word—Daniel had been killed in the line of duty.

Since then, no time had seemed right to tell Lily about that first letter three years before—and all the ones that had followed. Oh, there were moments—like this morning when Lily had asked, *Mama, why're you quilting in the heat of summer?*

Now Beulah's heart falls as she stares at the quilt pieces, and not just from all those missed opportunities with her daughter. It will be impossible to meet her self-imposed July 6 deadline. What's more, it strikes her that though she has plenty of fabric to make the quilt, it feels as though something is missing. Something that will tie the pieces together.

Her gaze shifts to the small notions table next to the treadle machine. Beulah opens the top, pulls out the tray that holds scissors and bobbins and threads and such, and sets the tray to the side of the sewing machine. Then she lifts the false bottom inside the table and stares at the letters, as if they might hold a clue about what's missing from the quilt in progress. She takes out the top letter, the most recent, starts to slip it out of its envelope—

Beulah jumps as the door creaks open, and there stands Jolene. Guilt pulses through Beulah, and she quickly puts the letter alongside the bobbin holder on the sewing machine.

Jolene stands in the doorway, hands clasped before her, dress sleeves pushed up to her elbows. Beulah notes that her granddaughter's hands and arms are clean, still wet from scrubbing up as best she could. But dirt smudges her sweet face, and her shoes are filthy, and they'll have to clean the steps and parlor of the dirt Jolene's no doubt tracked through from the barn.

Beulah's mild annoyance fades as Jolene pips, "I cleaned out Daisy's stall, and the fresh straw bed is so sweet that I about lay down to take a nap myself." Then Jolene's eyes well. "Do you think Mama means it? That I can't go to the park tomorrow, too?"

This is the first Beulah has heard about this additional penance for Jolene taking a big handful of mud and smushing it down on Micah's head last night. It had dripped into his eyes and made him wail in pain—a horrifying moment. But while Beulah agrees that Jolene needed punishment, missing the fishing trip and cleaning the mule's stall seems sufficient. Still, Beulah feels obliged to align with Lily. "I think she wants you to behave. You're the big sister, and—"

"But Micah was making fun of me! Said girls shouldn't go fishing, that it's unladylike and no one will ever like me. *And . . .*"—at this,

Jolene pauses, showing a bit of flair for the dramatic after all—"he said I'd never learn to fly a plane, either, because girls can't."

Jolene, who loves to read, had excitedly followed the newspaper coverage of Amelia Earhart being the first female passenger to cross the Atlantic in an airplane just a few weeks before. Jolene immediately exclaimed she'd someday fly across the ocean herself.

Lily grinned, scooped up her daughter in a hug, and blithely proclaimed, *Of course you will!* But Beulah had frowned at Lily for encouraging such a fool notion.

Now Beulah shivers at the thought of crossing the ocean on an ocean liner, what's more by air. She asks, "Did you tell your mama that Micah said these things?"

Jolene crosses her arms, sticking her hands under her armpits. "No. I'm always having to defend myself. And anyway, no one likes a rat."

Beulah gestures to her granddaughter to come in, and Beulah pulls her into her lap. *Oof, the child is growing up: slender but muscular.* Jolene nestles against Beulah's chest, and Beulah smooths her granddaughter's hair, a rich, deep brown-black hue. It will be fully black soon, like her father Daniel's had been.

"You're not being a rat if you tell the truth," Beulah says. "You should always tell the truth." Her heart pings as she says this, pricked by her conscience.

"But Mama wants me to be perfect, *all the time*. So I'm always getting in trouble."

Beulah gives her granddaughter a little conspiratorial grin. "Your mama was always getting into trouble with me. Why, her brother—"

"Uncle Roger," Jolene says confidently, though of course she'd never met her uncle, only heard the occasional mention of him.

"Yes, Roger. Why, the number of times she threw dirt at him, or pretended she was going to give him an apple but it was really a toad." Beulah stops, shakes her head at the memory of her daughter's antics.

"Did you make her muck out the mule's stall?"

"No, we lived in Kinship then."

"Like we used to," Jolene says. But a look of uncertainty crosses her eyes. "Mama acts like she always lived out here." They live in a farmhouse, the old Gottschalk place, a good five miles east of town, on twenty acres that Lily farms out for corn and buckwheat, though they have a sizeable yard and garden, and the back of the property dips down to Coal Creek. They'd moved here almost two years before.

"Your mama always loved the countryside better. Did you know, my parents had the farm next door to this one? Your mama loved coming out here. Fishing. Hiking. Hunting with her daddy. Just like she lets you hunt with her sometimes," Beulah says, a gentle reminder for Jolene that Lily really does love her and approve of her.

"I guess—she does do that," Jolene says begrudgingly. "But when Caleb and Micah are older, I bet she won't take me then—"

"Oh, I bet she will."

But Jolene starts crying. "What if she doesn't? Micah said yesterday that Mr. Russo is going to be our new daddy, and that Mama will have lots of babies, and when she finally has a daughter who acts like a real girl, she won't have time for me and you won't, neither, 'cause you'll like your new granddaughter better—"

"Oh, honey, while it's true that your mama and Mr. Russo do like each other—"

"I don't like him," Jolene says.

Benjamin Russo is always quietly kind and gentle with the children. But Jolene is wary of him, and Beulah can guess why. Micah was so little when his father, Daniel, died, he doesn't remember him. Jolene does. Daniel—with his hearty laugh, his ease in swooping Jolene up in a hug, filling a room no matter how big it was with his presence—will live on in Jolene's heart. And yet, as Benjamin grows in their lives and hearts, Daniel will fade and quiet in everyone's memories. Jolene may be yet too little to put this to words, but she is old enough to sense it.

Beulah strokes Jolene's hair again. "Your father is always part of you, honey. You have his hair, his outgoing personality—and he loved you so much. Still loves you. Besides, the rate your mama and Mr. Russo are courting, you'll be married up and have babies of your own before they get hitched."

Jolene giggles. Still, she persists. "What if they do get hitched? And have a baby girl?"

"Oh, sweetie. That won't take away from how they love you—or your brother. Or how I do. . . ." Beulah pauses. As her eyes prick with tears, she looks away from Jolene. Her love for Roger is never ending, as is her love for Lily, for Caleb Jr. For her grandchildren.

As Beulah considers how to best express this to her nine-year-old granddaughter, Jolene says, "What if . . . they have five? What if you have five more grandchildren?"

"Love isn't like that. It's not like there's only so much space in your heart. It always makes room for more family."

Jolene narrows her eyes, pinches her lips, looking just like Lily in her serious moments. "What if there are eleven?"

"Even if there are eleven."

"Eighteen?"

Good Lord, Beulah thinks. But she nods seriously. "Even if there are eighteen."

"What about . . . about thirty-two?" The seriousness slips from Jolene's face as she tries not to giggle. She knows, even at her tender age, that she's exaggerating for effect.

"Even then," Beulah says. "Listen to me, child—" She cups Jolene's smudged face between her hands. "Family is where you're always safe and loved. And you'll always be safe and loved with me, and with your mama. No matter what. Because love, well, it's . . . it's . . ." Beulah thinks of today's searingly bright blue sky. Of that March freezing gray sky four years ago. Of how Jolene yearns to fly. "Well, it's like the sky. Endless."

At last, Jolene smiles.

Beulah asks, "How about ham sandwiches and cherry pie for lunch? And you don't have to do any of the cleaning up after?"

Jolene lights up. Cherry pie is her favorite. "But the pie is for the picnic tomorrow—"

"I need to bake another one, anyway," Beulah says. It's true, with all the friends joining them for the picnic in the backyard, before heading over to the Meuse-Argonne Memorial Park for the big dedication ceremony.

Beulah's heart clenches at the thought. Lily's mentioned having to go over to Chalmer Fitzpatrick's a few times, something about MayBelle Fitzpatrick, Chalmer's mamaw, showing up at the courthouse with complaints about a drowned girl—though of course there isn't one. Has Chalmer said anything to Lily about . . . well, no. He'd promised he wouldn't. And if he had, Lily would not have held back from confronting her. She *must* tell Lily, today.

Jolene hops down, about to leave Beulah's room, but then she stops, stares at the hexagon pieces of cloth laid out on Beulah's bed. "What're these all from?"

Besides the pants and shirt he'd worn to work at the grocery, there are pieces from Roger's first pair of big-boy britches. From a suit he'd worn to church as a youth. His church choir robe. A suit he'd worn when he gave the graduation speech at high school. From random clothes she'd made or bought but can no longer specifically remember Roger wearing. She tears up at realizing that she can't remember all the specifics of each source of her hexagon pieces.

Beulah clears her throat. "From your uncle Roger's clothes. I'm making a quilt."

Jolene frowns, just like Lily does when she's perplexed. Beulah sighs. Jolene must also be wondering why her grandmother has opted to make a quilt in the thick heat of summer.

"Do you still have big-sky love for him?" Jolene asks. "Uncle Roger?"

Beulah's throat tightens and she can only nod.

"Maybe you could tell me stories about him, sometime?"

Beulah glances at the sewing machine, with the letter sitting out. She should put that away. And yet she's been hiding the truth for too long. *Oh God.* How is she going to tell everyone? At the very least, she should have told Lily right away. If she had, it would be so much easier now—

The floorboard squeaks. Both Beulah and Jolene jump and turn toward the open door. There stands Lily, leaning against the frame, offering them both a careful, conciliatory smile. "Cherry pie, huh?"

CHAPTER 3

LILY

Tuesday, July 3, 1928
Noon

Jealousy pangs in Lily's heart, seeing Mama and Jolene in such a cozy interaction. *Unbecoming,* Lily chides herself.

But of late, she'd felt Jolene—who'd always been quick to snuggle, eager for any attention, happy to be read to or cheerfully do a task for Lily—pull away.

Lily had rationalized it: of course there'd be more conflict between her and her children as they grew older. That had been the case between her and her parents—well, truth be told, between her and Mama. And grandparents are always kinder and gentler and more forgiving of their grandchildren than they had been toward their own children. Without a doubt, as far as Mamaw and Papaw Neely—Mama's parents, who once owned the farm next door—had been concerned, Lily could do no wrong. Even when Mama banished Lily to her grandparents' house to help with the large garden and household tasks—punishment for some sassing or wrongdoing—Mamaw and Papaw found a way to make it easier for her, even at times fun.

Now both Mama and Jolene stare at Lily with struck, almost fright-ened expressions.

"Mama, did you see the work I did in Daisy's stall?"

Lily takes note of the smudges—and the eager-to-please look—on Jolene's petite face. But then she notices Jolene's dirty boots, no doubt the source of the dirt tracked through the kitchen and parlor and up the stairs. She'd just cleaned those floors two days before.

"I did—and I also saw the dirt you tracked in," Lily says.

Jolene's face curls up, her mouth pinching, her eyes welling. Lily's heart crumbles.

"Come to think of it, I left some boot tracks. I'll take care of the steps and floor. . . ." Lily hesitates. Is giving an inch too much? Well, maybe. But seeing the relief in Jolene's eyes makes Lily smile.

Jolene runs over, throws her arms around Lily's waist, presses her head hard into Lily's abdomen. "Thank you, Mama." Then Jolene leans back, stares up at Lily. "But I'll help you. With that and anything else needs doing."

Lily smiles, smooths back the child's hair—so like her father's—then cups Jolene's sweet face in her hands and says, "That'd be right nice of you. The more we get done today, the sooner we can *all* leave for the park tomorrow."

Jolene's eyes widen with eagerness. "Mama! Does that mean I'm go-ing, too?"

"Yes. But listen, you're the big sister, and that means that at least until Micah's bigger, you have to do more than him to stay out of fights. All right?"

Jolene opens her mouth as if to protest, then looks down, nods.

"Go on downstairs, and set out lunch for us. I need to talk to your mamaw."

Jolene rushes from the bedroom. Lily closes the door, turns back to Mama.

"Thirty-two grandchildren, huh?" Lily says. "Even if . . . if things work out between me and Benjamin—" Oh, how odd that sounds to say. Yes, they'd seen each other since last fall off and on, at pie suppers, or barn dances, even exchanged a few chaste, careful kisses. Some might call that courting. But lately, since March, Lily sensed a reluctance in Benjamin, a holding back, which she chalked up to her work as a sheriff. She's made it clear that she will not give up her work, and she knows that such an odd role for a woman—what's more for a wife—gives Benjamin pause. Now Lily tries for a bit of levity. "I think I might be only ready for, oh, another dozen or so children. Not thirty-two."

Lily waits for Mama to give a quick smile, but Mama's smile is barely a flash, and she still looks sad. "Oh, you heard that? Nothing before?" Mama flushes bright red as she asks the question.

Lily lifts an eyebrow. "What were you discussing before?"

Mama looks over at the bed, covered with stacks of carefully cut hexagon quilt pieces. Lily studies them—*oh*. Pieces from her brother's old clothes. Some she recognizes; some she does not. But her heart pangs, just at the sight.

"I was telling her about Roger, about making a quilt from his clothes," Mama says.

Lily sits on the edge of the hope chest at the end of the bed. She studies the subdued hues and patterns of the pieces: tame brown and blue solids, plaids, a few stripes. Almost dull on top of Mama's quilt—pink florals, reds, whites, the bright colors and busy patterns Mama usually favors.

She touches a stack of blue cotton pieces. "Oh, this is from the shirt Roger wore the night he gave that oratory at his high school graduation." Suddenly she sees him as clearly in her mind's eye as if she's sitting in the stuffy theater of the Kinship Opera House, squished between Mama and Daddy on the hard, close seats, making faces at him in the dark even though she knows he can't see her from the stage, just like she had at their home, making him laugh, until Mama hollered at her, *Your brother being valedictorian is serious business, young lady.* In the theater, she'd suddenly been struck by how compelling he was. So scrawny and goofy—she could still outrun him without even getting winded—but smart. First, he told a joke on himself, an anecdote about his awfulness on the baseball field, and an apology for ruining the season, and a prediction that the team would henceforth improve. After winning over the audience with humor, he launched into his actual message: his worry about the hatred rising in the world, even striking here in remote Kinship at some of its citizens who had immigrated from Germany and Lithuania and other countries some called barbarous. His fervent hope that humanity would come to see how truly connected we all are—breathing the same air, having the same needs, holding such similar hopes and dreams.

Even then, the speech had struck her as too hopeful, too naive—but she had loved him for it. Roger had really come into his own, on that stage, and later that night, as they sat out on the front porch sipping lemonade and she'd told him as much—well, in a joshing, little-sister way, no need to get *too* mushy—he'd confessed to her—

Mama's soft gasp draws Lily's attention back to this moment. Mama's eyes are glistening, about to brim over. "I was wondering earlier—I couldn't remember where that shirt had come from. I know these are all Roger's old clothes, but there are so many that I can't recollect when he wore them, why I saved some and not others. I thought I'd never forget a single detail, but—"

Oh. Lily understands how Mama feels. Thinking in the moment that you'll always remember it, thinking you'll never lose grasp of moments with a loved one, that you'll hold such precious memories forever crystal clear in your head. But in another moment—months or years later— you realize that some of the earlier moments are fading.

Lily says, "But you remember lots of them, I'm sure."

Mama scoots forward, points to a dark gray coarse fabric. "This was from his first suit, for church. He was so proud of that suit."

Lily puts her hand over her mama's. "Mama, I think it's fine you are making a quilt of Roger's clothes—but why now? In the heat of summer?"

"I— I don't know— I just thought . . . it was time . . ."

"Does this have to do with the park?"

Mama meets Lily's eyes then, startled, wary. "Why—why would you think that?"

"Well, it's named after the battle Roger fought in, along with Chalmer, Daniel, Benjamin—too many others." For a moment, Lily thinks of poor Hiram Fitzpatrick from this morning, jumping at the sound of a door slamming, then disappearing into the woods. "And I was out there this morning."

Lily fills Mama in on MayBelle Fitzpatrick showing up this morning to complain yet again that she'd seen a dead girl floating in the man-made pond, on going back to the Fitzpatrick property, trawling the pond, and of course finding no more than fish.

"Oh—MayBelle is known for her sight." Mama looks worried.

Lily shakes her head. Mama, who prides herself on her intellectual pursuits at the Woman's Club, can revert with surprising quickness to the beliefs and superstitions of her own mother. "You've reared me to be a God-fearing practical Presbyterian"—a bit of a stretch, as Lily quite often finds more questions than answers or comfort in her faith—"and now you're telling me to take this seriously? I think poor MayBelle might be addled with dementia—or it could be that MayBelle senses something and has put it in a dream. Or maybe she remembers something from the past. . . ." Lily hesitates, recollecting MayBelle's sorrowful expression as she gazed across the pond. "Maybe she's seeing lost relationships, or has regrets over what should have long been repaired."

"Maybe," Mama says. "The family is known to have fractured years ago."

Lily nods. "I only vaguely know about that. Something serious enough that I thought Chalmer had nothing to do with his cousins, Hiram and Dorit. But they were at the house, apparently working for Chalmer and Sophia. Helping with the park, the house, taking care of MayBelle—who still lives alone in a cabin on the property. What do you know about the Fitzpatrick rift?"

Mama's lips twitch with a smile. "You're asking for my help in a case?"

Well now, Lily wouldn't say she has a *case* concerning the Fitzpatrick clan. There was no body in the pond. Chalmer and Sophia were tense with each other, enough to be disturbing, but not enough to call dangerous. And Hiram and Dorit being at the property, working for

Chalmer and his wife, could indicate a positive step forward. Yet something feels . . . off . . . to Lily.

Not that she's experiencing the sight, like MayBelle. Just something pinging at the back of her mind, warning her.

"I'd like you to tell me what you know of the Fitzpatrick family history."

Mama looks a wee bit disappointed at Lily not just saying, yes, she needs her help with a case. "Let's see . . . MayBelle was a Murphy. Large family, poor, scratching out a living on hardscrabble farms and working whatever trade they could find. Anyway, she married Norman Fitzpatrick—a good match for her, seeing as how Norman's granddaddy was one of the first settlers out here."

Lily shifts uncomfortably, swallows back a sigh. Must a woman's lot always be tied, one way or another, to the men in her life? True when the area was settled shortly after the Revolutionary War and too often true even now, in 1928.

"And Norman's brother Leonard, who was a lot younger than him, and they had a passel of siblings that passed on before they could wed and have children of their own, a hard lot for their mama—"

"Uh-huh, go on," Lily says impatiently.

Mama cuts her a sharp, chastising look that says, *Don't sass me, young lady.* But out loud she says, "Anyway, Leonard married another Murphy girl, a distant cousin of MayBelle's. Ida."

"All right," Lily says, "so we have two couples, Norman and Maybelle, who are much older—by how much?"

"I'd reckon at least twenty years. Norman and MayBelle had but one son. He and his wife—both deceased now—had two sons, Chalmer, who you know, and Michael, who lives up in Columbus. Meanwhile, Ida and Leonard had Hiram and Dorit. You know them pretty well."

Lily's stomach flips, just at the brief flash of memory of her run-in with Leonard and Ida ten years before. But Mama, as far as Lily knows, doesn't know about that, unless Daddy told her. She studies Mama's face, doesn't see the tension of worry that would surely be there if

Daddy had. "Hiram was at high school at the same time as Roger and me. Dorit is older. So, anyway, we have two brothers, each married, each with two children. The brothers are now both deceased, but their widows are still living." Lily swallows, remembering the relief she'd felt a few years ago, hearing of Leonard's passing—and the shame she'd then felt. But even dead, Leonard is still a spectre in her mind. "I haven't heard anything that explains a family rift."

"Well. Here's the thing. The land and money was divided evenly between the brothers, Norman and Leonard. But while MayBelle's husband, Norman, was careful with his inheritance, his brother, Leonard, was not. He gambled, got in debt, sold off portions of his property. Talk is he went to his big brother Norman for one loan too many, who finally in anger said if Leonard was so good at the poker table, why not have a winner-take-all game."

Lily's eyes widen.

Mama nods, her mouth set in a grim line. "That's right. And Leonard lost. Now, Norman did leave him and his family a small patch—which is where to this day Ida, Hiram, and Dorit all live. But the relationship between the brothers was broken, and bitter feelings on both sides passed down to Leonard's children, Hiram and Dorit, and even on down to Norman's grandsons, Chalmer and his brother."

Suddenly Mama brightens. "But if Hiram and Dorit are working for Chalmer and his wife, maybe the widows of the brothers have patched things up. Let bygones be bygones."

A lovely thought, but Lily doubts it. She flashes again on Hiram's parents, their hateful, angry faces that day outside of Daddy's grocery. So proud of their hate, carrying it like a torch.

Lily regards the quilt pieces. Mama still hadn't answered her question about why she's making a quilt from Roger's clothes now, in the heat of summer. She'd been eager to sidestep answering with the review of the Fitzpatrick history. "Well, thanks for filling me in. But—back to my earlier question. I can't help but wonder if this quilt has anything to do with Chalmer, or the park?"

Mama clears her throat. "Why would it?"

"Well, Chalmer wondered if you or Benjamin had told me something. He started to say what it might be, and then stopped when it was clear I didn't know what he was talking about—and when Sophia interrupted us. And then at the end of my visit, Hiram started to tell me something about Roger, too, but ran into the woods."

Mama's eyes turn to the sewing machine and notions table—uncustomarily littered, Lily notes, with notions and what looks like a stack of letters. "Well, um, Chalmer did talk with me a few times after church about his plans for the park. Asking me what I thought, and I said the plans and games area seemed fine. I reckon he could have talked to Benjamin, too. I— I guess I just got sentimental, you're right, because of the park. That's— That's why the quilt."

Lily's jaw clenches with frustration. Mama's explanation doesn't have the ring of truth.

And then her shoulders slump. She's gotten so testy of late with her dearest loved ones. "Well, all right then. I reckon I'll just have another biscuit for lunch. I just came home to check on you and Jolene."

Mama looks back at her, crestfallen. "You can't stay for a proper supper?"

Lily shakes her head. She wants to leave before she gets into another argument with either Jolene or her mama. "I need to get over to Rossville, check in with Marvena."

Mama's eyebrows go up. "I didn't know you were going over to see Marvena."

"We need to go over the plans for directing traffic tomorrow morning for the grand opening of the park. Chalmer's implied that it will be busier than I'd have thought. And it's possible that MayBelle is aware of a girl in the county in trouble but has forgotten where she heard it," Lily says. Marvena lives near Rossville with her daughter Frankie from her first marriage, her second husband, Jurgis, who is a coal miner and union leader, and Jurgis's mother, Nana. Marvena, recently a union organizer, knows the eastern part of Bronwyn County so well that sometimes Lily thinks her friend is closely acquainted with every leaf and branch and turn of stream.

"Well," Mama says, tentatively, "if you don't mind, maybe me and Jolene could go with you. I've been wanting to see Nana"—Nana has become one of Mama's best friends—"and I know Jolene would love to spend time with Frankie." Those two girls are best friends, too.

Usually, Lily gets annoyed when Mama tries to hitch a ride with her on her sheriff's duties. After all, they have Daisy the mule and the mule cart if Mama needs to go into town or anywhere else and Lily has insisted on teaching Mama to drive, even offered to buy her another automobile. Lily cherishes her time alone driving, using it to mentally sift through the tedium of cases—or, in this situation, the odd interactions at the Fitzpatricks'.

But maybe taking Mama and Jolene with her is a way to make up for her hurtful interactions with each of them over the past few days.

So Lily smiles. "If you really think Jolene would rather see Frankie than have cherry pie for supper. She'd have to have those ham and biscuit sandwiches on the way over."

Mama shrugs, trying to appear as if going over is neither here nor there. "Well, that would save me making a whole 'nother pie." In her next comment, her voice turns eager. "Go on, let her know. I need to tidy up in here."

Lily starts to leave but lingers in the doorway for a moment, staring back at the quilt pieces cut from Roger's clothing.

It doesn't take "sight" to know that Mama is holding back something about the park and Roger. Between Chalmer's comments and Mama's earlier reactions, that much is clear. And how is Benjamin involved? Lily's gut twists at the notion of any of them holding back truth from her. To her, that's just a form of lying. But why would they lie to her about anything having to do with Roger?

And yet she has her own secret about Roger.

Well, no use dwelling in the past. And she can just ask Benjamin if Chalmer had said anything to him about Roger or the park.

She looks at Mama, not making a move to tidy the sewing machine. Clearly waiting for Lily to leave. Lily shakes her head to clear it. She's being silly, worrying about MayBelle's visions, the tension between Chalmer and Sophia that probably wasn't nearly as bad as she thought, wondering about Mama's quilting and slight messiness, being too harsh with her daughter, Jolene.

Lily smiles at her mama. "I'm sorry about this morning, about bossing you around. I reckon this park, thinking about Roger in the war, really has shook me." Her eyes sting and well. "He was the better of the two of us—"

Suddenly Mama jumps up, rushes to Lily, reaches up, and cups Lily's face in her soft yet strong hands. Lily's eyes well even more at her mama's warm, gentle touch. "I know you still miss him. How you looked up to him," Mama says.

Lily nods, pats her mama's hand, walks swiftly away, dashing the back of her hand across her eyes. Time's a-wasting, and she has plenty to do before taking tomorrow off.

CHAPTER 4

※

BEULAH

Tuesday, July 3, 1928
2:00 p.m.

"Life is hard. Have tea," Nana says.

Beulah can't help but smile at her friend Nana Sacovech, who is a sprightly seventy-four years old, with as much or more energy than Beulah, and who says this so often that it's become an echo in her mind even when she isn't spending time with Nana.

Beulah and Nana sit on a backless, hard bench on the front porch of the Owens cabin, up in the woods on top of a hill just outside of Rossville. Tattered blankets and quilts are heaped behind them, but the sour smell wafting from the pile turns aside any notion of folding one up to use as a seat cushion. Besides, they're probably the sleeping blankets for at least some of the household's children.

Even without a back to the bench, or a cushion for her rear, Beulah is thankful to be resting her aching hips and knees after the trek over from the cabin on the hill across the holler where Nana lives with her son, Jurgis Sacovech, and his wife, Marvena Whitcomb Sacovech. Once Lily started conferring with Marvena about the possibility of a girl in trouble explaining MayBelle's persistent visions, Nana insisted *they'd just take a quick stroll to check on a local woman she'd been tending to.*

Now Beulah nearly snorts at Nana's notion of *a quick stroll.* But eyeing Suda Owens, perched on the edge of an old rocker with half a runner missing from the bottom, Beulah comprehends Nana's concern.

Suda shakes her head woefully. It's so hot that the strands of her greasy blond hair, sticking to her sweaty forehead, stay stuck. "No time for such niceties—even if'n I had tea in the house," she says, jostling one baby up and down on her knee, while holding a smaller, sleeping one in the crook of her arm.

Nana clucks her tongue and points at the basket at her feet. "I've brought along sassafras bark and some other herbs—mostly chamomile, some yarrow root—to build your blood right up. I'll brew it, so you don't have to worry about that. You've got some quart-size canning jars I can save the tea in?"

Suda lights up a little, and she nods.

"Now, which'n again is yourn?" Nana asks.

Well, it's pretty obvious, but niceties are important, especially in delicate situations. Without irony, Suda jostles the bigger baby she holds steady on one knee, the one with Suda's wide blue eyes, a spattering of freckles on his nose, and a wild shock of straw-blond hair that Suda and all the other Owens children—all daughters, ages two to eleven—share. The girls are in the side yard with Jolene and Frankie. Beulah had sent them off to help the older girls hoe the large garden and keep an eye on the younger ones.

The blond, older Owens baby opens his mouth in a protesting *oh!* but stops short of crying, suddenly focusing on Beulah and dimpling up with a smile. Beulah's heart softens irresistibly at the sight, and she wrinkles her nose at him, and he chortles.

But the tinier baby, with dark eyes and fuzzy brown hair, wails. Unceremoniously, Suda unbuttons her blouse and puts the tiny baby to her breast.

The blond baby on Suda's knee stares at Beulah, reaches for her.

Beulah goes to Suda. "Do you mind?"

Suda shakes her head, looks relieved as Beulah scoops up the baby boy. She settles down with him in the rocker. "What's his name?"

"Otto Junior," Suda says proudly, "for his daddy. First boy! We just call him Junior, though. Otto's already talking about how he can't wait to show him how to use a hammer and a nail—though Prudence, that's our oldest, keeps asking." She shakes her head—whether at Prudence or at Otto not being willing to show his daughter the tools of his trade Beulah is not sure. Then a sorrowful look shadows Suda's face. "You hear tell 'bout old man Hurley passing?"

Nana nods, looks over at Beulah, explains, "Tobacco farm, a few hollers away."

"Well, Otto made his coffin, of course." Suda glances toward a smaller outbuilding, by the barn. "Spends hours and hours working in his shop, but the money he makes, after buying lumber and such, well . . ." Her voice trails off. She doesn't want to spell out how thinly stretched are their means.

An eye-watering foul stench suddenly fills the porch. The blond baby on Beulah's knee has gone red faced and grunting, ridding his bowels and filling his cloth diaper.

"Well, Beulah," Nana says, unabashed amusement rounding out her tone, "I'll check on the girls in the garden, and then focus on the tea, while you help Suda tend the babies."

The front room serves as kitchen, sitting room, and sleeping area for Suda and her husband, while this room at the back of the cabin is for all of the Owens children to share.

It's crowded, with cots and two cribs and a changing table, where Beulah now works cleaning up Junior. A window in the side wall is open, and a decent breeze circulates around the room, sifting in the heavy scent of lilac growing along the side of the house, making tolerable the mingling smells of lye and waste from the diaper pail. In spite of the cramped conditions, the floor is swept clean and is topped with braided rag rugs, which don't show a speck of dust. They must have recently been beaten clean outside.

Suda sits in a brand-new rocking chair, runners safely intact—so much safer than its much poorer brother on the porch—not even a single squeak or sigh. One of Otto Sr.'s trademark pieces. It's touching, to think that he could have sold this rocker and just left an old one like the one on the porch back here for Suda. But he wants to offer at least this much of a nicety for his wife.

Beulah slides a fresh diaper under the now-clean Otto Jr. and neatly ties up the diaper corners. It's only been a few years since she'd diapered her own Caleb Jr.

She lifts Otto Jr. and gives him a tickly kiss on the cheek, and he dimples up and coos again. Beulah props him on her hip, turns toward Suda still wet-nursing another woman's infant.

"Thankee," Suda says. She looks down at the dark-haired infant in her arms. "This one's a little girl. So sweet. But I'm glad I finally had a boy. I'm hoping now that I have, we can be done with having more children. And if Otto can get on at the lumber mill—we heard tell there will be openings—then I won't need to help out by wet nursing. Oh, Otto makes a nice profit on his porch swings and rockers and caskets and such, but he works awfully slow—" She stops, a flush of shame coming over her face.

"Yes, I know he makes nice porch swings. I bought one for the farmhouse where I live with Lily—that's my daughter, the sheriff." Beulah can't keep a note of pride out of her voice. Suda nods; she knows who Lily is. "Well, we love our swing. Sturdy. Comforting."

Suda lights up. "Oh! That's nice. I can never keep track of who all he's sold to. Pert near everyone. Even the mamaw of the fella who owns the lumber mill."

"MayBelle Fitzpatrick?"

"Sounds right."

The baby briefly squirms, then resettles. Beulah asks, "So is it—usual? For folks to leave their baby here all the time?"

"Not if they live nearby. But this particular mom, she lives a far piece from here." Suda shakes her head. "Otto was fit to be tied, but I hushed him up good. She's paying plenty extra for round-the-clock care. And I ain't too proud to say I'm grateful for the money."

Her face lights up with hope. "I might use some of it to get me a wringer washer."

Junior leans his head against Beulah's chest. His eyes droop shut. "Awww," Beulah says. Then she nods toward the baby in Suda's arms. Suckling stopped, the baby's eyes droop. "What's that one's name?"

"Don't know. Reckon she don't have a name yet. I'm about to name her myself."

"How old is she?"

"About a month."

"And all this time the parents have never said even ideas for a name?"

Suddenly Suda looks down, as if shamed. She'd not been embarrassed by the natural process of feeding, by her own child's needs—but this question, for some reason, makes her turn red. "She—I mean they—they don't visit right often. Though she—they—send someone to check."

Suda abruptly stands, goes to the crib, and gently lowers the sleeping baby girl into it. She doesn't look at Beulah but says, "Do you mind keeping an eye on her to be sure she settles down, while I check on Nana?"

"Not at all," Beulah says. She hands over Junior, who fusses only a little in the transfer.

Beulah waits until Suda has left the room, then goes to the new crib. She stares down at the baby girl, already snoozing and blowing bubbles with each exhale. As Beulah gazes at the other woman's infant, she is struck by the feeling that she's missed an opportunity to learn something important. For the first time since Lily became Bronwyn County Sheriff, Beulah wonders how Lily does it—asks the just right, subtle questions to gather the information she needs. Or listens in a way that gets people to open up to her. It's the first time she's thought about Lily in her job beyond worrying about her safety.

There's a pinkish-red splotch on the right side of the baby girl's neck, as if a hand had been there. A strawberry birthmark that will likely fade completely or to almost nothing over time—otherwise, whoever the mother is might well come calling on Nana for some salve or other to help fade the mark. The little girl is flexing her hand open and closed and Beulah reaches down and lets the little baby girl grasp her finger. It's a tight grip. Roger had had a grip like that as a baby, like he'd never let his mama go. Lily, on the other hand, always seemed to be trying to wriggle away, eager and curious about the world.

Beulah blinks back tears. "Who do you belong to, little one?" Beulah whispers to herself. She feels a surge of worry and protection over the child. What will her life be like? The tiny baby reminds her that life is so fragile.

And yet someone had made sure that the baby has sustenance. Someone wealthy enough to pay for round-the-clock care. Was that why Suda had been so cagey earlier—the mama was wealthy? Wanted Suda to keep the baby secret?

But such a secret, Beulah well knows, can only be kept so long.

About halfway back to Marvena's cabin, Nana stops Beulah and the girls. She points to black raspberry bushes, blooming a mite early just off their winding path.

"Looka-there, girls." She pulls off her hat. "Think you could fill this? I can make hand pies for our picnic tomorrow."

"Oh, can we share them with Suda's kids?" Frankie asks, eagerly.

Jolene looks a little taken aback at the notion of sharing—not the hand pies, Beulah thinks, but her friend. Beulah's heart pings with apprehension. She tries to push it aside. Course Jolene will figure out she can share her friendship with Frankie with others. And oh, how those Owens girls had lit up with excitement as Jolene and Frankie told them what they knew of the new amusement park coming to the county. Even beset Suda's attention was drawn to the descriptions, a keen eagerness filling her face.

"Sure 'nough," Nana says now.

As Frankie and Jolene run back down the path to the black raspberry bushes, Nana hollers after them, "Watch out now, for poison ivy. But take your time. We need a break afore we go the rest of the way."

Beulah perches on a rough rock. Though the path back is easier than the steep climb up, she's exhausted. After both babies were settled, Beulah and Frankie and Joleen had helped the Owens girls set the cabin to rights, while Nana had carefully reviewed with Suda how to dilute the mix of herbs she'd just brewed down to a tincture.

Now Nana says, "You wanna spit it all out?"

Nana's long gray hair, loosed from the hat she'd just volunteered as a berry bucket, is in a comically wild tempest. Beulah forces her expression to stay serious, though. "I don't know what you're talking about."

"Oh, sure you do. What're you keeping swallowed down? You got that look on your face, pinched and sour apple green, and if you'd come to me looking like that, I'd normally think, well, her stomach's stirred up. She'll feel better if she just throws up whatever is ailing her, and then has a spot of chamomile to settle things down. But I reckon it's not a stomachache. It's something about that nice doctor man you've told me about, from church, ain't it?"

"Well, now, Dr. Twomey, he's right nice, and new to the town. He saw an advertisement in the Columbus newspaper about Kinship needing a doctor, and moved here without even laying eyes on the town before. . . ." Beulah pauses. At first, she thought that was insane. Now she finds it brave. Exciting. She'd never been outside of this county, other than long ago picnics over in Athens County. "Anyway, I'm just offering Christian charity—"

Nana chuckles. "Oh, Beulah, it's fine to have a little romance." The old lady waggles her eyebrows. "Are you worried about what Lily might think?"

"She thinks he's—to use her term—stuck up!"

"Well, huh. She can get right uppity herself at times. Maybe she feels a little threatened?"

Beulah turns this notion over. Well, it has only been four years since dear Caleb passed on. And Lily and her father had been close, of the same mind in many ways. Little Jolene earlier saying she didn't like Benjamin flashes across Beulah's thoughts. Maybe Lily is feeling some of the same trepidation Jolene has had. Beulah's heart softens. She should talk all of this over with Lily, too. Just because Lily's about to turn thirty doesn't mean she doesn't need a little reassurance about Beulah having plenty of love for all of her family.

Not, of course, that she's in love with Walter. No, with Dr. Twomey—they're not yet on a first-name basis. Beulah blushes at her foolishness—as if she's a young woman.

"'Cause in my opinion," Nana's saying, "Lily's taking too long with that handsome Benjamin Russo. Anyway, you can't wait on Lily's approval; you're younger than me, but not exactly a spring chicken—"

"Why, Nana Sacovech! Have you lost your mind, talking like this, or have you been dipping in Marvena's hooch?"

At that, Nana looks hurt. "Now, you know she's given up on all that. Again. Leastways, for now. Don't try changing the subject. Tell me what's eatin' you."

Beulah stares down at the ground. For a moment, she lets herself be mesmerized by the lush green clover, the frilly dots of white blooms. She should tell Nana. Get it off her chest, get advice for how to tell the others.

Beulah abruptly looks up. "It's about Roger. He has a daughter. Esmé Chambeau. She's nine. Roger had a relationship with a young woman while he was in France. Chalmer Fitzpatrick was hurt, and Roger tried to get him to a medic, but they got separated. 'In the fog of war' was how Roger put it in a letter to me. And they ended up at a farm, and there was a young woman, and well, one thing led to another over the next few weeks before they could reconnect with their unit, and he had an affair, and he was there long enough to learn the farm girl was pregnant."

Beulah stops, watches for Nana's reaction. But Nana doesn't react other than to reach down and grab a bit of wild mint and stick it in her mouth to chew on thoughtfully.

"All right," Nana says slowly, after she's finished off the mint. "We've both lived long enough to know these things happen. I reckon this isn't coming back to bother you just because of the Argonne park?"

Beulah sighs. "I didn't know about any of this until after Roger died. After, even, my husband died. I got a letter from the girl's grandmother. Charlotte. March, three years ago. Just a few weeks before Daniel died. Roger died before he could make things right. And Esmé's mother died in childbirth. Charlotte started having stomach troubles, and feared she wouldn't live long enough to finish rearing Esmé."

Nana arches an eyebrow. "And you believe this story?"

Beulah nods. "Charlotte included a love letter that Roger had left behind for the young woman, and a few he'd written after he went back to the front. They reference people—life here—in a detailed way. And he'd written a letter to me, for them to send, if, well, if something happened to him. And she hand-copied one of the letters he'd written to his unborn child. There were several letters, apparently, to the child and her mother that were on his person when he died." Beulah tears up. "I've been corresponding with Charlotte ever since the first letter from her. I like her, even from her halting style of writing. She learned enough English, from someone in her village, just so she could write to me about Esmé. And I've learned some French, too, from our correspondence. I think if we met in person we'd be fast friends. Anyway, a few months after I received the first communication from Charlotte, I talked with Chalmer Fitzpatrick, who confirmed that Roger and he had been at the Chambeau farm, that he'd known about Roger's affair and child. Chalmer said he'd gotten Roger's letters for the child back to the Chambeaus. We didn't bring it up again, and he's the only person I told. A few months ago, I talked with him again. . . ." Beulah trails off, unsure how to phrase the next part of the story.

Nana nudges her on. "All righty then. Why talk with him about the situation, after all these years?"

Beulah stares into the deep woods, hearing the girls giggle as they collect black raspberries. She doesn't have much time, she reckons, before they return. "Because Charlotte revealed that her illness has taken a turn for the worse. She only has months to live—at best. I asked for her to send Esmé here. To live with us. I wanted Chalmer's help to navigate the paperwork and arrangements to get Esmé here safely."

Beulah looks back at her friend. "Esmé came over, with a chaperone, by ship. It arrived in New York yesterday. They are on their way to Columbus, where they will spend tonight and all of the Fourth, then arrive in Kinship, by train, on the morning of July 5."

Nana studies her for a long moment. "Have you told Hildy? Or Lily? Any of this?" Her tone reveals that she already knows the answer.

Beulah shakes her head and then drops her head to her hands. Sweat and tears sting her eyes. *He was the better of the two of us*—Lily's comment from just a few hours ago—echoes in Beulah's mind. As much as she'd teased him when they were kids, Lily had idolized her big brother. Hildy, who had been engaged to Roger when he went off to war, had certainly idolized him. And since his passing, Hildy, who is a lifelong close friend of Lily's, had become in recent years like a sister along with Marvena. For the past few years, Hildy has been courted by Tom, Marvena's older brother, who works in the mines over in Rossville, where Hildy is the schoolmarm. Hildy has become a mother figure to Alistair, Tom's son from his first marriage, especially touching since Alistair's mother died in childbirth fourteen years ago. But through it all, Hildy has stayed close to Beulah, closer even than she might have been as a daughter-in-law.

Perhaps everyone except Beulah herself had idolized her son Roger. Oh, not that he hadn't been good, and kind, and smart. He had been all of those things. But Beulah also knew what a romantic he was, how he could be caught in the moment and not think of future consequences, a dreamer. She recollects again the letter he'd written to her that Charlotte had forwarded in that first packet of correspondence. He'd been full of hope for a peaceful future after the war, for himself, for the world, and promised that he'd find a kind way to tell Hildy the truth, and hoped that Hildy would understand. And he'd been confident that Lily would come around, understand later, if not right away, why he'd stay in France after the war. . . .

Now Beulah shakes her head. So idealistic. Romantic. Flawed and human. She sighs. Thinks maybe one of the greatest gifts a mother can give a child is to see and love that child for who they are, not who they want the child to be, no matter what anyone else might think.

She'd tried to do that for Lily, even if Lily doesn't see it that way. Defending Lily against even the smallest slights at the Woman's Club or church meetings, even when Lily's not in attendance, about Lily's unusual job, as if her daughter is a novelty and not dedicated to protecting and serving the people of her county.

Beulah looks up, meets Nana's gaze. "As I said, I've told Chalmer, out of necessity. And now I've told you. I know I need to tell Lily and Hildy, but—" All the excuses about not finding a right time, or having the moment thwarted by circumstances beyond her control, start to rise to her lips, but then she blurts out the truth. "I— I guess I wanted to—protect them."

Nana tilts her head to the side, cocks an eyebrow. "Protect them—or protect how they see Roger? And how they'll see you, for holding back this news for so long?" Though the words are harsh, Nana's tone is gentle, kind.

"All-all of that." The enormity of it breaks over her. Tears course down Beulah's face.

Nana comes over, puts her arm around Beulah's shoulders. "You have to tell the truth. Before Esmé arrives."

Beulah starts to shake. "Tell Lily, when we get back to your cabin?"

"No. You'll tell Lily you and Jolene are spending the evening with us. And you will tell Hildy first. And then you and Hildy will tell Lily."

Beulah's eyes widen. "Oh God, Hildy . . ."

"Hildy is strong. And it will be better for you and Hildy to tell Lily together."

For a moment, Beulah's mind eases.

"Mamaw!" Jolene hollers, and right behind her Frankie shouts, "Nana!"

Beulah and Nana both immediately pivot their attention to the girls. Beulah hurries toward them. "Girls, are you all right?" Her heart pounds. Had they been hurt?

But then she sees that they're flushed with excitement, not fear.

"We saw her again," Jolene announces.

"The lady we saw at Prudence's house," Frankie adds.

"Prudence?" Beulah asks.

"Suda's oldest girl," Nana explains.

"Anyway," Jolene says, a mite impatiently, "we saw the lady off in the woods when we were working the garden. Prudence and the other girls pretended we must be making her up."

"But she was clear as day," Frankie says. "She had on a blue dress—"

"And a white hair bow," Jolene puts in.

Beulah stares at the pair. That was the description Lily had shared of old MayBelle Fitzpatrick's vision of a young woman floating in the pond on the Fitzpatrick property.

"She didn't want us to see her, Mamaw," Jolene says. "At the Owens place—"

"And just now, in the woods," Frankie says. She looks at Jolene, suddenly scared. "Do you think she was following us? She looked mad that we saw her—"

"She more'n likely didn't want to be seen visiting the Owens place," Nana says.

Was the woman they'd seen the mother of the baby Suda is wet-nursing? Or someone the mother had sent to check up on Suda and the baby?

"But why?" Frankie asks.

"Well, because, well—life is hard sometimes." Nana stumbles over her words.

"And we need to get back to your mamas," Beulah says. Maybe the woman the girls just described is simply a coincidence with the woman MayBelle saw in her vision. Still, just in case, she should tell Lily about this. She sighs. Another necessary conversation, nosing its way in front of the more needful one. "We'll have tea."

CHAPTER 5

ESMÉ

Tuesday, July 3, 1928
7:10 p.m.

Dear Child, the letter starts.

Esmé nearly giggles at the opening—*Child.* Such a funny way to start a letter.

But Papa—Roger McArthur—didn't know if she would be a boy or girl. What Mama would name her. Mémère had explained all that.

Esmé keeps reading. It's hard, because she doesn't know English very well yet, though it is easier to read than to speak. And her stomach is churning from the long jolting train ride from New York City to this new city—Columbus, Mémère had told her. And from Madame Blanchett glaring at her the whole way. Since they arrived in New York, Madame has never let her out of her sight—even standing by the doorway when Esmé had to go to the bathroom down the hall from the small room they'd stayed in last night.

She hasn't even let her go to the bathroom on the train, though Madame herself seems to have become uncomfortable, from the way she's been squirming. Madame hadn't allowed them any food or drink since getting on the train, and Esmé's stomach is growling.

But they have to spend just one night in Columbus, and one day—a big holiday, July Fourth.

Then finally, they will get on the train and arrive in Kinship on the morning of the fifth. Esmé can't wait to arrive, partly out of growing curiosity about her father's family. But partly because she can't wait to never again have to see the glaring Madame Blanchett. Esmé hasn't decided yet if she'll confess such an ungenerous thought to either grandmother.

For now, she's reading her father's letter again, to practice her English in her head and to distract herself from Madame's glares, and from the dueling needs for both a bathroom and food and drink.

I hope I get to meet you soon after you are born, Papa's letter continues. *I've only known your mama for a little while, but I already know she is a kind and lovely person. I was trying to get a fellow soldier to help after he was wounded when we lost our way and stumbled on your mama and mamaw's farm—* "'Mamaw'! That's a funny word," Esmé thinks. *Your mama was the first person we spotted, coming out of the mist that morning, and she immediately saw that we needed help—*

The train jolts and Esmé lurches forward. She looks out the window. The train is pulling into another station, another city. Columbus.

"Esmé," Madame Blanchett says.

Esmé looks at her chaperone, on the seat across from hers.

"I have to find the facilities," Madame says, in French. A few nearby passengers stare. "But you will be a good girl, and wait here?"

Esmé nods, though she is confused. Why is Madame smiling at her and speaking in a singsong voice? And why is she grabbing her embroidered bag and taking it with her?

But before Esmé can ask any questions, Madame is hurrying away, down the aisle.

The train finishes pulling into the station.

Esmé folds the letter from Papa and puts it in her bag.

People are getting off, and soon Esmé is alone in the train car. Should she get off, too? Is Madame on the platform, impatiently waiting for her? Esmé's heart pounds. She doesn't want to do the wrong thing, but what if she is supposed to get off and by staying on she goes to the next stop—wherever that is? Then she will be lost, will miss going to Kinship, and she will have no idea what to do next.

She must make a decision.

That's what Mémère always says when they are faced with a tough situation. Money woes on the farm. An animal getting ill. Mémère getting sick. Tears spring to Esmé's eyes, even as she hears Mémère's voice in her head: *We must make a decision.*

And so she does. She picks up her bag, starts to hurry off.

But then there is a man, a short man in oversize overalls and a big floppy hat, like a farmer. And he is coming toward her, blocking the way Esmé needs to go to get off the train.

And suddenly he grabs her.

Esmé tries to jerk away, but he holds on, dragging her roughly.

Esmé's next decision takes no thought and comes from the gut: she must get away. She screams for Madame, twists, squirms, flails.

CHAPTER 6

LILY

Lily stands near the front of the crowd of at least a hundred people, gathered on the dance floor and pressing toward the stage.

The crowd murmurs with anticipation, in awe of the red, white, and blue bunting on the wooden backdrop to the just-finished stage. A sign over the backdrop reads: *Meuse-Argonne Memorial Park,* and just below the lettering is a white curtain. On either side of the stage hang U.S. flags, their thirteen stripes and blue fields of forty-eight stars sifting in a soft wind.

The breeze isn't enough to cool Lily or any of the other people. Sweat dampens the underarms of her dress, the back of her neck, and her swooped-up hair feels at risk of falling down from its bun.

She wishes she could break free of the crowd, escape to the cooler woods surrounding the dance floor—though, truth be told, given the traffic this morning, there must be plenty of people at the other features: the fishing pond, the archery range, the games area. In the distance, she hears the rat-a-tat of gunfire at the shooting range.

Lily spent the morning, with the help of Marvena and the other deputies, keeping the flow of traffic moving and making sure people parked or tied up their beasts well off Kinship Road. Lily makes a note to talk with Chalmer about clearing an area at the entrance for parking. She'd started to tell him when he came down to see how it was going at the entrance, but when she saw how excited he was for the park to finally open, she decided this wasn't the right time. He'd reminded her that he wanted her whole family at the dedication, then looked at Marvena. *You, too,* he'd said, and rushed off. Marvena's reply to Lily's questioning look was a shrug, and *Frankie's been asked to sing.*

Now Lily yawns as she looks around for her family and for Marvena. They'd gotten separated as they took care of directing traffic.

Lily hadn't slept well last night. After Mama and Jolene came back from their trek with Nana and Frankie to check on a wet nurse whom Nana is tending to, Jolene had proudly presented her half of the black raspberries that she'd picked, and begged to spend the night at Marvena's for more time with Frankie. Mama said, *'Fraid I put the notion in her head; I've a mind to stay over myself.* Lily had been surprised; they hadn't packed a change of clothes, and Mama isn't usually so spontaneous. But Lily can't tell Mama what to do, and after denying Jolene the fishing trip Lily had pity on her daughter and gave in.

After Frankie and Jolene ran off to wash and sort the black raspberries, Mama told Lily about the girls thinking they'd seen a young woman in the woods near the Owens cabin, a young woman dressed in a similar way to MayBelle's description. Marvena again quickly reassured Lily that, as far as she knew, there were no young women in trouble in her part of the county. So that odd anecdote didn't, to Lily's thinking, explain either Mama's wanting to spend the night at Marvena's or her worried expression.

Not long after Lily returned to her own home, Benjamin arrived with the boys in tow. They'd brought catfish from a successful fishing trip, and Benjamin had helped Lily clean the fish, dredge them in flour and cornmeal, and fry them up in bacon grease. She'd put together coleslaw as a quick side and whipped up cobbler for dessert from Jolene's black raspberries.

While they ate and then cleaned up, Lily'd found herself gazing at Benjamin and wishing the boys had spent the night away, too, so she and Benjamin could be alone. When he'd caught her glance and grinned widely, she'd flushed bright red, knowing he was thinking the same.

Of course he'd left after dinner. She'd settled the boys down for the night, then went to bed herself. But she'd tossed and turned throughout the night—so much on her mind. MayBelle's visions and portents. Remembering Roger. The sense that Mama is holding something back from her. The coming, busy day at the park. And Benjamin . . .

Someone jostles into Lily—"oh, sorry"—and brings her back to the moment. Lily glances around, looking for her family. And then she spots Benjamin.

She nearly gasps at the sight of him—tall, lean, in a summer linen suit—how does he manage to look so neat and unrumpled in this heat?—his dark shock of hair, unruly even under his hat. He's talking to a group of other fellows, miners he's befriended during his work in the region for the Bureau of Mines, assessing safety practices.

As if he senses her gaze, he turns from the conversation. Their eyes catch just for a moment over the jumble of people in the crowd passing between them. The crowd shifts again and she loses sight of him but sees Marvena, in her slouchy brown hat, who's worked her way to just in front of the stage. Of course she'll want to be up close to see Frankie, and probably the rest of her family is up there, too.

Lily starts working her way through the thick crowd and feels a hand falling on her shoulder. Lily spins quickly and sees that it is Benjamin. Her heart quickens.

"Lily," he says, and for a moment all the sounds from the people surrounding them mute and fall away. "I just saw your family up by the stage. Jolene and your mama are saying they want to spend another night at Marvena's, and now the boys want to as well."

Well, of course they do. They'd fussed about it *not being fair* that they didn't spend last night over, and they love spending time with Alistair, Marvena's nephew. If she relents to their request, she'll be alone tonight—*oh*. Benjamin is gazing at her with a mix of hesitancy and hope.

"Well, that only seems"—Lily reddens, stammers out her next word—"fair."

"I enjoyed our visit last night. But it was hard to talk with the boys clamoring around. I— I could drop by this evening—"

"Yes," Lily says, her heart quickening. "I'd like that—"

Their words overlap, and then they both stop.

For a long moment, the rest of the crowd falls away and Lily sees only Benjamin.

But then harsh words ring out from just a few yards away: "Stay the hell away from me, you crazy old woman!"

A tall, scrawny woman shoves her way through the crowd, while MayBelle follows after her. MayBelle's head bobs forward and back, the fluff of her gray hair swirling around, loose from her bun, in long strands, like a crazed hen—which would be funny, except that her eyes are focused and dark and seem to dig into the other woman, who is red-faced and sweaty. She stops, causing people in the crowd to jostle into her. Someone curses in annoyance.

Lily recognizes the woman, but it takes a moment for her to place her. Oh, Ida Fitzpatrick—mother to Hiram and Dorit.

Lily's stomach turns at the sight of her; the last time she'd seen Ida Fitzpatrick had been on the main street in Kinship in front of her father's grocery, not long after Roger and Daniel and Chalmer and Hiram and the other men had gone off to fight. Ida had trudged proudly alongside her husband, Leonard, leading a mob who'd tarred and feathered poor Mr. Gottschalk, the previous owner of the farm where Lily now lives. He was a German immigrant who had not bought war bonds. The mob had brought Mr. Gottschalk into town on a mule cart, Mrs. Gottschalk sobbing and running alongside the cart as her husband moaned in pain. The mob stopped in front of Lily's daddy's grocery, expecting her father, who sold war bonds, to join in with the horrific treatment of Mr. Gottschalk. But even though a terrified nineteen-year-old Lily begged him to back down, her father stood up to the mob. Lily had then helped get Mr. Gottschalk medical help, but she'd seen the disappointment in her father's eyes over her wish that he'd cower before the mob for the sake of his own safety. She'd never forgotten that look, or the look of mindless hate coating Ida and Leonard's expressions.

Now, Lily lurches forward, shoulders her way through the crowd, jostling people out of the way to get to Ida and MayBelle.

She ignores Ida. "MayBelle," Lily says, "are you all right?"

MayBelle looks up at Lily. The old woman is so tiny that she is overshadowed by Ida. Her eyes are a pale gray, and yet there is a sharpness to them. "She won't listen to me. No one will. I told her, I got the sight, I seen the girl a-floating—*her* girl—and she's gotta do something. I got the sight—"

Her girl—MayBelle must mean Dorit.

"The sight! The sight!" Ida snarls, flailing her arms out. She smacks the arm of a passing woman, and the man with her hollers, "Hey, watch it," and Ida turns, fists forming, as if she's eager for a fight.

"Mrs. Fitzpatrick, I suggest you remain calm," Lily says.

Ida turns toward Lily and stares down at her, her face crunched and curled with cruel lines. Lily holds her ground. She is not nineteen, fearing for her husband's and brother's lives in the Great War, and her father's, too, on the main street in Kinship. Now she will not cower.

"You think you're so tough—Lady She-riff?" Ida splits her title into two words. Her forefinger flicks up like a switchblade and hovers just over Lily's badge.

"If your finger so much as brushes me, I will bring you in for assault."

"You think you can do that?"

"Yes," Lily says. "Now, what is the issue here?"

"She keeps pestering me about her stupid sight." Ida looks at her sister-in-law. "Did you have the sight that your husband would steal this land from my husband?" She turns back to Lily. "It's bad enough that my children both work for high-and-mighty Chalmer, but now she keeps bothering me with her fool ramblings—"

"If you feel so strongly about Chalmer, why are you here? It might be better if you headed home—"

"Is it any of your business why I'm here? Am I obliged to tell you?"

"No, of course not—"

Ida leans forward, towering over Lily. "Oh, you think you're as tough as your daddy was?" Her voice is a low rumble. "He thought he was so high-and-mighty, defending German pigs, when my boy was over there, fighting—"

"So was my husband. My brother. Your son—"

"Oh, but my boy don't get a whole park in his honor, does he."

Lily blanches. *Oh.* She did not know, until this moment, that the park would be dedicated to her brother. That was why Chalmer was eager to know she and her family would be here. And working here, Hiram must have heard that the park would be dedicated to Roger. That was what he'd tried to tell her yesterday. And he must have mentioned it to his mother and sister.

"Welcome, welcome, everyone!" Chalmer is up on stage and his voice booms through a bullhorn over the crowd. "I know you're all excited to be here today. . . ."

Lily turns to MayBelle. "Come on. Don't you want to get closer to the stage?"

Gently, Lily guides MayBelle forward, leaving Ida seething behind them in the crowd. Benjamin joins them, and they all make their way forward, joining Marvena and her family, Nana and Jurgis, Hildy and Tom and Alistair. Micah and Caleb Jr. and Jolene are just on the other side of them.

"Where's Mama and Frankie?" Lily asks Marvena.

"Your mama took Frankie up to the main house, to have some quiet before the presentation," Marvena says. "Right nice of her."

Next, Lily looks over at Hildy, wondering how she will feel when it's announced that this park will be in memory of Roger. She does a double take, seeing her friend's expression. She looks sad, hollow eyed. Has someone already told her? Does this spur doubts about her relationship with Tom? But no, Tom has his arm around Hildy, tenderly.

In the distance, the rat-a-tat of the gunfire at the shooting range draws Lily's attention, and she wishes someone had told the people there to stop while Chalmer's dedication of the park is ongoing. He goes on, thanking various people for their support on his project.

"Sheriff Ross? Where are you?" Chalmer looks over the crowd. "Ah, there you are. Come on up. Bring your children and your little brother, too. Come on, we all want Sheriff Ross and her family up here."

The crowd cheers.

Reluctantly, Lily makes her way to the stage, with the children—Jolene, Micah, and Caleb Jr.—following her.

As Lily mounts the side steps, she notes just to the left, behind the bunting, Mama and Frankie and Sophia. Dorit rushes up to Sophia, bringing her a blue hat, which Sophia hurriedly puts on. With them is a young woman whom Lily doesn't recognize at first, and then she realizes it's Pearl Riley, a young woman who lives by herself in Kinship—a spinster, as people say.

Pearl's face is tearstained and wracked with emotion. No wonder Lily didn't recognize Pearl; at Woman's Club meetings she is usually so quiet and composed, only whispering occasionally with Sophia.

Beneath her fancy hat, Sophia's expression is cold, frozen, as if she is holding herself rigid lest she crack into a thousand pieces. She stares at Chalmer.

There's that pinging sense again. What is going on with Chalmer and Sophia—and, possibly, Pearl?

Offstage right, Hiram shifts nervously from one foot to another. He's wearing the same work clothes Lily had seen him in yesterday. He holds a rope, connected to the white curtain at the bottom of the sign. There's a twitchiness to him. Lily gives him a quick reassuring smile, but Hiram doesn't notice. He's got that stare again, across the stage as if at some spot miles away. Or, Lily thinks, maybe years distant in the past.

Chalmer turns, looks at Mama. He doesn't seem to notice his wife, Pearl, or Dorit. "Come on out, Mrs. McArthur. And our special guest!"

Mama and Frankie come out onstage.

"And of course, I must have my darling wife," Chalmer says, without a bit of irony, "by my side. Come on, Sophia."

Stiffly, Sophia comes up, takes her place by Chalmer's side.

Chalmer beams at the crowd. "We are so glad to welcome to our dedication the McArthur and Ross family. You all know Sheriff Lily. And of course her children—Jolene and Micah. And dear Mrs. Beulah McArthur, Sheriff Lily's mama, and Caleb Junior."

Lily and Mama share a look. It is so strange, and uncomfortable, for them to be in the limelight. Roger had taken to the stage easily, naturally, in plays and oratories in high school, and Daddy had been gregarious in greeting and helping customers at his grocery, but Lily and Mama prefer working in the background, one-on-one with others in the community.

Lily hears voices rising behind her to the left. She glances offstage, sees Pearl and Dorit arguing about something. Dorit grasps Pearl's arm as if holding her back. Surely Pearl doesn't mean to rush onto the stage?

Chalmer lifts his voice over the commotion. "Now, we all know what losses these two stalwarts of the community have suffered—first Mr. McArthur working to save trapped miners back in the Widow-maker collapse of '24. And before that, they lost someone, a hero, Roger McArthur, whose efforts in the war can't ever be fully known—"

At that, Lily's eyebrows go up. Chalmer's face suddenly flashes with real emotion, his eyes misting over. What does he mean?

Then Chalmer's expression clears, and he returns to his usual show-man persona. "And so I am pleased to announce that this is not just the Meuse-Argonne Memorial Park—it's the Roger McArthur Meuse-Argonne Memorial Park!"

He gives a cue, and Hiram tugs the rope, pulling back the curtain and revealing the bottom of the sign: *In Memory of Roger McArthur.*

A murmur goes through the crowd. Heat rises in Lily's face. She loves her brother, misses him still, and always will, but this just feels wrong. There are so many veterans in the crowd. So many people who'd lost their brothers and neighbors and husbands and sons. This park should be dedicated to all veterans.

Suddenly a loud boom comes from the shooting range, and every-one startles. Then Hiram rushes onto the stage. His gun is pulled and he screams at Chalmer, "You can't hurt her; I won't let you hurt her!"

Lily starts to tell Mama to get the children off the stage, but Mama is already hustling them down the stage steps. Mama glances at Lily as if to say, *come on,* but Lily shakes her head. Mama looks scared and then resigned—she knows Lily won't leave the scene until she's calmed Hiram and contained the situation. Mama pulls the children off the stage with her, just as Hiram startles again and runs from Chalmer to the left side of the stage. Chalmer takes this opportunity to exit stage right, pulling Sophia along with him, even as Sophia stares wildly at Hiram.

"Hiram, stop," Lily cries. Now, only she and Hiram are on the stage. Hiram freezes. He still holds his gun drawn.

Several men from the crowd start to rush onstage to grab Hiram as Marvena hollers for them to stay back.

Hiram stares down the steps, behind the bunting, and Lily follows his gaze. Pearl and Dorit have disappeared from where they'd just been standing at the bottom of the steps, out of sight of the crowd.

"Hiram, put your gun away," Lily says. "If you put it away, I won't have to bring you in." Well, she can't really bring him in for having a gun or even holding it in a crowd. But she wants him to put it away before he uses it. He'd just threatened Chalmer, and she doesn't understand what he meant about Chalmer hurting *her* or who *her* would be, but for now, Lily just wants Hiram to calm down.

"Hiram, look at me."

He slowly turns, faces Lily. He still holds his gun. Lily spreads her hands wide from her sides. "Please put your gun away, and then we can talk somewhere quiet."

Hiram gazes past her, eyes locked on something miles away, and maybe years ago, that only he can see.

"Hiram," Lily says more gently as she walks up to him. "Hey—look at me. Look at me. Roger would want you to look at me."

At that, he turns his eyes, glazed, toward her. But she can see that using Roger's name has had an impact on him. She walks up to Hiram.

"Listen, I'm not sure what's spooked you, but Chalmer is not going to hurt anyone. I won't let him. But first, you need to hand me the gun."

Hiram's hand lowers. Now the gun is near Lily's abdomen. She hears someone gasp, a woman crying, a man cursing. God, she wishes they'd hush.

She steps forward, heart in throat. If the gun goes off accidentally or otherwise, she'll be shot in the gut. But she must have Hiram's trust. "Please. Hand me the gun. We can talk this over. You can tell me whatever you need to, but in private, all right, not here?"

Suddenly Hiram's shoulders slump, and he hands her the gun.

"Thank you," she says softly, as she tucks his gun in the waistband of her skirt. She glances at Chalmer, cowering at the bottom of the stage steps. Well, a lot of help he'd be in an actual confrontation. She calls to him, "Please go on with the dedication."

Then she takes Hiram's elbow, gently nudges him to leave the stage.

Lily and Hiram sit on the edge of the dock, feet dangling just over the water. Just below the surface, a catfish languidly swims by. It's relatively quiet down by the pond. They're the only ones here, as the dedication continues. From a distance, Frankie's sweet voice drifts to them through the bullhorn, singing "God Bless America." The sound makes Lily smile. It seems Frankie's voice just gets sweeter and stronger every time she sings.

Lily looks up at Hiram. He still has that distant gaze, and she doubts he hears Frankie. Lily recognizes that long glassy stare. She'd seen Daniel go into it every now and then, after he'd wake up from some nightmare that would send him thrashing and crying out, until he'd wake up, stare like that. Such episodes happened less as time passed. Lily'd heard tell of shell shock, and studying him—the pasty paleness of his face, the sweat on his upper lip, the hollow distance in his eyes—she thinks he's experiencing something like that. Is it possible, ten years after the war? Has working on the memorial brought it all back to him?

Scruffy beard stubbles his jawline, and underneath that his narrow cheeks are pitted with acne. More than time has ravaged his face to look much older than his thirty-one or so years. Yet to Lily, his expression is that of a scared young boy.

But Hiram has always, Lily reflects, looked scared, about to jump out of his skin at the least provocation. Lily digs back in her memory. Roger and Hiram had been friends, but then Roger was popular with everyone. Still, Lily finds a few hazy memories of Hiram coming over to their house after school and Mama always setting an extra spot for him. Daddy always offered to take Hiram back to his house after dinner, but Hiram would always walk, his insistence almost panicky. And Lily hadn't thought much about it then, how hard it must have been for Hiram to come into town for school each day—well, most days, and as he got older, he missed more days than he attended. He'd dropped out after tenth grade.

Lily says so softly that her voice is a near whisper, "Too bad we didn't bring our fishing poles, huh, Hiram?"

He does not look at her.

She puts a hand on his arm, ever so gently, but he still jumps. Then, he does look at her, a bit wild-eyed, but he is finally focused on the moment, on her.

"Hiram, can you tell me what happened? Before you . . ." She pauses, wanting to phrase this accurately, but not accusatorily. "Before you came up onstage?"

"There was gunfire. I thought—I thought—"

"It startled me, too," Lily says. "Someone should have told the boys down at the shooting range to stop during that time."

Hiram looks at her at last, his eyes wide. "It was—just from the shooting range?"

"Yes. Part of the park."

He hangs his head again.

"Hiram," Lily says. "Please look at me."

Slowly, he looks up.

"It is all right," she says. "It would be easy to be startled by that sound. To not be sure where it was coming from. . . ." She pauses, considering how to best phrase her next question—why did the sound make him grab his gun, go after Chalmer? Did he think Chalmer was shooting?

But before she can ask, Hiram's gaze intensifies on Lily. "You are kind, like Roger. Well, *now* you are kind."

She tries to think—what does he mean, *now*? And then she recollects how she was one of several girls—except for Hildy, who never mocked anyone—who had laughed at Hiram when he tried to express that he felt sweet on Lily. She turns red out of shame, though she was only thirteen at the time.

Oh, and hadn't he then turned his attention on Hildy? But once he knew that Roger and Hildy were sweet on each other, Hiram had quickly backed off. Had she been unkind to him about his interest in Hildy, defensive of her best friend? Probably.

"I am sorry that I was ever unkind to you, Hiram," Lily says. "I wish I had been kind."

"Roger was always kind," Hiram says. He's staring again at the wall. "Even—over there. Roger, Roger, he—"

Hiram stops, and the back of Lily's neck prickles. She senses that he has something he wants to tell her about Roger, the same something he'd started to tell her yesterday morning but then abruptly stopped.

"Would you like to talk about Roger?" she says. "Chalmer referenced something happening over there. What did he mean, 'whose efforts in the war can't ever be fully known'?"

Hiram says nothing.

"I like hearing stories about him."

Hiram remains quiet.

"Or I could tell you a story about him," she says.

His face lights up and he gives a small nod.

Lily takes a deep breath. Suddenly all her memories of Roger tumble one over another, like pebbles tossed in a fast-rushing stream. She plucks out just one.

"Once, I brought home a tiny frog from a visit to our grandparents' farm. I think I was, oh, six or seven," Lily says. About the same age as Micah and Caleb Jr. are now. "So Roger would have been around eight. Well, of course Mama wasn't going to let me keep it in the house. I snuck out one of Mama's good candy dishes, and made a little nest for the frog, with twigs and grass, and dug up some worms for food."

Lily smiles, shakes her head at her younger self. "Well, of course the frog was gone the next morning. Mama was so mad that I'd used her candy dish that I had to wash it and all the dishes in the kitchen. And I wept and wailed the whole time. And Roger, well, he came and helped me wash the dishes, even though he knew Mama would be mad at him for helping me. . . ." Lily pauses, considers. Her eyes mist over. "I'd like to think I'd have helped him like that, but truth be told, I'd have probably just left him to the task and teased him later. But not Roger. He just kept reassuring me that the frog would be fine, while we washed all those dishes."

Hiram looks at Lily with wonderment. "You do not seem sad," he says, "when you talk about him."

Lily gives a small smile. "I think the sadness is still there—for me. For Mama. For Hildy. For lots of people. But the sadness is nestled down in a corner, staying mainly out of the way so we can remember Roger in other ways."

And yet sorrow fills Hiram's face. He is still overwhelmingly sad about Roger. Has he been all along? Or has the park triggered something in him?

"I'm happy to listen to your memories about Roger," Lily says. She feels certain that she won't learn anything new about Roger—or will she? This park, and its dedication to Roger, seems to have triggered something in Hiram. "There was something you wanted to tell me yesterday, about Roger. I'm sorry I got distracted. Do you want to tell me now?"

For a long moment, Hiram stares at her. The silence around and between them thickens and leavens, makes it hard to breathe. There *is* something—Lily can see it in the flash behind his eyes. And something else, too. He is *afraid* to tell her.

"All right, if you don't want to talk about Roger, that's fine. But Hiram, what did you mean when you hollered at Chalmer, that you wouldn't let him hurt *her*?"

His eyes go flat, blank.

"Who is 'her'? Sophia?" She waits. "I sensed tension between them yesterday. They were sharp with one another."

Hiram stares past her.

"All right then—should I be worried about MayBelle? I saw her earlier. With your mother."

At that, Hiram looks up, startled. Wildness sparks his eyes.

"MayBelle was telling her about the young woman she keeps seeing in a vision, floating here in this pond. From what she said, she's worried about your sister Dorit. Do you know anything about that?"

"I— I don't know—" Hiram sounds as if he is choking.

"Given how much your mother hates Chalmer and MayBelle and all of your uncle's part of the Fitzpatrick family, can you tell me why she's here today?"

Hiram shrugs.

Lily takes a deep breath, trying to retain her patience. "Offstage, I saw your sister Dorit. A woman named Pearl Riley—she's an acquaintance through the Woman's Club; that's how I know her—and she looked upset. Did you mean you won't let Chalmer hurt one of them?"

Hiram stares down at the fish. "I— I have feelings for Pearl. I've let her know. But she seems to want Chalmer, even though he's married to that uppity woman, and Dorit tells me I need to stop being so foolish, that Pearl will never want the likes of me." He looks up at Lily. "I'm sorry I overreacted to the shooting. Can I go now?"

Lily sighs. She's not going to get any more out of him, at least in this moment. "Yes—but I'd like to keep your gun for a bit, if that's all right." Not that she's really giving him a choice.

Hiram considers a moment, then nods and hops up. "I don't hear Chalmer talking anymore. I'd better go apologize, see what he needs me to do."

In the next moment he's gone, down the path back to the stage and dance floor. Lily sits alone by the pond, feeling somehow as if she's been sitting here alone all along. She stares down into the pond.

Just fish.

She remembers something else from school days about Hiram—the time all the teacher's chalk went missing. When the teacher demanded from the front of the classroom if anyone knew who took it, Hiram had immediately fessed up.

Not believing Hiram would come up with such a prank on his own, the teacher asked who had put him up to it. But Hiram wouldn't say, even when the teacher whipped the back of his legs, in front of the whole classroom, with a willow branch switch.

I won't let you hurt her! . . .

A delusion of some sort? Or is Hiram really worried Chandler is going to hurt a woman? Is MayBelle worried, too?

Lily rises to her feet, starts back to the park. Should she have pressed Hiram harder? But he had all but clammed up on her. All she can do now is stay at the park, see what she might observe. Ask Chandler directly what Hiram might have meant.

Most of the crowd has dispersed from the stage area and dance floor to the other features of the park. The stage is clear. She doesn't spot any of her family.

A light touch on her elbow makes her turn around. It's Benjamin, gazing down at her with concern. "Is everything all right?" he asks.

"For the moment," Lily says.

"That sounds ominous. Might I distract you by asking you to dance? At the end of his presentation—which was gracious, by the way, and I'll have to fill you in—Chalmer announced there'd be a band here shortly after suppertime. And square dancing . . ."

But Lily already is looking away from Benjamin, searching for Chalmer. "I don't have time for worrying about dancing, Benjamin," she snaps. "I need to find Chalmer, ask him a few questions. Did you see which way he went?"

She hears the disappointment riding in Benjamin's voice, just on one word: "No." She doesn't need to look at him to know his face will be covered in disappointment, too. She hurries off to find Chalmer.

CHAPTER 7

⋙

BEULAH

Wednesday, July 4, 1928
1:40 p.m.

"Well now, ain't that something. I reckon Jolene takes after her mama."

Beulah startles at the sound of Nana's voice. She realizes that her thoughts have wandered off and that her hand has clenched into a fist around her handkerchief, which she'd just been using to pat off the perspiration on her forehead and neck. Now, as she sits with Nana on a bench near the games area, her fist presses to her heart.

She relaxes her hand, pats her face again. The area is shady, yet humid. The canopy of the trees holds in the heat, which feels as thick as a wet blanket draped over them. But the children—Frankie, Jolene, Alistair, Caleb Jr., and Micah—are all having a grand time at the ringtoss game. Well, at least Jolene is. To the consternation of the younger boys, her rings are landing perfectly over the necks of the milk bottles set up at the back of the booth. Even through the crowd, Beulah hears Frankie and Alistair cheering her on, while Caleb Jr. and Micah wail, "That's not fair. She's gotta be cheating!"

Beulah smiles at the children's shenanigans, even as she blinks back tears.

"You all right?" Nana asks.

"Yes. Just so much excitement, about this park, and I guess I didn't expect—"

Well, there is a lot she didn't expect. She didn't expect this many people to turn out on the park's debut on July 4. She didn't expect to feel this overwhelmed by emotion or that Chalmer would dedicate the park to her son. He'd told her after the dedication ceremony that he'd meant it as a special surprise, a thank-you to her. Beulah's not sure what he's thanking her for—after all, he's helped her organize Esmé's immigration.

Her hand goes back to her chest. She hadn't gotten to tell Hildy last night—Hildy and Tom had been out to a barn dance. And so of course she hasn't told Lily yet, either.

After the dramatic dedication, they'd all regrouped for their picnic, and while most everyone had enjoyed the meal and gathering, Lily had eaten hurriedly, then run off, saying she needed to talk with Chalmer and hadn't been able to track him down. And Benjamin had been un- usually quiet, saying little more than, *Thank you, Mrs. McArthur, for a lovely meal*, at the end of the picnic, and *I'll be taking my leave.* Marvena had brought up the square dance scheduled for later, and Benjamin said, *Sounds fun, but Lily is, as usual, busy.* An uncharacteristic tinge of bitterness darkened his words, and as he walked off, Beulah cast a questioning look at Marvena, who'd replied with a shrug. A glance at Hildy didn't elicit any insights as to whether Lily and Benjamin have been quarreling; she looked sad, while Tom kept glancing at her wor- riedly and patting her arm.

"Well, I thought the day might be emotional, but not quite so dramatic," Beulah says.

Nana nods. "Do you know the young man who pulled his gun on Mr. Fitzpatrick? Way Lily calmed him down"—Nana's tone heightens with admiration for Lily, and Beulah has to admit, she admires how her daughter had handled the situation—"I reckoned she knows him?"

"Hiram Fitzpatrick," Beulah says. "He was a friend of Roger's in high school. Well, everyone was a friend of Roger's. Hiram, though, always seemed to especially admire Roger. Hiram only went the first year or two—can't quite recollect—to high school."

"Well, that's a sight farther than most folks get," Nana says.

Beulah grunts in agreement. Most were lucky to get through eighth grade. It strikes her—is Hildy worried about her teaching post? Has word gotten around that she and Tom, well, sometimes spend the night at one or th'other's house in Rossville? Or is he wanting her to finally marry him and she's worried about not being able to teach as a married woman? Beulah sighs. And here she is, about to tell Hildy the news of Esmé. But no, she can't postpone any longer. She's waited too long as it is.

"Yes," Beulah says. "I don't know him well, though I do remember when he, and several of Roger's chums, came to a supper I made for the boys going off to war. Roger, Daniel, Chalmer, Hiram, several others. They were all so nervous—except Daniel, of course, who always put up a tough front. And Hiram. I remember it struck me as so odd, that Hiram—always skittish and quiet—seemed relieved to be going off, as if he couldn't wait to get away. I thought maybe he was putting up a front, too, like Daniel. I asked him if he was all right, and he said . . ." Beulah pauses, swallows hard a few times. "He said, if he was in Roger's unit, he knew they'd be all right." She swallows again. "I hung on to that. Daniel, Chalmer, and Hiram came back. But Roger didn't." She wipes her eyes with her handkerchief. "I've only seen Hiram now and again in town since he came back. He came back—different. Not quite able to carry on, like Daniel and Chalmer. At least, on the outside, they seemed fine enough. But Hiram, well, I think he always has worn his heart on his sleeve."

Nana pats Beulah's arm. "Life is hard. And for some situations, there's just no tea."

Beulah closes her eyes for a moment, willing herself to rein in her emotions.

"Mrs. McArthur?"

Beulah opens her eyes, sees Suda Owens and her four daughters. The eldest daughter holds her little brother, while Suda holds the baby she's been wet-nursing, contentedly asleep, though the strawberry birth-mark looks more pronounced in this heat.

"Sorry, I didn't mean to disturb you," Suda says.

"Don't worry, dear; we're just taking a rest. It's a scorcher today."

"Don't I know it," Suda exclaims. "My feet feel like they're boiling over my shoe tops."

Suda and her brood are all hot and sweaty, and it hits Beulah that they'd all trekked here by foot from all the way over by Rossville—a good six miles.

"But the girls, after hearing all about this from your young 'uns begged and begged to come. And they wanted to hear Frankie sing. She's so good." Suda leans a little closer, and Beulah catches a whiff of talcum powder beneath the woman's sweat. She'd neatened up as best she could for this big event. "Truth be told, I wanted to come, too, and, well, I shouldn't share this but—" Suda leans forward. "And Otto even came with us. He's been talking about trying to get on at the lumber mill. Plus, Mr. Fitzpatrick has so many openings, he'd hired his feuding cousin, Hiram. And now, after the shenanigans on the stage, looks to me like there'll be another slot."

Beulah frowns, partly in displeasure at this unkind talk about Hiram, though now everyone from one corner of the county to the next will be gossiping about Hiram's attack—and how Lily diffused it. Her frown is also from wondering how Otto—with no truck nor automobile—will get all the way to work at the lumber mill, another five miles from here.

Well, no use adding to this woman's troubles. Let her have a bit of hope. Beulah switches her frown for a smile. "Well, other than poor Hiram's—shenanigans—I hope you're having a good time."

Prudence, the oldest girl, holding little Otto Jr., steps forward. "Ma'am, do you know if those games cost anything?"

Beulah's heart goes to downy feathers over the eagerness on the girl's face. "Not today," she says.

The girl looks up at her mama expectantly. Suda sighs, balances the baby in her arms, reaches out for Junior.

"I'll take him," Beulah says. "Though I hope he won't need me to change him again."

Prudence laughs as she hands over Junior.

"Go on then," Suda tells her daughters, who run over to join the other children.

"Well now, that's a heap of trouble waiting to happen," Nana says. "I can take the other baby if you'd like to go keep an eye on them."

As Suda lights up, it occurs to Beulah that Suda would like to enjoy the game booths, too. But Suda hesitates. "I—shouldn't. I don't think his mama—"

"Well now, I've tended many a child and helped birth quite a few," says Nana. The affront in her voice, as if her skills as a midwife and healing woman are being called into question, is put on just to shoo Suda off to have a bit of fun.

Suda pauses a moment longer, then carefully hands the baby to Nana. Then Suda hurries over to join the children. A moment later, they see her at another booth, this one for darts, and hear her giggling with glee even though she keeps missing the board.

"Look at us," Nana says. "A pair of old hens, keeping watch over the chicks."

Beulah laughs. "Poor Suda. She needed the break. How did you hear about her?"

"I hear a lot of talk, when I go round to tend folks that can't get to a doctor. And that's quite a few in Rossville. No doctor in town, and it's hard for most folks to get all the way over to Kinship to see your Dr. Twomey."

Beulah flushes red. "He's not *my* Dr. Twomey. But— I can put in a word with him that it might be nice to make a weekly visit into Rossville. If'n you don't think it'll trod on your turf."

"I'll keep an eye on him, make sure he knows what he's doing. Thought we might see him here today?"

Beulah's heart gives a little dip. She'd hoped he'd be here, too. "He's visiting his son and his family, up in Columbus, for the day."

"Well. I need to meet him right soon, make sure he's fit to be calling on my best friend."

At that, Beulah tears up. They'd only known each other three years, meeting under tragic circumstances after Marvena lost her older daughter, but yes, Nana had become her best friend, understanding her better than the women Beulah'd known all her life. She gives Nana a gentle elbow—not too hard, since the bench is narrow and they're both holding babies—and starts to speak up in Dr. Twomey's defense.

But then Pearl Riley rushes over. Her expression is fraught, her face still tear-streaked. Shortly after the whole group had arrived at the park this morning, Chalmer had spotted Beulah and Frankie and told them to go wait in the cool of the house. At the front door they were let in by Dorit Fitzpatrick. For a while, they sat in the parlor with MayBelle Fitzpatrick, who kept nodding off—even with curtains drawn and windows opening and a decent breeze, it was stuffy in the house. They awkwardly accepted glasses of lemonade from Dorit, who appeared to be working as a housekeeper. Frankie's eyes were wide, taking in the fine furniture and, most particularly, the baby grand piano. Beulah had been impressed, too—it was probably the only baby grand in the whole of the county.

Sophia had at first been startled to see them, then quickly composed herself. She told Frankie to go ahead, check out the piano. *Do you play, dear?* Sophia had asked. *A little,* the child said, *if'n I've heard the melody afore. There's a spinet at the church we go to.* At first, Frankie, though charming in her red hair bow and the blue-and-white-checked gingham dress Nana had made just for today's occasion, nervously poked at the keys. But then, as if even a few bluntly played notes were sufficient to calm her nerves and lure forth her true talents, Frankie began playing and singing "Amazing Grace." MayBelle stirred and stared transfixed at the child. For a moment, they listened to her play—marveling at Frankie's natural musical gifts, to be able to pick out a tune on a piano or guitar, with no training, and her sweet, simple voice.

But then the door to a study situated at the back of the parlor flung open. Chalmer yelled, *Just go!* And a young woman's voice drifted out, strained and pleading, *Please, you have to listen; you promised—* And then Chalmer stepped out, followed by Pearl Riley, the quiet spinster who comes faithfully to the Woman's Club and Kinship Presbyterian Church.

Frankie stopped playing and stared, wide-eyed, at Pearl.

Pearl gazed around the room and turned bright red. Then she rushed out.

Chalmer had muttered, *I'll take care of this. Sophia, get them to the stage, all right?*

Of course, dear, she'd replied, her voice like ice crackling in the hot room. He'd already left before she could finish. Sophia snapped at Dorit that she should go find Sophia's blue hat and bring it to the stage, then come back to the house to keep an eye on MayBelle. *We wouldn't want her to get hurt at the archery area or shooting range,* she'd said, her tone saying the opposite.

By the time Beulah, Frankie, and Sophia got to the side of the stage, Pearl was standing there, too, her face tear-streaked. And Chalmer was on the other side of the stage, preparing to make his grand entrance.

Now Pearl stares down at the baby in Nana's arms. "What are you doing? Why do you have her?—" She reaches as if to grab the baby, but Nana holds the little infant protectively. "Just keeping an eye on her for Suda. Why don't you sit a spell, dear, cool off—"

"No—no—I saw Suda and her brood here earlier, in the crowd. They can't be here—"

"Why not, honey?" Beulah asks. "It's a lovely July Fourth; everyone's celebrating—"

"Where is Suda?" Pearl looks around wildly.

Just then, a large beefy man in bibbed overalls tromps up to Suda, who is still delighting in being terrible at darts, even with Jolene now giving her pointers. He grabs Suda by the elbow, says something to her, and drags her over toward Nana and Beulah. The Owens girls reluctantly follow, while the young ones in Beulah and Nana's charge stare after them, startled.

Prudence, the oldest Owens girl, takes her baby brother from Beulah, while Suda collects the other infant from Nana.

"What are you doing here?" Pearl hisses at Suda.

"I just . . . we just . . . wanted to have fun." She sniffles, trying not to cry.

"Fun," the man says, as if spitting a curse word. Otto Sr., Beulah guesses. He's red-faced, sweaty, angry. And shaking. "Who has time for fun and games? And why'd I waste my time coming here? And after all the money I've spent at the damned lumber mill, that high-'n'-mighty Chalmer Fitzpatrick thinks he's too good to take me on full-time." He glares at Pearl. "And you. Putting fool notions in my woman's head, that high-'n'-mighty Chalmer Fitzpatrick is lookin' to hire good laborers."

"Please," Pearl says, glancing around nervously. "Just—just go."

"Well, he looked down his skinny nose at me, sneering after I said where we live. Asked why'd he want to hire someone who ain't got a way to get to work? Said I owe him still for some of the lumber I've bought—true enough, but I said I could work it off. And he told me I oughta just work the mines; I'd get further ahead on scrip than on my own sorry business—"

Suda gasps. "No—no. We're doing fine, you can make more rockers and porch swings, the older girls can help you, and I can, I can find a way to help more women—"

"Please. I'm sorry Mr. Fitzpatrick was unkind," Pearl says. "He's just nervous today, with his park opening and all—" She stops, tearing up.

Otto glares at Pearl. "Men like him, acting like they're better than everyone else, don't get nervous. They're just jackasses. Someone oughta put him in his place."

With that, Otto and Suda and their brood wander away. When they've disappeared from view, Beulah turns back to Pearl, wanting to ask if she is truly all right, if she needs someone to talk with. But Pearl has disappeared, too.

Nana shakes her head. "No tea for some things. Though I hope Suda is drinking the concoction I brewed for her."

"She looks stronger today—" Beulah starts.

Jolene is by her side, tugging on her sleeve, pointing off in the direction Pearl had disappeared. "Mamaw, that lady—she's the one me 'n' Frankie saw in the woods. Near the Owens cabin."

Though today Pearl is wearing a pink-flowered dress, not the *Alice in Wonderland* blue MayBelle had described, Lily's words come back to Beulah: *MayBelle said, "There's a girl floating facedown in Chalmer's pond."*

Beulah shudders. It's hard to imagine on a day as bright and hot and blue as this that MayBelle's words could come true. Yet a chill drapes over Beulah like a fine, ensnaring net.

She stands up. "Come on. We need to find Lily, tell her about all this."

CHAPTER 8

LILY

Wednesday, July 4, 1928
8:00 p.m.

Lily sits alone on her front porch, staring out at orange and pink fingers of dusk tucking away the last of the harsh bright sharpness of day. She watches as a nearly full moon rises in the clear sky, rendering the cover of night a velvety deep violet. On a small table, the glowing orb of a coal-oil lantern is a tiny, flickering counterpoint to the moonlight. Fireflies twinkle over the mowed field aproning her cabin, earthbound cousins of the heavenly scattering of stars.

The heavy scents of grass and earth and full-bloomed brashness of trees and shrubs and forest flowers are tamped by the cooling touch of nightfall, the smell of a coming summer thunderstorm. The earth sighs and softens into its sleep, the hush a respite after the insistent cries and caws of the day. But then the sounds of night rise—an owl hooting, crickets and katydids taking over from daytime cicadas the nighttime shift of summer song. Into the nighttime medley, Lily adds her own sounds: a long weary sigh, the squeak of the runners of the rocker like a fiddle bow on the porch slats as she moves to and fro.

There is comfort in this rhythmic rocking, in the melding of night sounds and her sounds, in the relieving coolness of a moonlit night.

And yet Lily is outraged by what she's learned moments ago. She makes herself backtrack, play out the timeline leading up to the shocking discovery.

A scant hour ago, she had finally gotten Chalmer to step aside from his mingling with park patrons and asked him if he knew why Hiram had attacked him onstage, if he knew what Hiram meant by hollering, *I won't let you hurt her!* No, Chalmer had claimed, he didn't.

Then Lily had tracked down Mama sitting on the edge of the dock, keeping a careful eye on the girls, Frankie whooping and giggling over catching a bluegill on her line, yet unsure what to do with the wriggling fish until Jolene patiently and expertly showed her how to hold the line a few inches above the fish's mouth, grab the fish with her other hand, and then carefully twist the hook out so as to throw the fish back.

Mama filled Lily in on an encounter with Pearl Riley in the Fitzpatricks' parlor before the dedication ceremony, and then later in the games area with Pearl and a wet nurse, Suda Owens. Told her about Otto Owens resenting Chalmer for not hiring him on at the lumber mill.

But, as Lily watched her daughter expertly show Frankie the delicacies of fishing, Lily impatiently wondered what any of this had to do with Hiram's outburst—unless Hiram was sweet on Pearl and Pearl was having an affair with Chalmer. Foolish—but none of Lily's business. Unless Hiram had a more violent outburst, his shenanigans today were best forgotten, and Mama's news was nothing more than gossip. And the Owenses' straits seemed to have naught to do with anything other than their own worries.

It's been a long day, ready to head back home? Lily had asked. Her dismissiveness, too hard to disguise given her weariness, came through in her tone, and Mama looked a mite hurt.

Then Mama had demurred—the boys were all down at the shooting range with Tom and Jurgis and Marvena. Nana and Hildy were taking a walk and talking to some friends. Everyone was still having a good time—there was still the pig roast and baked beans and such for supper, and square dancing, and besides, Mama said, *I know everyone's going to want to stay late and visit after. If it's all right by you we can all spend another night at Marvena's.* She added something about helping Nana with jarring dried herbs the next morning.

Lily drove home by herself, deciding to savor rare quiet moments of being alone—even though that meant tending to the evening care of the animals by herself. But on the twists and turns of Kinship Road, her stomach twisted and turned, too—and not in response to the curves Mama always yelps about, fussing that Lily takes them too fast. Something felt off.

As she pulled down her gravel lane it struck her: Mama, usually direct in speech and gaze, had avoided looking her in the eyes ever since their chat yesterday about the quilt Mama is making from Roger's old clothes. Could Mama still feel sour about their spat yesterday morning? But Lily shook her head at this notion. It's not like Mama to hold a grudge.

Once Lily arrived at her farmhouse, she'd foregone going inside right away for a quick trip to the outhouse. Then she'd tended to the animals: making sure the chickens were secure in their henhouse for the night, feeding her mule, Daisy, checking on a litter of kittens just born to one of the farm cats—yes, all three pink noses were there, and the kittens snuggled up to their mama—and putting out kibble and fresh water for Sadie, her bloodhound, who was supposed to be her tracking dog and served as such but was spoiled like a pet.

Then she grabbed the big basket she keeps in the mudroom and did a quick check of the garden, pulling up a few green onions, plucking a few tomatoes, and picking a mess of green beans, all near-on past their peak freshness. They'd drop off and spoil if they weren't harvested right quick. Even a day away from the farm meant all the routine tasks added up.

Yet by the time she'd filled the big basket and found herself pausing to take in the night pulsing with lightning bugs and the chorus of crickets underscored by the lazy thrum of bullfrogs down by the creek that runs behind her property, Lily's sense of ease had returned.

She even hummed to herself as she put the produce by the kitchen pump sink. Then Lily headed upstairs for a sponge bath at the bathroom's pump sink, changed into house slippers and a lighter dress. It felt good to shake off the grime and weariness of the day, to look forward to a light meal of leftover corn pone, one of those tomatoes sliced and salted and peppered. But as she headed down the hall, she caught a whiff of a coming rainstorm sifting in through the open upstairs windows. So she'd turned around, closed the windows in her and the children's bedrooms, and gone last into Mama's bedroom.

As she closed the window, just over on Mama's sewing machine she saw the envelope—a letter addressed to Beulah McArthur, General Delivery, Kinship, Ohio. From a Charlotte Chambeau, Sainte-Menehould, France.

Even as a voice whispered at the back of her mind: *This isn't your business; ask Mama about it later,* Lily watched her hand, as if compelled by some force competing with her inner voice, reach for the envelope. Quivering, while picking it up, and then in pulling out the letter.

Her eyes had teared as they wildly darted over the single page, taking in the truth.

Now, sitting on the porch, supper forgotten, her eyes are scratchy and dry. She's read the letter over and over by the light of the portable coal-oil lamp on the table next to the swing.

She's tempted to go back upstairs. Surely there are more letters. Hadn't there been a stack of papers on the sewing machine, an uncharacteristic mess for Mama? Now tucked away, probably in the notions table. Yet Lily stares across the yard, unable to move.

And besides, this singular letter spells out the truth: Her brother had a daughter. Esmé. And the girl—her niece—is coming here to Kinship, tomorrow. There's no need for further snooping. Lily must go to Mama, confront her. Why has she not told her about this before? For God's sake, with all the time they spend together, there've been opportunities aplenty.

Lily refolds the damning letter, tucks it in her pocket, douses the coal-oil lamp's light by turning down the wick. Just as she rises from the porch swing, Sadie trots up the steps. The bloodhound nudges Lily's hand.

"What's wrong, girl?" Lily asks. "Someone betrayed you, too?"

Lily's eyes prickle. Sadie whines, as if in sympathy—but of course, the dog is just lonely.

Lily sits back down on the porch swing, scritches the soft silky spot between the dog's floppy ears. Sadie jumps up next to her, the heft of the bloodhound setting the porch swing in motion, but Lily doesn't protest as she normally would. If Mama were here, she'd admonish Lily for spoiling the dog by letting her up on furniture. But God only knows what Lily would say to Mama if she were here. Yes, it's best that the storm of her emotions—shock, anger, betrayal—swirls within her while she's alone.

Sadie nudges forward, big forepaws and head on Lily's lap.

"Damn it, Sadie, I don't need comforting," Lily says, but there's no snap to the admonishment. Her eyes sting—oh, for pity's sake, now she's crying like a spoiled child herself. But she gives herself over to it, closing her eyes, just for a moment, just for a moment.

Lily startles awake, blinks, rubs her eyes. There's a crick in her neck, from falling asleep with her head dropped forward. She rolls her head, takes in the darkness. A few moments of shut-eye had turned into several hours. Clouds dart over the moon, which had been full two days ago, high in the ink-dark sky. Lily reckons it must be near on midnight, past eleven anyway. The air is cooler, lighter, released of its heavy humidity. She'd slept through the rainstorm. She briefly wonders if the storm had cleared out the park earlier than the stated closing time of ten in the evening.

She hadn't even felt the swing jolt when Sadie jumped down at some point during her nap. The hound stands at the top of the steps, alert. A figure moves toward them. But Sadie doesn't growl or yelp. Even in the scant light, Lily sees the friendly whipping of Sadie's tail.

Puncturing the scent of night air and lilacs and dark earth is another smell—tobacco. And another scent, distinct, comforting, unnameable, except it's—*Benjamin.*

Even with the hard day past and ending with shocking revelation, Lily's heart leaps. A smile widens her lips. By the time Benjamin's ground out his cigarette in the yard, come up the steps, greeted Sadie, and scratched her head, Lily's relit the coal-oil lantern.

She stands; he approaches her. As the space between them tightens, thoughts of other people completely vanish as Lily's heart thumps and her breath quickens with the realization that this is the first time that she and Benjamin have been alone—not just on a walk together, where passersby can spot them, or chatting in the vestibule of church—but truly alone together.

He's waiting—the next movement is up to her.

Lily puts her arms around him, leans into his chest, relishing his arms tightening around her waist. Tension seeps from her shoulders, her back; even the crick in her neck dissolves.

She tilts her head so that she looks up at him. Their lips brush, and her breath quickens at the feel, at the taste, of him. Their kiss deepens; their embrace tightens. Lily rues the layers of cloth between them, wishes they would just dissolve, that they could feel skin on skin.

As their kiss tapers off, Benjamin gazes down at her. She cannot look away from the heat and intensity of his eyes. He puts his hand gently to the back of her neck, and she nestles her head against his chest, and they sway like this in a slow private dance, like she'd agreed to dance with him after all instead of brushing him off at the park. But it's better, swaying here, with no one else around and only the slowed sounds of crickets and an intermittent owl hoot.

"I couldn't stop thinking about you, how we left it," Benjamin says. "I should have seen you were busy, working, and not pushed about the dance tonight. I went back to the park, hoping you'd still be there, but your mama and the others said you'd headed home. So I did, too—but I still couldn't stop thinking about you, and so I came here, I guess to apologize, to—"

He traces his finger, gently, over her cheek.

Oh, to claim the sweetness of the night for herself and for Benjamin. A flash of how the next morning could be—waking up in the still cool morning, on the warm tousled sheets of her bed, the scent of him enveloping her—stirs Lily's imagination.

You don't have to apologize. I shouldn't have snapped at you. And you don't have to go tonight. If you don't want to . . .

That's what Lily wants to say, the words that come to her mind, and almost to her lips.

Instead, she bursts out, "Did you know? About Roger's daughter? Did Mama tell you?"

Benjamin pulls back, a frown flexing his brow.

Lily suddenly wishes she could retract the questions. Why is she ruining this moment with Benjamin?

Yet she presses on, propelled by some impulse that she can't name or understand. She grabs the letter from her pocket, thrusts it at him. "I found this. In Mama's room, after I got home. I wasn't snooping, I was just closing up the windows, the coming rain, and I found this—"

Benjamin has taken the letter but isn't reading it. Instead, he guides her as she babbles on her way back to the porch swing, as if he's helping someone who has just had a great shock. And, she supposes, she has. Tears well again.

After she sits back down, Benjamin joins her on the porch swing. Their bodies are no longer touching. He reads the letter. In the lamplight, she sees his hands are shaking. Because he's as shocked as she was?

But then he looks over at her, and she sees no surprise in his eyes. His hands shook simply at the notion of her having learned the truth in this way. Suddenly the gap of a few inches feels like a great gulf.

"I wish Beulah had told you," Benjamin says.

For a swift moment, Lily is confused—and then she realizes he is of course referring to Mama by her name. It is just odd, hearing him refer to Mama by her given name, not as Mrs. McArthur, and the familiarity, the intimacy, of using her mama's name like that strikes at Lily's heart. It tells her they've been having conversations that she is not aware of.

"You knew?"

"Not from Beulah," Benjamin says. "From Chalmer. He came to me several months ago, asking for advice. Your mama wanted Chalmer's help in getting everything in order for Esmé to immigrate. But Chalmer ran into roadblocks, asked me if I had any contacts who could help him sort things out—and I did. I wanted to convince her to tell you, but Chalmer thought it would be best to leave that up to Beulah, so she is not aware I know about Roger's daughter. Anyway, Chalmer didn't want your mama to know I was helping him."

"Why not?"

"Well, that's Chalmer. He wants to be the hero of every story," Benjamin says. He gives an abrupt, bitter laugh, cryptically adds, "He was like that on the front, too."

Frustration simmers up in Lily, quickly boils into a sudden, fierce anger. "Daniel kept things from me. Things he thought I could not handle. He protected me because he thought that I was not strong. Never gave me the chance to show him otherwise—"

Suddenly Benjamin turns, twists, kisses her—but lightly. On the forehead. Almost brotherly. "No, Lily," he says. "He never thought you were weak. He did, though, worry that you expected too much of others. Too much perfection."

Lily pulls back, recoiling, suddenly hurting. She hears the criticism in Benjamin's voice, Daniel's criticism echoing from the past into this moment.

"So Mama thought I saw Roger as perfect, that I would reject his daughter—"

"Your niece, Lily," Benjamin says.

"Yes, niece. I know that, Benjamin. I can do the calculations of family bloodlines, dammit." Even in the dim light she can see a flash of hurt cross his face. But she presses on. "What of Hildy? She needs to be told. My God—did you, did Daniel, know that Roger had . . ."

Benjamin grabs her hands, not harshly, but firmly. "I barely knew Roger and Daniel and Chalmer at that point in the war, Lily. Chalmer was their ammo man. I was an assistant gunner for someone else. But I was aware that Chalmer was badly hurt. Roger tried to get him to the medic, and Daniel came over to our squad for a bit. They were gone a long time—turned out, Roger and Chalmer got separated from our platoon, and spent it at the Chambeaus' farm. Mind you, I didn't know any of this until Chalmer told me a few months ago. And I don't think Daniel ever knew. After—after Roger died, and I became Daniel's assistant gunner, he only talked about what a good man Roger had been. How he looked up to him. I think if he'd known, he'd still have looked up to Roger, but I think he'd have also told me about Roger and his daughter. He'd have certainly told you once he got home."

Lily puts her head down to her hands. Would Daniel have told her? She'd learned of secrets from his past after he died, secrets she was sure he'd have never told her. Benjamin slowly rubs her shoulders.

Ah. At his touch, her anger and confusion recede. Perhaps the night is not lost for them.

Another wave of questions rises within her. Why hadn't Mama told her? How long had Mama known? She thinks again of the other letters upstairs, but no, it would be better to ask Mama directly, get the truth out of her before Esmé arrives—good Lord, tomorrow afternoon.

But that's tomorrow. She and Benjamin could still have the night to themselves.

Suddenly Benjamin pulls his hand away. Sadie howls. Lily sits up, alert.

Another figure is approaching. She'd been so lost in thought, in the conversation, she hadn't even heard the automobile pull down her lane.

As a man comes to the top of the steps, Lily hushes Sadie. She recognizes the man, though she can't quite place his name, as a farmer who lives just down the road, a half mile or so from Chalmer's place.

"I've been sent for you, Sheriff Lily." The man's voice quivers.

Lily's heart flips—*oh God*. Had something happened to one of the children? To Mama?

"What's happened?

"There's been a death. Maybe murder. Over at the new park. At Chalmer's place."

CHAPTER 9

※

BEULAH

Thursday, July 5, 1928
12:30 a.m.

Beulah sits on the front porch of Hildy's cabin, rocking to and fro on the porch swing, sturdy and strong, the signature handiwork of Otto Owens. Theirs is just like it, painted with the same blue milk paint. So many porch swings like this on so many porches, and yet each one seems so personal, so intimate. Porch swings meant to last a lifetime and into the next generation and the ones after that. Several lifetimes of contemplation and serious conversations.

Too bad about Chalmer refusing to take Otto on for a steady job that would surely give him better pay and yet leave him some time for woodcrafting.

Maybe she should say something to Chalmer—but then Beulah pushes the notion aside for now. She has enough to contend with here, with her own brood.

Beulah's rested here for quite a spell, after insisting Marvena and Jurgis drop her off. A rainstorm had come through a half hour or so before the park closed up at ten o'clock.

You sure you'll be all right? Marvena had queried.

Don't you worry, Nana admonished, giving Beulah a scant sideways look. Nana knew what Beulah must do.

I'll have Tom bring me up, or else I'll spend the night here, Beulah said. Her voice had wobbled on that assertion. After she tells Hildy the truth, Hildy and Tom might not be so readily inclined to proffer favors. Or even speak to her.

Beulah brushes away sudden tears at the thought. As much as she's worried about how Lily will react to the news of Esmé, Beulah realizes she's worried even more about Hildy's reaction. Beulah had long ago embraced Hildy as a future daughter-in-law. Though that possibility died along with Roger, Beulah still embraces Hildy as if she's kin, and knows Lily does, too. Likewise Tom, and his sister, Marvena, and all of Marvena's family—Nana, Jurgis, Alistair, Frankie. They've all become close, and Beulah doesn't want a falling-out among them.

If there is a rift, Beulah rebukes herself, it won't be Esmé's fault. It will be her own, for not telling the truth about the child as soon as she knew.

Hildy's made her home—part of her recompense as schoolmarm—a place of pride. Moonlight, now bright and clear since the rain has passed, shines down on an apron of violet-hued phlox covering the small yard rising from the edge of the runty footpath that leads to the Rossville schoolhouse, where Hildy teaches from mid-September to mid-May.

Beulah inhales deeply, taking in the lingering scent of rain, and then sighs. Hildy has made more than a cheery home here. She's made a full, lovely life. And Beulah's about to lob a grenade right into the middle of it.

But maybe Hildy suspects something? She'd been so quiet at the park, even avoiding her. Had Chalmer told her?

Headlights flash up by the road. An automobile door opens, shuts. Footsteps coming to the house. Hildy.

"Yoo-hoo," Beulah calls, as she lights a coal-oil lamp Hildy's left out on a small table near the porch swing. "It's me, Hildy."

Hildy looks surprised as she steps up on the porch. "Mama McArthur," she says. "We've all had quite a long day, and I thought you were staying with the children up at Marvena's? But you're welcome here, I have lemonade in the springhouse out back, and oatmeal cookies. . . ."

"Oh no, that's all right. I just—I need to talk with you." Beulah glances toward the road. "Tom and Alistair—"

"At Tom's house," Hildy says with a wan smile. Though Hildy and Tom are quite close and Beulah isn't so naive to think that Tom doesn't sometimes stay here, or Hildy at Tom's, the couple aren't married. Tom, a coal miner, lives in Wessex Mining Company housing with his son by his first wife, who'd died fourteen years before in childbirth. But the community won't accept a married woman as a schoolmarm, creating a conundrum for Hildy. Just as remarrying would further complicate Lily's role as sheriff, already tricky.

Hildy sits down next to Beulah. "If this is about how distant I've been lately—" Hildy starts bravely. And then she bursts out sobbing.

Beulah puts her arm around the young woman. Hildy's wracking sobs ease.

"Oh, my dear, what is so troubling you?" Beulah asks. It must be something dire—and she doesn't think it's word of Esmé getting to her before they can talk. Nana wouldn't turn such news into gossip, and she can't think of a reason Chalmer would have told Hildy. He's promised not to tell anyone just yet.

Hildy sits back up. She pulls a handkerchief from her skirt pocket and wipes her face. "I'm afraid you'll think ill of me, and I couldn't bear that."

Beulah's heart squeezes with guilt over carrying this secret for so long, and fear that Hildy will be the one who has cause to think ill. She pats Hildy's hand. "Honey, you know you can tell me anything."

Hildy's always had a tender heart, but the past few years have brought her enough troubles that she has toughened up a bit. Yet now, even in only moonlight, Beulah sees the dark circles hollowing out Hildy's eyes, sorrow tugging down her usually bright expression.

Hildy takes a deep breath. "You know I love Tom. And . . . and I think you're all right with that. Remember when you said, a few years back, that Roger would want me to go on living, be happy?"

Beulah swallows a sudden lump in her throat. Nods.

"Well, the only reason we haven't married at this point is that I don't want to give up teaching. Tom says it's ridiculous—the company won't let me go just because I'm married. But I'm not so sure. And even so, it would be seen as unfair by many of the families here, if Tom was earning company scrip, but I was also working."

Beulah nods again, understanding. Wessex Corporation, as with all aspects of Rossville, is in charge of the school. Add to that the fact that so many of women's decisions hinge on their status in regard to the men in their lives—whether fathers, brothers, husbands. Or, in Hildy's case, a lover.

"But here's the real issue. Even though we're not married, well. I was pregnant, Mama McArthur. At the beginning of this year. And then again this spring." Hildy's chin quivers. Beulah holds her breath. "I lost both children early on. No one knows except Tom, and Nana, who after the first loss tended to me."

Well, by rights Beulah should be shocked at Hildy's having been pregnant out of wedlock. But truth be told, she understands. Hildy and Tom are in love. The strictures of society, she's come to understand, rarely bind human nature from true passion. But Hildy also wants to teach. How cruel to have to choose. And how cruel to suffer these losses.

"I'm so sorry, Hildy," Beulah says.

Hildy looks relieved at Beulah's sympathy. "There's someone else who knows, besides Tom and Nana. After my second loss, I went to Dr. Twomey." A quivering smile teases Hildy's lips. "Nana said you talk a lot about him, that you think highly of him, and I should trust him, from what you've said. And I can see why. He's a kind man." The smile drops from Hildy's face, and another sob wrenches forth. "And—oh—it turns out that I cannot have children. He believes, from my symptoms, that I have bleeding cysts on my ovaries. He says it's a condition that some women have always had to deal with, but there are new studies about it. He said I have endometrial adenomas—that's the proper name for it."

"Oh, Hildy, I'm so sorry," Beulah says again.

"Tom says it's fine, I can be a mother to Alistair, and I love the boy, though I know I can't and shouldn't ever replace his mother, but I would have liked to have a child, and oh—"

Beulah wraps her arms around Hildy's shoulders. "This is hard. And Tom wants you more than anything. But this is hard."

They sit like this for a time, wrapped in the heavy hot stir of a bare breeze, the thick scent of hollyhocks, the occasional nighttime chirrup of katydids and crickets.

Hildy straightens up, wipes her eyes. "I'm— I'm sorry, here you are sitting in the dark—you must have come for some purpose."

Beulah stands up, walks to the porch rail, gazes over the phlox. A sudden rush of memory, of receiving the blunt telegram that came from the War Department about her boy, starts to overcome her, but she pushes it back for now. In spite of the lingering heat of the day, a thudding cold rushes over her as it had when she and Caleb read that telegram together, collapsing into each other in the doorway, barely able to make it to their sofa.

There is just no way to ease into shocking news.

Beulah turns, squares her shoulders, faces Hildy. "I'm so sorry to share this now, right after what you've just told me. But there hasn't been a good time to tell either you or Lily, not over these past few years, or recently—"

Hildy's hand flies to her mouth. "Oh God, Mama McArthur, are you all right? I thought Nana meant when she said you talk a lot about Dr. Twomey that you were sweet on him—"

Tears prick Beulah's eyes. "Oh, Hildy, I'm fine." She swallows, makes herself go on, though suddenly her fear echoes Hildy's—that the younger woman will think ill of her. "This is—this is about Roger."

And then she tells Hildy the truth: about Roger, about his wartime love affair, about Esmé, about corresponding with Esmé's grandmother Charlotte, about the need for Esmé to come here.

For a long moment, Beulah and Hildy regard each other, and in that moment Beulah knows that she will never forget the struck stillness of Hildy's face, how her expression went rock hard.

"Roger died before he could let you know, Hildy. Before he could let us know. Then one day, a letter came to me. A little over three years ago. From Charlotte, Esmé's grandmother. It arrived several months after my Caleb died. Charlotte explained the situation, that her daughter had passed away in childbirth, that Charlotte herself was not well. She included a letter that Roger had written to us that was found on Roger. Chalmer had gotten all the letters that Roger carried back to Charlotte. At first, I was disbelieving. I thought to talk with Daniel, since he'd served along with Roger, to see what he knew. But before I could find my courage, he died."

"And you never told Lily?" Hildy's voice is taut as a thread pulled through quilt pieces, as she puts the whole story together.

Beulah shakes her head. "There never seemed to be a right time. And I was afraid that Lily—"

"Would see Roger as less than perfect?"

Beulah swallows hard, blinks back tears, holds her breath as if this will hold back emotion. She nods.

"And that's why you haven't told me?"

Beulah nods again.

All these years, Beulah hasn't told Hildy, certain that she would be distraught by the truth that Roger had had a lover while in France, and a child.

How foolish.

Hildy might be surprised by Roger's choices. But her greater sense of betrayal is with Beulah withholding the truth. Assuming Hildy to be too weak to manage the truth when, really, Hildy—though quieter and seemingly more conventional than either Marvena or Lily—is just as strong as they are.

"But you've told Chalmer Fitzpatrick."

"I didn't know him well, except I did know that Roger looked up to him. Chalmer is a few years older, and had coached him in baseball." Beulah considers. Her boy had been terrible at the game, but Chalmer was always calm and encouraging. "I asked him directly. Charlotte mentioned Chalmer by name in her first letter. And he confirmed that all this was true. When— when he and a few others buried Roger in a graveyard near Charlotte and Minette, Chalmer brought them the news, and told them how to write to us here in Kinship—if they wanted."

Beulah suddenly chokes up, has to swallow hard to continue. "I've corresponded with both Charlotte, and my granddaughter, over the past three years. They have not asked for anything, but when Charlotte wrote to say she wasn't well at the beginning of this year, and that there were no relatives who could take in Esmé, I knew what I had to do. I enlisted Chalmer's help this past spring to complete paperwork for Esmé to immigrate here."

Beulah drops her head, thinking about all the telegrams and paperwork that had been required. She could not have navigated the process without Chalmer's help.

Suddenly the emotions Beulah has held at bay come rushing forth. The telegram from all those years ago comes back to her in the form of Caleb's shaky voice echoing in her memory: "*We regret to inform you that Roger McArthur died in battle in service to his country.*"

Before Beulah can stop them, sobs wrench out of her.

Then, in a swift graceful movement, Hildy rises from the porch swing and comes to Beulah's side, and wraps her arms around her.

"Come on, Mama McArthur," Hildy says. "I need to take in what you've told me. But now it's late, and you need some rest. You can have my bed, and I'll sleep on the sofa, and in the morning, we'll both feel better, and talk some more."

CHAPTER 10

⫷

ESMÉ

Thursday, July 5, 1928
1:10 a.m.

Esmé cannot sleep. She is itchy, on this straw bale, and too hot in the barn, even though it is the cool of night. What's more, the barn smells bad. It has not been cleaned out in a while for the mule and the two dairy cows.

Disgusting, these smells, not just the odor but that they indicate the people here don't care about their poor animals. And the way the older woman treats the poor dog, who sleeps under the porch, kicking at it, making it whimper. Esmé has watched through the slats in the barn.

She wishes the dog would escape. It's not tied up, like she is. After the man had wrestled her off the train and into his truck, she'd sat quietly. He hadn't said anything, and she couldn't read his expression under his wide-brimmed hat, pulled low. But she knew better than to try to jump out of the truck.

When they first got here, the man had pulled her into the barn and she'd again kicked and hit, afraid of what he might do. Well, he'd gotten angry and smacked her across the face and then shackled her ankle to a post in the barn. He still hadn't said anything.

Later, the man came back, this time with no hat, and he was friendlier. He brought food and told her he was sorry about how he'd treated her earlier, but she'd understand soon enough.

She'd wondered, briefly, if this was the family that Mémère had sent her to—but surely not. That mean old woman, kicking at the poor dog, couldn't be her *grandmère*, could she? Mémère had corresponded with her for years and told Esmé how nice she was from her letters, helped her read the letters. And Grandmère hadn't said anything about an uncle—just about an aunt. She had yet to meet her aunt.

Now Esmé opens her bag—the man had looked through it when they first got here and seemed to think there wasn't anything in it that would pose a threat—and pulls out the letter from her papa.

She'd been able to stretch far enough to reach a coal-oil lamp on a bench, and a pack of matches, and she'd waited this late, thinking surely no one would be up, to light the lamp so she could read further. She needs to feel that connection with her papa.

. . . Your mama was the first person we saw, coming out of the mist that morning, and she immediately saw that we needed help and she tended to us without asking any questions. Then your mama and mamaw let us stay for a month or so at the farm, while my friend recovered.

I suppose I should have left him at the farm, to heal, but at first I told myself I needed to watch out for him. Truth be told, your mama struck me as an angel. I found myself thinking that maybe I had to come halfway around the world and into this terrible, cruel fighting to find out what love really is. Love beyond friendship.

But it will be a long time before you understand what I mean. Right now, I want you to know that no matter how terrible or cruel the world around you seems, there are good people.

Suddenly the door creaks open. Esmé startles, tries to stuff the letter back into her bag, but it is too late. The man is here and he snatches the letter from her.

Oh, why had she been so foolish as to light the coal-oil lamp? The light in the barn must have drawn his attention. She'd thought everyone surely must be asleep. Esmé scoots back as far as she can from him, as if that will keep him from hitting her. She stares at him, her eyes begging him not to destroy the letter.

But he doesn't destroy it. He reads it, quickly, by the lamplight.

And he mutters her papa's name, twice, like it is being forcefully yanked out of him. "Roger, Roger—"

And then he carefully folds the letter and puts it back in her bag. And he says, "I am going to take you somewhere. Somewhere safer, all right? But you must promise me to stay there until I come for you. While I try to figure out what to do next."

Then he undoes the shackle and helps her stand up. He douses the lamp and takes her by the wrist and pulls her out of the barn.

She stumbles along behind him, twisting her wrist, unable to break free. She glances back, suddenly wishing she could rescue the dog and they could run away together.

Then she's stumbling along behind the man, and the house and barn fall out of sight, and he lets go of her wrist.

At first, Esmé stops in her tracks, stunned he's let go, thinking she will run.

But then she understands why he's let go. In the scant moonlight, she sees that the forest twists and grows around her, trees leaning in, brush around her ankles. If she tries to run, she will be snagged and fall.

Esmé walked in the Meuse-Argonne once with Mémère, just before leaving to come to the United States. She'd seen the splintered and charred remains of forest in some places, the thick growth remaining in other spots. It was important for her to see, to know the history, Mémère had said, to not forget.

This hilly forest is like that one. She would soon be hopelessly lost. Tears spring to her eyes. She must make a decision. Should she take her chances with running, with the hope she'd find someone to help her instead of getting completely lost, or worse? Or follow this man who for some reason, a day or so after kidnapping her—Esmé has lost track of time—has decided to free her from the barn and take her somewhere he says is better.

An owl hoots in the distance. The sound is strangely reassuring.

Esmé chooses to follow the man.

CHAPTER 11

LILY

Thursday, July 5, 1928
1:30 a.m.

Lily rows the canoe across Chalmer's large fishing pond. Under the bright eye of the nearly full moon, a woman floats facedown in shimmering, rippling water. Lily lets the canoe drift to a near stop, shines her flashlight on the figure. Blue dress. Dark hair fanning out.

Lily gives an involuntary shudder. Just as MayBelle had envisioned.

She looks over at Marvena, sitting on the bench seat behind her, holding a flashlight over the water. Between the light of the flashlight casting up and the moonlight casting down, Marvena's face is oddly lit, and yet Lily is sure she sees sorrow in her friend's eyes. Marvena had lost her older daughter several years ago, and her body had been found in Coal Creek, not far from Lily's farmhouse.

"What do you think the best way to do this—" Lily starts. At the same time, Marvena says, "Get alongside her, so I can grab her arm—"

Soon they manage to turn the woman over in the water.

"Pearl," Lily says softly. Then: "Can you hold her, and I'll row us in."

Marvena grunts her assent, leans to the side, but not so far as to tip them, and holds tight to Pearl's arm.

As Lily rows back to the dock, she shudders, thinking how just hours before, not even a full day, their daughters Jolene and Frankie had been in one of the canoes, maybe this one, fishing in the bright day. How Mama had gossiped about Pearl running after Chalmer as he came out of his study, how Sophia had barely reacted. How Mama had later seen Pearl talking with a wet nurse—Lily can't quite bring forth the name.

She thinks how quickly life can turn from light to dark, thinks how hurt need only find us once to then echo through the rest of our lives. Lily wishes she could comfort Marvena. Wishes for a different outcome for poor Pearl. Wishes Mama had told the truth about Roger and Esmé a long time ago.

On the dock, Benjamin stands, holding a coal-oil lamp. Lily keeps her gaze on his silhouette, thankful for his presence.

An hour or so ago, the Fitzpatricks' neighbor had explained that Chalmer had come to his house with the news that something had startled Sophia from her sleep and when she'd gone outside to investigate she'd found a baby on their doorstep. She'd heard movement, down by the fishing pond, and when she went to check she saw a form floating in the pond and another figure running away. After she alerted Chalmer, he'd driven to the neighbor's, told him to fetch Lily.

Odd, that Chalmer didn't come himself, Lily'd thought, but she'd sent Benjamin to fetch Marvena—not the most conveniently located deputy, but the one she most trusted—and she'd gone on to the Fitzpatricks', approaching the house with caution.

There she'd found Chalmer out on the front porch, armed with a shotgun, on the watch. Multiple coal-oil lamps burned on the front porch and inside windows. He'd told her that he'd instructed Sophia to barricade herself upstairs in their bedroom, arming her with a pistol. Then he'd gone to fetch his mamaw from her cabin, just in case whoever Sophia saw running tried to take refuge there. He'd secured MayBelle upstairs with Sophia, then quickly gone to the neighbor to send for Lily's help, and finally he'd taken up watch on his front porch.

His words and his voice were calm. But there was something wild, loosed from deep within, in Chalmer's gaze. The same ravaged look

Lily had seen in Hiram's eyes much earlier in the day, the look she'd seen upon occasion in Daniel's eyes.

By the time Chalmer had finished this explanation, Lily decided to wait for Benjamin to return with Marvena. When they came back, more quickly than Lily'd expected, so Benjamin must have driven at breakneck speed around the hilly curves, Nana was in tow.

Heard tell a baby's been found, Nana said. *Thought the child might need some tending.*

Marvena had shrugged and shaken her head, as if to say, *Can't tell Nana what to do.*

Nana had stayed at the house with the Fitzpatricks and the baby, while Lily, Marvena, and Benjamin came down to the dock.

And now Benjamin ties the canoe to the side of the dock, securing it so it won't tip. Lily and Marvena lift Pearl's body into the canoe. With clothing soaked through, even a woman so slight as Pearl is heavy and difficult to move. Benjamin kneels on the edge of the dock and helps lift Pearl the rest of the way onto the dock.

For a long moment, sounds overlap. Their raspy breathing. The gentle splashing of water onto the dock. The distant sound of a hoot owl. The hushed, nudged whispers and rustles from the woods. A cacophony oddly counterposed to Pearl's silence.

"Shine your flashlights down on Pearl," Lily requests.

Marvena and Benjamin comply. Pearl's forehead is deeply bashed, on the left. Her eyes are still open, glassy. Though tempted to pass her hand over Pearl's eyelids to shut them, Lily forces herself to study the injury, to look for clues.

"I reckon she could have fallen near the pond, hit her head on a rock, rolled in," Marvena says. "Mayhap running away after leaving the baby?"

"But according to Chalmer, Sophia saw another figure running away, after she'd already spotted a body—Pearl—in the pond." Lily shakes her head. "I don't recollect any rocks this big in the land around the pond. Chalmer would have made sure there were no big rocks for visitors to trip over. We'll look just in case, but—wait. One of you bring your light closer, focus on her neck."

Lily'd thought she saw a dark hue imprinted around Pearl's neck. As Benjamin retrains his flashlight on Pearl, Lily gently sweeps aside the young woman's dark hair. Sure enough, there's dark bruising around Pearl's neck. That had to be a human's doing.

And in the whites of Pearl's glassy eyes are red flecks, as if tiny blood vessels had burst. Lily makes a mental note to ask the undertaker and Dr. Twomey about this. Hopefully Dr. Twomey will help her, though he hasn't signed on officially as county coroner—a fact that irritates Lily. He's the only doctor in the county seat, for pity's sake, and he'd brushed aside her perfectly polite inquiry as if he is just too good for such work. Using some uppity excuse about coming to Kinship to be semi-retired.

So now Lily—in case Dr. Twomey brushes her aside again—does her best to think like a coroner might. The bruises on Pearl's neck imply someone choked her. Even if Pearl had fallen, bashed her head, and rolled into the pond, those markings had to come from someone else.

Such a deliberate way to kill someone. It's not an in-the-heat-of-the-moment murder, like a shooting or a stabbing could be. And the method suggests that poor Pearl trusted whoever had killed her, allowing him to get close to her.

It would also not be a quick death. The awful moments of gasping for air, not finding it, wanting to inhale, to breathe, more desperately than anything you'd ever wanted . . .

Oh God. The memory rushes over Lily: being caught under the water near the Kinship Tree, desperately wanting to gasp for air, knowing that her mouth and lungs would fill with water, that she would only make it worse for herself. But Roger had pulled her free.

Lily pulls in a deep, cleansing breath, admonishes herself to focus.

She again regards the bash on Pearl's forehead. Had the bash come before, or after, she was choked? The wound was no longer freshly bleeding. Perhaps the bruises are from earlier, not the actual cause of death. It's possible Pearl was bashed in the head, knocked unconscious, then dragged into the pond and left to drown.

Lily lifts Pearl's hand—already Pearl's body is stiffening—and looks at the fingertips, prune wrinkled. She's been in the water for several hours. Lily calculates. It's been well over an hour since the neighbor came to her house, and it had to take him a good half hour, maybe forty minutes, to arrive.

Lily looks up at Marvena. "What time did the park close?"

"Ten," Marvena says. "But the rain came through, scattered most people, an hour or so afore that."

Lily switches her gaze to Benjamin. "Do you know what time it was when you came to my house?"

Benjamin clears his throat. "Half past midnight. Thereabouts."

"So later than I thought," Lily says thoughtfully. She's constructing a timeline, trying to hold the details in her mind. Itching to make notes. But first things first.

"Benjamin, I need you to help me get Pearl into the back of my automobile," Lily says. "Marvena, walk the perimeter of the pond. See if you—"

"Can find a rock or something to explain that bash in Pearl's head?" Marvena asks flatly. "I'm on it."

Twenty minutes later, Lily sits on the edge of a chair in the Fitzpatricks' parlor. Benjamin has joined Marvena in the search for any weapons, or items that could serve as weapons. The bodice of Lily's dress is still damp from dealing with Pearl. For the first time, she realizes she's still in a thin, sleeveless dress she ordinarily deems only suitable for around her house.

Sophia sits on a fancy sofa, staring down wide-eyed at the baby she holds, swaddled in a soft, clean blanket. She seems completely unaware of the others in the room; besides Lily, Chalmer, on the opposite side of the love seat, and Nana and MayBelle on side-by-side chairs.

MayBelle dozes in and out, moaning now and again. Each time she does, Nana pats her arm reassuringly and MayBelle settles.

Chalmer swallows, his Adam's apple bobbing up and down, as he nervously regards Lily. "Who—what—"

"Pearl Riley," Lily says.

Chalmer's eyes well, and his face goes slack and pale—and yet, Lily notes, he does not look surprised.

The baby fusses, twists. Lily notes a flash of pink on the baby's neck. A birthmark.

Sophia coos at the infant, "Well, that explains you, now doesn't it?" Then Sophia looks up at Lily. "I know Pearl and my husband had a— friendship. And she's been gone the last month or so. I guess she had the baby, decided to dump her on our porch step. Must have run the other way in the dark when she spotted someone—then tripped and fell. A shame, really."

A shame? The poor girl is dead! And from what Lily has observed, not from simply tripping and landing the wrong way.

MayBelle moans, sorrowful. Nana pats her hand.

"You'll need to get the cradle down from the attic for now. And I'll order some new furniture. We can put it in my room. . . ." Sophia hesitates as Chalmer stares at her. Perhaps, Lily thinks, Sophia suddenly realizes how callous her request is in this particular moment. But then Sophia frowns at her husband. "Well, what are you waiting for? If you're nervous about getting it down yourself, get Hiram to help you in the morning. Oh, and I want to hire Dorit as live-in help. I can't tend your mamaw and your baby at the same time."

Sophia looks at Lily. "Well, I assume this baby is Chalmer's. Isn't that the way unwed mothers do—leave the baby at the doorstep of the father? Too bad she tripped and fell and drowned in that fishing pond. I never wanted Chalmer to add a pond—certainly not one so close to our house."

As Sophia returns her gaze to the baby, her expression softens. Yet Lily suddenly wants to snarl at Sophia, *What has happened to you?* Sophia has been so mousy all these years, and in encounters with her at the Woman's Club, Lily had wished Sophia would find some kind of spine and stop playing the lonely outsider. But now Sophia is going too far. A young woman is dead, and even if the baby is Chalmer and Pearl's, what is the point of making a display of harshness?

Lily clears her throat. "Your neighbor summarized events for me, but I want to hear what happened, from your point of view." Neither Chalmer nor Sophia says anything. "Sophia," Lily says harshly. "I need you to tell me what happened this morning, in the moments before you found this child on your porch."

"Oh." Sophia looks up at Lily. "I'm not sure what jolted me awake— Chalmer and I have separate rooms, you see," Sophia says primly, "so it wasn't him tossing and turning. I guess I was sleeping lightly, still keyed up from the day. I went outside to see what the noise source was—"

"About what time?"

Sophia looks perplexed. "Well, I didn't pause to check the clock on my side table. I guess around eleven thirty? A little before or after?"

Lily quickly calculates: The park closed at 10:00, though she surmises that many people would have left before that due to the rainstorm. Even those who lingered after the rain started would not likely have been at the fishing pond in the rain. Sophia discovered the baby, the floating body, and someone running away around 11:30. That allows for an hour window, hour and a half at most, for Pearl's murder, shortly after she'd left off the baby. Had someone followed her to the Fitzpatricks' house? Or simply been on the property anyway for the festivities?

"You weren't scared?" Lily turns her attention back to Sophia. "Nervous? Didn't want to wake up your husband if you thought you heard something odd?"

Sophia looks taken aback at the notion. "No—no, I wasn't scared. You hear all kinds of things, living in the middle of the country, you know that. Anyway, I thought if I wasn't going to sleep for a while, I might as well get some fresh air. And then I found this little baby, wrapped in this blanket, left in the woodbin."

"On the front porch?" Lily asks. Wasn't that where the neighbor had said the baby was reportedly left?

"No, by the side door."

"You went outside through the side door?" Lily asks.

"What does it matter which door I went out of?" Sophia says. "Yes, I went out the side door. And that's where I found the baby, and saw the body floating in the pond, and someone running away."

"You weren't frightened at seeing someone running away?"

"Could have been someone lingering overlong at the park—maybe fell asleep in the woods, at the games area, or in one of the old railcars that Hiram is converting to lodging—though I can't imagine anyone wanting to stay in one, and I don't like the idea of people spending the night on our property. Anyway, I figured it was a loiterer, who noted the body in the pond, too."

"At the same time you did?"

Sophia shrugs.

Lily looks at Chalmer. "It appears that Pearl didn't accidentally fall in and drown," she says. "She appears to have been strangled. Or attacked until unconscious and then left in the pond to drown."

"Oh God," Chalmer cries out.

Nana moans.

Lily looks back at Sophia, who does, at last, look appropriately horrified.

"You can see the pond clearly from the side door?" Lily asks.

"Check the view from the side door if you don't believe me," Sophia says. "I came back in with the baby, woke Chalmer, told him what I just told you. He took over from there."

Lily looks at Chalmer, who nods.

"Any idea of who might have wanted to kill Pearl?" Lily asks. Of course, the obvious guess as to the murderer would have to be either him or Sophia. But why send for Lily right away? If one of them killed Pearl—out of revenge or in a moment of emotion—why not wait, let her body stay out in the pond until the morning, let someone else discover her? Or why not move the poor woman's body to the woods or even take her to the river and dump her there?

Eventually, someone would wonder—what happened to Pearl Riley, the quiet old maid who lives in her deceased parents' house in Kinship?

And people might talk—how did a baby happen to show up at the Fitzpatrick household, right about the time Pearl disappeared from town? But they might assume Pearl had left the baby to be reared by the father and that she had taken off to start life over.

Of course, questions would later arise about her abandoning her house and its contents. But eventually, if Pearl didn't pay the property taxes and couldn't be located, her property would become the county's and be auctioned off. And once that was done, soon enough Pearl would fade from memory, and eventually the child would be accepted as belonging to Chalmer and Sophia.

"No, no," Chalmer is saying. He shakes his head, wide-eyed. Still in shock. "I had no idea she is—she was . . ." His voice trails off.

"Pregnant?" Sophia asks, a crisp snap to the word.

"She doesn't have the shape of someone recently pregnant," Lily muses. "It's hard to imagine how she kept a baby unnoticed in the middle of Kinship—"

"Amazing what women can do, when they have to," Sophia says matter-of-factly. "Take me. I reckon we'll just have to raise this child. She's Chalmer's, after all. And he's always wanted children. Blamed me that we couldn't have any. Sometimes that happens."

"You're all right with this?" Lily asks.

Sophia shrugs. "What choice do I have? I can't live on my own, and wouldn't want to. Any divorce settlement I'd get would be paltry." She smiles. "What choice do any of us women have?"

More than Sophia is implying—though of course there are strictures—but Lily and Hildy and Marvena have all challenged those limitations. Sophia, though, seems, well, not content, but at least willing to abide.

"One choice is that if Chalmer denies the child is his, the baby can be put in an orphanage."

A slight gasp escapes Sophia, apparently surprised by this possibility. But Chalmer shakes his head. "No. I do not deny the child. I'm— I'm just—we need to get some rest now, if that is all right? If you don't have any more questions?"

"Not for the moment," Lily says. She glances at Nana. "I reckon we should take our leave. Find Benjamin and Marvena."

Nana nods.

Lily stands, crosses to Nana, offers an arm to help her to her feet. "We'll exit through the side door." She cuts a glance at Sophia, but the woman is already back to staring down at the baby. Chalmer slumps forward, head in his hands, elbows on his knees. MayBelle's sleep has deepened to soft snoring—a slumber that is nevertheless peaceful. Now that her prediction has come true, perhaps she is simply wrung out of emotion.

Lily thinks, *What an odd tableau.*

Minutes later, Lily's thoughts have already shifted to a different aspect of the troubling night. She and Nana stand outside the side door—the door that less than forty-eight hours before, when Lily was here with MayBelle and trying to dispel her visions of a young woman drowned in the fishing pond, had burst open with Hiram running out and his sister, Dorit, following him.

They'd been quarreling. Lily casts her mind back, recaptures the moment: *Hiram, we need to talk about this!* Dorit had cried. And his shouted response: *I told you—leave me alone!*

It had, in the moment, seemed a nonsensical tiff. But now, as Lily stares down the path—just as Sophia had said, she can see the fishing pond glistening under the moonlight, the dock, the approximate area where Pearl had been floating—she has to wonder if there was a connection between the siblings' fight and the events that have since unfolded.

Nana tugs at Lily's arm.

"Lily," she whispers, "I've seen that baby before."

Lily stares down at the older woman.

"You notice the strawberry birthmark on the baby's neck?"

Lily nods.

"Well, me too. Same baby as at Suda Owens's place."

Lily gazes blankly at Nana.

"The wet nurse. Suda Owens. Me and your mama went there, day afore yesterday. I brought some herbs for tea to help build up Suda. She was nursing her own baby, and that little one. Your mama didn't tell you about this?"

Lily thinks back—earlier she'd remembered her conversation with Mama on the dock while Jolene and Frankie were fishing in that pond. Mama filling her in on the encounter with Pearl Riley in the Fitzpatricks' parlor before the dedication ceremony and then later in the games area with Pearl and a wet nurse. Suda Owens. And Mama told her about Otto Owens resenting Chalmer for not hiring him on at the lumber mill.

"She mentioned Suda earlier today," Lily says. "But no, she didn't say you all had been to the Owens place. Course, there's a lot Mama hasn't mentioned of late. Or even over the past several years."

"Well, you should talk to Suda," Nana says. "See if the baby she was wet-nursing isn't gone—I'm telling you, this is the same baby. Mayhap Pearl—poor woman, may she rest in peace—said something that can help you out."

Lily's lips curl in an amused smile. Seems like everyone wants to be her deputy, one way or another. But Nana is right.

"And the girls—they told us they saw a woman in the woods near the Owens place. I bet it was Pearl—"

Lily's smile switches to a frown. "You took the girls with you and Mama to the Owens place?"

"Well, yes. Two days ago, when you came over to talk with Marvena, and we all went on a herb- and berry-picking walk. Lily, they just helped the Owens girls with the garden. They all had a right nice visit—"

"Lily!" Marvena calls from beside the automobiles. Benjamin stands beside her.

Lily and Nana walk toward them—Lily itching to run, but Nana needs to amble along and Lily can't bring herself to trot off from the older woman. What if Nana trips in the dark?

Benjamin holds something. Marvena trains her flashlight on it: a man's work shirt, wrapped around an item. "We didn't find any big or jagged rocks that Pearl might have fallen onto," Marvena says. "But we did find this. Right by the edge of the pond. On a big flat rock, perfect for sitting on and fishing from. About a quarter of the way around the pond."

Benjamin unfurls the work shirt. In it is a big, heavy wrench. Under the light of Marvena's flashlight, Lily sees the blood on the edge of the wrench.

"This work shirt, the wrench, could be anyone's," Lily says. "There have been men working in and around these woods for weeks, leading up to the opening of the park."

Oh, the park in her dear brother's name—tainted by the blood and death of a young woman.

"There's paper folded up inside the pocket," Benjamin says. "We heard it crinkling, but we haven't pulled it out or looked at it. Thought that was best left for you."

Lily glances up, sees the deference and respect in Benjamin's eyes—he understands that he's on her turf. Even on this awful night, Lily's heart takes a moment to soften with gratitude.

She refocuses and pulls out the paper. Two simple pages:

> Dearest Pearl,
> I love you and think of you all the time.
> There must be a way we can be together.
> Please, can we just meet and figure out a way?
> [Then the second page:]
> You are ever in my heart and soul.
> I think of you with only fondness, and will abide by your wishes.
>
> > Yours,
> > Hiram

Cold denial rushes over Lily. No. Simply, no. Not Hiram.

But then after angrily rushing at Chalmer on the stage—*I won't let you hurt her!*—he'd briefly admitted to Lily his crush on Pearl. And Hiram has a history, as Lily'd recollected yesterday, of being a bit obsessive about his crushes.

Could he have found out about the baby, realized how serious the relationship really was between Chalmer and Pearl, taken his anger out on her? Lily had taken his gun. But he'd apparently found another weapon.

CHAPTER 12

BEULAH

Thursday, July 5, 1928
9:30 a.m.

Inside the Kinship train station, Beulah sits on one of the four benches—the one closest to the exit to the platform—legs crossed primly at her ankles, hands on top of her handbag. She wears her best Sunday-go-to-church dress—a new pale blue one that she'd made just for this day—and a crème-colored hat and matching gloves. And her sensible, but good, brown shoes, which she'd meant to polish this morning, but there hadn't been time.

After a quiet but cordial breakfast, Hildy had gently said she needed to talk with Tom and that Beulah must tell Lily about Esmé. Hildy had driven Beulah back to the farmhouse, but Lily wasn't there. Hildy had checked on the animals while Beulah had a quick washcloth bath, changed clothes, and repinned her hair into a neat bun. Hildy reported that the animals were fine, although Sadie the bloodhound wasn't on her line, so Lily must have been called away.

At the train station, just as Beulah was getting out of Hildy's automobile, Hildy put a gentle hand on her arm. *It will be fine,* Hildy'd said, kindness warming her eyes. And Beulah had squeezed Hildy's hand, grateful for the young woman's grace. She'd briefly wished Hildy would come in and wait with her for Esmé but then quickly realized that was expecting too much and at this tender moment it would be cruel to ask for Hildy to wait with her to greet Roger's daughter, especially after Hildy had just revealed she is unable to have children of her own.

Now Beulah is nervous and sweating. She wishes she could get up and pace around, though the red clapboard station is the smallest building in Kinship, with the possible exception of the Sears, Roebuck catalogue ordering office. Smaller, even, than the new ice-cream shop. At most, a third of the size of the grocery store. So there is very little pacing-around space, and besides, already Mr. Pennington, the stationmaster, is eyeing her curiously from behind the ticket counter.

Beulah realizes she's jiggling her right leg up and down. She stomps her foot so forcefully that the sound of her heel coming down on the polished hardwood floor echoes.

She's the only one in the waiting area. The next train—Esmé's train—isn't due in for another forty minutes.

Beulah catches her leg jiggling again, the heel of her shoe tapping on the floor. The metal clasp at the top of her pocketbook digs into the palms of her hands. Sweat trickles down her scalp, but she leaves on her hat, fearful that her bun will explode in a flurry of bobby pins, leaving her fine, sandy gray hair a straggly mess.

Mr. Pennington comes out from behind the counter. He stands before her, arms crossed. Apparently, her tapping has raised his ire.

"Is there something I can help you with, Mrs. McArthur? A ticket perhaps?" Mr. Pennington asks.

"What? No! Why would you think that?"

"Well, you are admirably dressed for church. And this is a Thursday." He glances around searchingly. "Though I don't see any bags."

Beulah clicks open her purse and pulls out the printed train schedule, folded many times, so it is soon going to rend in half. This morning, while getting dressed, she'd quickly gotten it out of her notions table drawer, along with a telegram confirming Esmé's travel schedule, and two photos. As she'd tucked these items into her purse, she'd noted that her bedroom window had been shut, whereas she'd left it open—no doubt Lily securing the house before last night's rain. But the letters, telegrams, photos, were all as she'd left them in the side table. A brief flash of worry had crossed her mind—the hours since Lily had come to her room to apologize for their squabble and tell her about MayBelle's vision had flown by in a blur. But of course she'd tucked everything away, before leaving with Lily and Jolene to go over to Marvena's on the afternoon of the third, hadn't she? Yes, she was sure she had.

Now Beulah points to a spot on the schedule. "I— I'm waiting for the ten-ten train from Columbus."

"Ah, someone special is coming in then, for a visit?"

Beulah ignores the question. "Is it still on time?"

Mr. Pennington points to the arrivals board.

Oh. Beulah hadn't noticed that earlier. She, herself, has never traveled on a train. But she quickly deciphers that yes, the train is listed as being on time.

Then he points to the clock. "It's not going to arrive for another thirty-five minutes."

"I can tell time, Mr. Pennington," Beulah says crisply. "I will wait here. Might you open the door, though? It is so warm."

"No. Too much dirt gets in, and that makes the evening cleanup harder." But he gives her an assessing look and takes pity. "I can open the window, though."

After he does so, the sounds of the town filter in. Mr. Pennington goes back to the ticket counter, and for a moment Beulah closes her eyes. She tries to hear the sounds as if this is her first time coming to Kinship. Tries to imagine how it would be to see the town, the countryside here, for the first time. To breathe in the scents.

But she can't imagine. She's lived here her whole life.

Beulah opens her eyes, then clicks open her purse. On impulse, when she'd grabbed the schedule and the confirming telegrams she'd also grabbed a photo of Esmé and Madame Blanchett, taken a few months ago, and two of the many letters she'd tucked away. Now she pulls out the more recent of the two letters she brought with her:

Dear Grandmère,

I am looking forward to meeting you and all the family at once in the town of Papa's home. The trip will be much exciting, and I will have stories. I hope I am not sickly on the big ship. Here is a photo of me and my chaperone. So you do not mistake us. Do I look like the other ones?

Love,

Esmé

Grandmère—Beulah had quickly understood that was French for "Grandmother." And it still sounded foreign and odd to her. Would she get used to hearing that when the others called her Mamaw?

Next, Beulah pulls out the photo, peers at it as she has so many times. There's a kindness of spirit to Esmé's eyes, and a slight hook at the top of her nose—attributes from Roger. A gentleness to her round face that must come from her dear, deceased mother. But also a steadfastness to her expression, a stubborn set to her jaw, that reminds Beulah of Lily. Yes, there's a lot of her Aunt Lily in Esmé, she can see.

Then Beulah looks at the other letter, from Charlotte Chambeau, Esme's maternal grandmother, written in English. Over time, Beulah had learned French terms from Charlotte. For example, Beulah had learned that the French term for "granddaughter" was *la petite fille.*

My dear Beulah,

I have entrusted Madame Blanchett for this trip to accompany Esmé. Madame is odd, I must warn you, but reliable, and our priest agrees she will do as a chaperone. Esmé will be fine in her company—I would just say please do not judge the French or our village by her, and do not feel you need to extend hospitality more than a few days if that. She is eager, I understand, to join with relatives in Saint Louis. And she has been well compensated.

I would wish that we could meet in this life, for my friend—I hope I may call you that after all of these years

of correspondence—I believe we would enjoy one another's
company, and I would love to meet your family—Esmé's family.
Esmé is all the family I have left, and so I am glad she will be at
last with her dear papa's family.
Roger was such a good young man, so I know all of you must
be good, too, and will welcome her warmly. Please pray for my
soul and let Esmé know once more that I love her very much.
I have told her that I will see her again—she does not know of
my illness, or its depth at least, or I fear she would not go on
this trip—and I will, but I hope it will be many years for her,
but a blink of time for me.
Enclosed please find Esmé's itinerary.

> *With gratitude,*
> *Charlotte*

At that, rereading, Beulah's eyes well. She had meant to write her back and say of course she could call her friend. Oh, Charlotte would fit well with Nana, too.

Beulah reviews the schedule—the departure on the SS *Île de France* from Marseille, the days on the ship—she'd paid for second cabin passage on the ship, the first cabin prices being too dear, even from the savings she'd inherited from her husband. She hoped the room and the food had been satisfactory. And what must it have been like, seeing Lady Liberty in the harbor, majestic and powerful, when they arrived on July 2? And then that night in the New York hotel that Chalmer had helped her arrange—along with all the paperwork for Esmé to come as an immigrant. Arriving very late in Columbus on the third at another hotel, spending the Fourth in Columbus. Hopefully Esmé's chaperone had taken her out to enjoy a meal and festivities in the big city. Esmé could tell her all about it, Beulah thinks. And finally, after one more night in Columbus, the rest of the journey on this morning's train to Kinship.

The breeze coming in the window seems to only stir and thicken the heat of the waiting area of the station, like a soup cooking down on the stove. Beulah puts away her letters, schedule and photo, tucking them alongside two carefully pressed and folded handkerchiefs, and her coin purse and tiny bottle of smelling salts.

People start to come into the waiting area. Beulah glances at the clock—soon, soon, Esmé's train will arrive. Beulah smiles, her heart surging.

Suddenly there's the screeching sound of the train pulling into the station.

Beulah stands, swipes at the wrinkles on her dress, smooths her hair.

She steps forward, past the people coming into the station, a few to await the next train out, a few, like her, in anticipation of greeting visitors. Loved ones.

Beulah walks against the current, out to the platform. At last, at last, she is going to meet Esmé.

Roger's daughter, she thinks.

My granddaughter.

Ma petite fille.

Fifteen minutes later, Beulah stands on the open-air platform all by herself, her heart thudding hard, as if it is trying to beat its way out of her chest. She clutches her purse so tightly that the clasp digs painfully into her hands. Heat roils over her—from the passenger train, from the sun—and she can barely pull in a full breath.

A porter emerges from one of the train cars, a black man in a sharp navy outfit with red trim and a matching hat. He's humming to himself, a low baritone, but stops and does a double take when he sees Beulah.

It's only then that she realizes she's sobbing. She must look a frightful mess.

"Ma'am? May I help you? Do you need your luggage—"

Beulah rushes to him. "No, no, I'm looking for a girl, nine years old, who should have gotten off the train—"

"Oh." The porter looks relieved. "Well, ma'am, there was a family with a girl about that age, got off among the first people." He smiles.

"She was excited about visiting her grandma, talking about a new park and ice-cream shop—"

"No, no, that wasn't her." Beulah had noted the family getting off among the first people to disembark and had even briefly smiled, wondering if Esmé and the child had chatted on the ride from Columbus.

But she's not smiling now. Beulah gasps, trying to hold back a sob. "She would have been with a chaperone, an older woman. Let me show you this—" Beulah opens her purse to get out the one photo of Esmé that she has, but her hands tremble so badly that she dumps the contents of her purse to the ground.

The porter immediately kneels to gather up her purse and items, just as the conductor steps out the door of the caboose, about to head up to the engine, but stops short when he sees the sobbing Beulah and the porter.

"Ma'am!" The conductor rushes over. "Is this man assailing you?"

Fear flashes over the porter's face as he looks from Beulah to the conductor, understanding clear in his young face that his fate rests in her word. In spite of being terrified that Esmé hasn't gotten off, Beulah feels a flash of anger on behalf of the porter. Two years before, Lily had had to deal with the white supremacist WKKK, the women's KKK. And her granddaughter, Jolene, whose father was half-Indian, half-white, has been taunted at school for being "mixed blood." Beulah'd seen her husband stand up to those who hated German immigrants. And she'd already worried that Esmé would be teased for being French.

"Oh for pity's sake," Beulah bursts out. "He's helping me. And I'd appreciate it if you would as well." She turns to the porter. "Please hand me that photo."

She takes the photo, shows it to the conductor. "He merely saw that I was upset, and that I'd dropped my purse in getting out this photo. I'm looking for this girl and woman. They should have arrived, gotten off with everyone else—"

The conductor doesn't even glance at the photo. "It's not my job to take note of everyone on the train. I'm sure they've gotten off—"

"They didn't," Beulah snaps.

"Well, that's not my problem," the conductor says.

He starts to brush past. Beulah grabs at his sleeve. He looks down at her hand with a frown. Beulah says, "Please, can't we check, just let me walk through—"

He pulls his arm away, gives her a stern look. "I can't let you on without a ticket. You don't have a ticket, do you?" He smirks. "And I don't think you have time to buy one before we pull out again—"

Beulah squares her shoulders. "Let me do a quick walk through. There is a child who should have gotten off here, with a chaperone, and they haven't. They could have simply fallen asleep. Or there could be something wrong—perhaps at the last station—"

Mr. Pennington, the stationmaster, comes out onto the platform. "What seems to be the problem, Mrs. McArthur?" His brow furrows. "Should I fetch the sheriff—"

"Now, there's no need for that," says the porter. "She hasn't done anything—except ask to walk through to look for—" He stops as the conductor gives him a stern look.

"A friend," Beulah says quickly. She knows how fast word spreads, and if Mr. Pennington tells his wife over his lunch break it will get back to Lily before she can talk with her about Esmé. "A friend, who I hope just fell asleep on the train."

"Oh, let her walk through," says Mr. Pennington. He looks at the conductor with a twinkle in his eye. "No need to upset the sheriff's mother."

The conductor holds his hands up. "All right, all right, though I'd be in my rights to keep her off. I don't think he has any jurisdiction here."

At that, Beulah smiles for just a moment. "She. My daughter is the sheriff."

The conductor looks shocked. A smile flashes on the porter's face, but his serious expression quickly reassembles as he opens a door on a train car for Beulah.

Beulah follows the porter from car to car, her heart sinking as he holds her elbow and helps her off the train and back down to the plat-form. She'd seen neither Esmé nor her chaperone.

A short time later, Beulah is in Dr. Twomey's office at the back of his residence. His sign had been turned to *Closed*—odd, but Beulah didn't give that more than a moment's thought as she banged on his door anyway.

He'd come to the door, first looking annoyed and weary. Darkness circled his hazel eyes, his sandy gray hair was askew, and his clothes—dress shirt, pants, suspenders, but no jacket or tie—were rumpled as if he'd just been sleeping in them. Yet he'd opened the door to Beulah, ushered her through to his parlor.

As she had the night before for Hildy, Beulah had explained every-thing about Roger, Esmé, the travel arrangements and chaperone, even how Lily still doesn't know about Esmé. Now Beulah perches on the edge of one of the sofas.

"I've been to the telegraph office—no word. The post office—no let-ter," Beulah says. She's sweaty and red-faced and overheated. Her heart is racing, palpitating. She's still clutching the top of her purse so hard that her knuckles are white. "Oh God, oh God, what could have hap-pened, what have I done?—"

Suddenly she's sobbing again. Dr. Twomey leaps from his chair and joins her on the sofa. "Mrs. McArthur, just breathe. Slowly. Count three in, and three out."

He pulls her purse from her hands, puts it on an end table. He mo-mentarily steps out of the parlor, then comes back with a glass of water.

Beulah tries to take it, but her hand shakes so hard that she can't.

Dr. Twomey says, firmly yet kindly, "Mrs. McArthur, you're over-heated. And I don't want you to pass out from heatstroke. Take a sip."

He sits next to her and helps her take a drink.

"Let's get you out of this hat, too," he says, gently removing it before she can stop him. He puts it on the side table, next to her purse.

As Beulah calms and cools down, she realizes that she can smell her own sweat. Her hair collapses from its updo, falling to her shoulders.

"Oh God, I'm sorry, I'm a mess—"

He smiles. "Well. As a doctor of thirty years, I can certainly say I've never seen any people who are a mess."

Despite herself and the situation, she laughs a little. She takes the glass of water from him. Her hands have settled enough that she can drink some more. And, she admits to herself, it feels good to take a moment to calm down. To breathe. To be soothed.

She drinks the rest of the water, then stares into the empty glass. "I need to find Lily. Get her help. I should have told her before, but a time never came that seemed suitable."

"I see."

She thinks she hears flat disappointment in his voice. But then he puts his finger to her chin, gently tilts her head back up. His kind hazel eyes reassure her.

"Well," he says, "it would have been better if you had talked with her before now, but I can understand why you put it off. Your daughter is a smart, fierce woman. Great attributes. Just like her mother. But she is also, well, a little scary."

A strangled half sob, half laugh wrenches out of Beulah.

"Now, I'm guessing Esmé and her chaperone just missed the connector in Columbus. It would make sense to telegraph there and inquire—"

Beulah nods. Of course. Why hadn't she thought of that, done that? She'd been too upset, that's why.

"And then I'm sure you'll find they're there, and I'll drive you up to Columbus," Dr. Twomey says. "And I've no doubt that once Lily meets Esmé, all will be well."

Beulah is not so sure, but she nods. Worries about Lily's reaction can wait. The most important thing now is to find Esmé.

CHAPTER 13

LILY

Thursday, July 5, 1928
9:30 a.m.

As she drives on the winding roads over to where Hiram lives, Lily focuses on both the twists and turns and the revelations she'd uncovered at Chalmer's.

Sadie, the hound, wedged between Lily and Marvena, yelps and slides into Lily's thigh as she takes a curve a mite too fast.

"You throw us in a ditch *again*," Marvena snaps, "and we ain't going to get to Hiram's to put Sadie's nose to work!"

"One tiny mishap," Lily says, "and you're not going to let me forget it." They'd ended up in a ditch—which Lily still blames on ice and snow—on a case this past winter.

"Well, we gonna talk about it?" Marvena asks.

"My driving skills are fine."

"Not that."

"All right. I'm finding it hard to believe that Hiram—"

Marvena heaves a sigh. "I don't mean we ought to talk about Hiram, leastways not right this minute, either. How are you *feeling*?"

"Like I want to find Pearl's killer," Lily says. "And I'd rather it not be Hiram. Not that we often get what we want."

"Lily, on top of everything else, you've learned about this niece of yours, Esmé, coming into Kinship—and all our lives—right about now. That Benjamin knew about Esmé, about your mama's plans, for weeks now. And your mama has known about Esmé for more than three years—since right before Daniel died."

Dammit, Lily thinks. Why had she fessed up everything she'd learned to Marvena? Because she was exhausted.

After leaving the Fitzpatricks, she'd sent Benjamin back home—asked him to rest up in case she needed him to help with her family later—and she and Marvena had taken Pearl's body to the funeral home. They'd awoken Dr. Twomey, who thankfully had returned several hours before from visiting his son in Columbus, and who examined Pearl's body and confirmed Lily's suspicion: Pearl had been choked to death—the neck bruising and blood spots in her eyes attested to that. Or at least she'd been choked or knocked out long enough to lose consciousness, so her killer could shove her into the pond so that drowning would finish her off.

Lily had wondered if it was possible that Pearl had been killed elsewhere, then her body brought to the pond to make it look like she'd drowned.

Possible, Dr. Twomey had allowed, but even going off only Pearl's physical condition, he'd place her death between 9:00 and 11:30 last night.

Lily and Marvena had then talked to the neighbors on either side of Pearl's modest home—no, they hadn't observed Pearl coming back from the park the night before. But then they hadn't observed her leaving, either. Nor had they heard any ruckus. Yes, that was her Model T—it had been her parents'—parked along the street. Pearl had inherited both house and automobile from them.

So, Lily reasoned, Pearl had either walked to the park or gotten a ride from someone else. But the neighbors had not observed Pearl getting into an automobile with anyone else. She must have walked to the park, not returned to her home.

Pearl had left her back door unlocked, and so Lily and Marvena had quickly and quietly walked through. The home was small, neat, tidy—no signs of struggle, nothing out of order, which fit with the neighbors saying they had heard no ruckus.

Lily had wanted to go straightaway to the Owenses, find out if Pearl had been there the night before and taken the baby. Or go to Hiram's . . .

Marvena had calmed her down: *If Hiram's guilty, he's already likely run, Lily. And if he ain't gonna run, he'll be there tomorrow. And we're more'n likely to get shot at either place, assuming we can find them in the dark, if'n we show up in the middle of the night.*

Another swath of rain came through, and by then it was nearly three in the morning. So they'd gone back to Lily's house and sat down in the parlor with cups of tea—Nana would be pleased—to talk over what happened.

And somewhere in the midst of all of that, Lily found herself telling Marvena the truth about Roger and Esmé.

Now Marvena adds, "And you and me both know how you are about people holding things back from you. Specially people you love. So, how are you?"

The question hangs heavy between them, making muggy air even more sodden.

The question is especially hard coming from Marvena. Before Marvena and Lily were friends, Marvena was friends with Daniel. And then they were, for a time, lovers, until Daniel and Lily met. Yes, Lily knows Daniel was physically true to her—but he kept secret from her such a large portion of his life. Not only Marvena but also that her first daughter—may she rest in peace—might have been his.

But—this secret Mama had kept from her, which Benjamin, too, had kept hidden for the past months. That hadn't been to protect her because they thought her fragile. That had been to protect *themselves* from her, or at least, from what they perceived as her expectations of perfection.

Lily pulls to a stop at the turnoff to the dirt lane that leads up to Hiram's place. This morning, they'd gone back into town and Lily got a warrant for Hiram's arrest and looked up where Hiram's mother's property is located. Sadie whines, gives Lily's hand a nudge. She pets the hound in the silky spot between her floppy long ears. And then she looks at Marvena.

Marvena stares at her, waiting, eyes wide.

"Truth be told, Marvena," Lily says, "I'm overwhelmed. What if Hiram has gotten away—or isn't Pearl's killer? What if we don't find out who is? And as for Roger having a lover in France, having a daughter—well, of course I'm going to welcome my niece."

How had Marvena just put it? *Esmé, coming into Kinship—and all our lives . . .*

Suddenly tears fill Lily's eyes from the humbling realization that she is so, so lucky to have a friend like Marvena. Something that three years ago she would not have foreseen.

"But I want Hildy—God, Hildy has to be told—to be all right. And as for Mama and Benjamin—well, hell. You and I ended up overcoming our differences, so I'm sure I will with them—" Lily sniffles. She quickly pulls a handkerchief from her pocket and puts it to her eyes. "Damned hound, shedding like crazy. I need you to get outta the automobile, Marvena."

"What? You're kicking me out 'cause I asked you how you're feeling?"

Lily chuckles, tucks her handkerchief away. "No, I gotta back the automobile up the lane, or the automobile will stall out, high hill like this."

The door creaks as Marvena opens it. "Sure—I'll walk up and holler at you to guide you. . . ." She pauses, gives Lily a wry grin, but with a little twist of sadness. "I bet you were a little pill testing your big brother every time you could."

Lily makes herself smile. "Sure was."

"I wanna talk to you, Sheriff."

Lily jumps at the harsh voice, turns, looks out the windshield. Then she does a double take at an old, scrawny man in overalls, standing on the other side of the road, sucking on a pipe. He looks as if he's materialized from the woods.

But then Lily notes a small shanty, set just a little ways back, on the other side of a narrow plank bridge over a thin creek, the bridge just wide enough for foot traffic or maybe a well-disciplined mule.

Lily gets out of her automobile, walks to the edge of the road, while Marvena keeps a watchful eye. "Yes, sir?" Lily says. She forces back a smile at the old man's expression, drawn up in outrage.

He pokes the stem of his pipe toward her automobile. "You talk to that boy. He's always racing down the hill in that truck of his, like he's gonna crash plumb into my house. Just did it t'other day."

Lily recollects rattled Hiram from yesterday afternoon at the dock, how he'd kept his eyes cast down. It's hard to imagine that Hiram is a man who'd race down the hill in his truck. On the other hand, he'd attacked Chalmer in plain view of a full audience at the park's dedication. And in the back seat of her truck is a shirt that might be his and a wrench that he might have used in Pearl's murder. The letter—addressed to Pearl and signed by Hiram—that she'd found in the shirt is carefully folded, put away in her tote.

Lily looks back at the old man and respectfully says, "I'll have a word."

That seems to be sufficient to soothe the old man's concerns. He nods, says "I'd be much obliged," sticks his pipe back in his mouth, and walks back across his tiny footbridge.

Lily turns toward Marvena. "Ready for this?"

Marvena nods.

After yet another dangerous switchback, they come at last to a narrow but flat spot. Lily cuts the engine and sets the parking brake. She gets out of the automobile.

Both women take a moment to catch their breath—Marvena from the trek and Lily from the tension of backing up the hill. Her heart is pounding so hard it feels as though it is up in her throat, and yet she is strangely calm, as if her pounding heart is merely a fluttering bird.

Then as Lily gets out of her automobile and pats her leg to let Sadie know she should come out, she says, "Ida, Hiram's mother, is a hothead." She retrieves her tote bag, containing the work shirt, wrench, and letter. "We will have to approach carefully—and be ready."

"You aren't afeared that Hiram'll run when he knows we're coming?" Marvena looks perplexed as she watches Lily leash Sadie, lest the hound run off after stray scents of squirrels or chipmunks. She's already got her nose to the ground, snuffling. The women and the dog start walking away from the automobile, up the rise.

Lily shakes her head. She wants to believe he's innocent of Pearl's murder, but wanting doesn't make it so, and if he's guilty he has to know Lily will be coming for him. And if he is, would he have tried to run from the county by now? Would either his mother or his sister try to cover for him or protect him?

The women walk the rest of the rise, their tread and the padding of Sadie's paws adding a soft undertone to the rising chittering of June bugs and crickets.

At last, a clearing and an old log-and-mortar cabin come into view. Parked under a wooden roof on stilts, built out of the side of the cabin, is an old black truck, with an open roofless carriage and a cracked windshield. No wonder, Lily thinks, Hiram careened fast down the curvy lane. The weight of the truck alone would send it pummeling down the side of the hill. And putting on the brakes too hard would burn them out.

Tricky.

Just like this visit.

Lily hollers, "Sheriff Ross, here." She hesitates, wondering if she should mention Marvena. Looks at Marvena, who gives a quick shake of her head. *Right. Good to have the element of surprise, if necessary.* "I just want to talk to Hiram." Lily's voice bounces off the cabin, reverberates.

The cabin remains quiet, a stillness quickening around it in the clearing. But smoke rises from the chimney. A breeze flutters a white curtain in the open window. The scent of breakfast—eggs, bacon—lingers in the air.

Marvena slides a questioning look at Lily, gestures with a swirling motion to ask, *Should I go round back?* Lily nods and hands Sadie's leash to Marvena. Then she hands over her tote with the shirt, wrench, and letter.

Marvena nods her understanding: *Look for Hiram in the outbuildings behind the cabin. Have Sadie sniff the shirt.* If the shirt is really Hiram's, Sadie will be able to track Hiram on the property, assuming Hiram's there.

The hound has quieted, as if she, too, knows this is the time for stealth. Marvena takes a slow, silent step back and disappears into the woods as if she'd never come along at all. Lily shakes her head in wonder—how is it that Marvena can do that?

Lily waits, counts a few beats, giving Marvena time to slide around to the back. Then, hand at the ready if she needs to grab her revolver, she steps forward. Her hands shake, so she tells herself to calm down. She has had plenty of encounters that feel like stepping along a knife's edge.

But not with someone like Hiram. Not a friend, so much, but someone from her community who—whatever he has or has not done—is fragile. Someone who needs protecting, or at least respite. Based on her brief encounters with both Ida and Dorit over the last few days, he's likely found neither protection nor respite with them. He's only yoked himself to family obligation. As has she—but she has love in return. Loyalty given is only valuable if loyalty is repaid.

Lily stops. The front door creaks open. A woman steps out. Dorit.

"Dorit, it's Lily Ross. I need to talk to Hiram—"

"He ain't here."

"You know where he is, then? I need to talk with him—"

Ida lurches out of the house, shotgun pulled, roughly pushing her daughter out of the way. Lily quickly ducks behind a wide oak tree.

"Get the hell offa my property, woman," Ida yells.

"I'm here as the law," Lily calls back over her shoulder. "To talk with Hiram."

"You ain't entitled, not without a warrant," Ida says. "I know my rights."

"I got a warrant."

"For what?"

"He's a murder suspect," Lily says.

The air goes stiff, silent. Lily can almost feel the pulse of the rising heat of day throbbing around her. She carefully peeks out to the side of the tree. Dorit and Ida are stock-still. Somewhere from a nearby tree a crow calls out.

"Mrs. Fitzpatrick, please lower your gun, let me come talk to Hiram—" Lily calls.

"Not here."

"All right, let me talk with you, then. If you can tell me what you might know of his whereabouts since last night, or now, it'd go easier on you and Dorit—"

"You're here for *him*, not us—"

"I can also haul you in as accessories. That means—"

"I know what that means. I ain't stupid."

A long silence. Lily wheels around from the tree, hand by her holstered revolver in case she needs it, but Ida has lowered the gun. And Dorit has disappeared from the porch.

Lily takes a few cautious steps forward. "Where's Dorit?"

"Went back inside, putting up green beans," Ida says. "That all right with you?"

"Sure," Lily says. So long as she's not warning Hiram.

"So, who'd he kill? Chalmer, after all? Haven't been that proud of my boy in years. Wish he'd shot that bastard dead, right there in front of everyone."

And then Hiram would have gone to prison for murder—maybe two if he really is guilty of killing Pearl. Chalmer would be dead. Witnesses would be traumatized and possibly others hurt, or worse. How could Ida hold so much hate that it makes her this callous to her own child, and to others?

Then Lily wonders—could Ida have put Hiram up to killing Chalmer? Failing that, had he killed Pearl, maybe out of jealousy? Or to hurt Chalmer?

"Would the land have then gone to you?"

"What?"

"My mama reminded me of the rift between your husband and Chalmer's father."

"No. The land would go to his wife—that snotty Sophia, I reckon. Else to that stuck-up brother of his, living up in Columbus."

"Since you hate Chalmer so much, why were you at the park yesterday?"

Ida frowns. "Thought you were here to interrogate my boy."

"I am," Lily says. "But until he shows himself"—or Marvena rousts him out of hiding—"I'm curious. Much as you hate Chalmer, why go to the park?"

Ida wipes the back of her hand across her nose. "Bad enough Chalmer's granddaddy took land that should've been split; now Chalmer's got my boy working at his lumberyard and park—and Sophia has Dorit cooking and cleaning, like there ain't plenty to do here. And they're behind on getting paid. So I went to get what's mine."

"You mean *theirs*. You went on the biggest possible day to demand *their* pay."

"I let 'em live here, don't I? Roof over their head, food on the table. They owe me."

Lily tilts her head, studying Ida's snarled-up, angry face. Then Lily takes in the log-and-mortar cabin, the lean-to, the chickens clucking in the distance, the scruffy expanse of cleared land that's so poor the stalks of tobacco are stunted and wilted. Well, it's true—Ida's living on the worst part of the Fitzpatrick property. But she could have sold it, probably even back to Chalmer, and moved on with her life.

Instead, Ida is more than willing to enjoy the money her children earn working for Chalmer and Sophia, even as she keeps stirring the old feud.

Disgust rises in Lily. There is no scent or sight to suggest that Ida has been drinking. Nothing to give Lily cause to look around the property with the hope of finding a reason to haul in Ida—and she can't take someone in for pure meanness.

"Thinking my place is not much, aren't you?"

"Thinking Hiram has had a hard row to hoe—"

"'Cause a' that war?" Ida shrugs. "Maybe. He's been squirrely ever since he came back from that war—course he always was too fussy. Sad all the time. Like it was a big awful thing. He and the other boys were over there, what, a few months? Not even a year?"

"That's about right," Lily says, "for the boys that came back."

"Oh, that's right—your brother didn't make it back. But now he has a whole park devoted to him—good old Chalmer." Ida grins, digging her point home.

Heat rises in Lily's face.

A large shepherd stirs under the porch, leaves its shelter and shade to trot up to Ida, but she kicks at it. Ida misses, but the dog cowers and whimpers anyway, and its eyes are on Lily. It trots over, and Lily kneels. Poor thing is panting, too skinny, and she wishes she could, as she scratches behind its ears—one of which is split, as if by a knife—take Ida in for how she treats this dog, but there are no laws about that. Fleas jump up from behind its ears and Lily hops up quickly. The dog startles, trots back under the porch. She feels bad, but she doesn't want to take fleas home to her animals.

Ida laughs. "Yeah, I see you're all sympathy, till you see something's a little gamey. You sure have gotten big for your britches—or should I say your skirt, what with that sheriff's star. Thinkin' you're high-and-mighty, just like your daddy."

Lily fixes a hard gaze on Ida, but the mean woman laughs. "Oh, I remember. You were a scared little bitch, when we brought that traitor, that German, into town." She cackles. "Oh, how he howled, and jumped, funniest sight, all tarred and feathered. Your daddy thought he was such a do-gooder, speaking up for that man—"

"His name was Mr. Gottschalk."

"Whatever his name was, my husband got some of the boys to round him up because he wouldn't buy bonds; he was a traitor, and traitors need to be dealt with, and, and we was doing it for Hiram, knowing he was over there fighting—"

"No, you were doing it because—"

Ida's fists clench and she yells, "Get off my property." She grabs her shotgun.

Lily pulls her revolver. "Sit down and shut up. I'm here as law and I'm not leaving until I know if Hiram is here or not."

Dorit rushes out of the cabin. "Mama! Please!" She quickly pulls the shotgun from her mother's hand. Dorit gives Lily a pleading look. "Mama has had a hard life—"

"Haven't we all," Lily snaps.

Suddenly a hound dog howls. Sadie.

A moment later, Lily jerks her gaze to the right of the porch, spots Hiram walking with Marvena. But she doesn't have a weapon pulled, and his arms aren't up. Sadie trots alongside, calmly. Hiram's coming voluntarily.

Lily holsters her revolver.

Marvena glances at Sadie, nods.

Lily's heart falls. She knows what that nod means—Sadie had traced the scent of the work shirt that had been wrapped around the wrench to Hiram. Between that and the letter, there is plenty of circumstantial evidence.

As they come closer, Lily sees that Hiram's face is red and tear-streaked.

"Found him hiding behind the tobacco barn," Marvena says.

Ida and Dorit give each other alarmed looks.

"Filled him in," Marvena adds.

Hiram looks at his mother and sister. His voice is calm, firm, flat. "Go inside. I need to talk with Sheriff Lily. Alone."

A few minutes later, Hiram sits on the bottom front porch step, Lily and Marvena standing before him. Sadie has curled up on the ground for a snooze. Ida and Dorit have retreated inside. Lily has the feeling that this is the first they've listened to Hiram's wishes in a long time. With the dull stirring on this hot morning of thin curtains in open windows, Lily doubts their conversation is very private.

Hiram's expression is stolid. He looks as he had in those moments after his outburst at the park—staring a thousand miles away. His hair is tousled, and he's wearing just an undershirt with his pants. His feet are bare. His forearms rest on his knees, his hands clasped as if in prayer.

"Hiram?" Lily finally says softly, trying to call him back.

After a long moment, he looks up at her. "Told you I had a big crush on Pearl. But more'n that, I knew about the baby. Knew she was pregnant when she left with Soph—with Mrs. Fitzpatrick—to tend to her aunt down in Virginia."

"How did you know that?" Marvena asks.

"Pearl told me. We became friends again, working for the Fitzpatricks. She told me that the baby is Chalmer's, but that Mrs. Fitzpatrick didn't know. When they first came back, I asked Pearl what happened to the baby, and she said she'd had it down in Virginia and came back before Mrs. Fitzpatrick, who'd dismissed her after finding out Pearl was pregnant out of wedlock. Said Mrs. Fitzpatrick called her all sorts of names, claimed she couldn't have a woman like Pearl working for them.

"When she got back, Pearl left the baby with the wet nurse. She didn't want people to know she'd had a child out of wedlock, and how would she take care of a baby by herself? I told her I'd marry her, tell everyone the baby was mine, and help her take care of the baby, but she—she just wanted Chalmer to help her take care of the baby. Or pay her to give the baby up for adoption. She was trying to decide which—she hadn't told him yet about the baby."

So the shock Chalmer displayed about the baby last night was genuine, Lily thinks.

"I followed her after she left the park," Hiram says. "She didn't go back to her house."

Well, that fit what the neighbors had told Lily and Marvena earlier.

"She trekked all the way over to the Owens place," Hiram goes on, "where she'd been paying Suda to take care of the baby, got the baby, brought her to the Fitzpatricks, and left her on the side porch. I surprised Pearl as she was leaving—she didn't know I'd been following her all this time—asked her what she was doing. She said she'd had enough, she was leaving the baby with his father, and she was going to leave town, start over. I begged her to change her mind, told her I— I loved her." Hiram's eyes water, his expression finally crumbling in hurt and pain. "Told her I'd make a good husband, a good father, it was a chance for both of us, and I wouldn't—she didn't—even need worry about me touching her. In that way. And . . . and she laughed at me, and suddenly I— I hit her. And knocked her down, and she rolled into the pond and I— I ran away."

"You hit her," Lily repeats flatly. She looks at Marvena.

"I just told him that Pearl had been found, murdered, her body in the fishing pond." Marvena glances at the tote she still holds. "Sadie here took a sniff of the shirt we found, but I had it all tucked away by the time Sadie tracked Hiram."

Lily regards Hiram. So Marvena had wisely not revealed Pearl's exact injuries or the existence of either the wrench or the letter. "You hit her," Lily says again. "How?"

Hiram looks startled. "With—with my fist. And I— I may have grabbed her. Shoved her. I don't know, Lily; it's all a blur. Just like when I'd get riled up . . . over there." He means in battle in the Great War.

Well, maybe it was a blur. Or maybe he just doesn't know the specifics because he didn't kill Pearl and he's covering for someone.

Chalmer? Ida?

Lily has incriminating, although circumstantial, evidence and his willing confession. Hiram's violent behavior at the park dedication is also incriminating. She has no choice but to bring him in.

Yet Lily squats, so she and Hiram regard each other eye-to-eye. "Hiram," she says softly. He starts to look away, but she says his name again, more harshly, and he looks back at her. "You can tell me anything. You don't need to cover for anyone. Hiram, the baby is safe"—true enough for now—"and we can't do anything for Pearl, but help yourself. Save yourself—"

"Oh God!" Hiram's voice comes out in a great strangle. He lifts his fists and pounds them against his temples. Lily grabs his forearms. He is strong, especially in his distress, and she cannot lever enough force to stop him from hitting himself in the head. "Oh, Roger, Roger—"

Lily startles at hearing her brother's name. She drops her grasp, stumbles back, sitting on the damp ground. Marvena rushes to her, helps her up as Lily cries out, "What about Roger?"

Suddenly Dorit is back out on the porch. "Hiram!" she shouts. She drops to her knees by her brother. She sits next to him, one arm around his back, another on his shoulder, as he rocks and hits himself, his levering fists coming close to hitting Dorit, but she doesn't flinch, and Lily realizes that Dorit has done this many times before. Slowly, his rhythmic hitting stops, slows.

Dorit looks up at Lily. "If you're taking him in, could he please have a shirt and shoes?"

"Of course."

Dorit nods. "They're in his room, back of the house."

"I can go—" Marvena starts.

"No, you keep an eye on them," Lily says.

She goes in the house, passes by Ida, sitting in a rocker in a corner, hands clasped in her lap. She stares at Lily.

In Hiram's room, Lily picks up shoes, a shirt, a comb. As she crosses the front room, Ida's laugh is low and mean.

"Well, thankee, She-riff, for taking the trash away. That boy ain't never been right, and th' war is just an excuse—"

Lily stops, fixes her with such a hard stare that she stops midsentence. She crosses to the table between her and Ida and sets aside Hiram's items.

Then Lily suddenly thumps her fists on the tabletop, keeps her hands there, leans forward, staring down at Ida. Her grin drops from her face, and she shirks back, alarmed, like the bully she is. Satisfying, but Lily wishes it were Hiram standing up to her.

Wishes she had stood up to her and her husband back then.

Back then she was nineteen.

Now she is just shy of thirty.

And she's learned a few things about how to walk tall and hold her place in this world.

"That man, who you and your husband tarred and feathered and shamed in front of my father's store? Mr. Gottschalk wasn't a traitor. He was just a man with debts who couldn't afford a war bond at the time. And no, Mrs. Fitzpatrick. You didn't torture him for Hiram. He'd never have wanted you to do that. Hiram hated bullies. You did it, because your husband was a bully. And you are, too."

Moments later, Lily drives as slowly as she can down the winding path back to the bigger road. Sadie sits beside her, and Marvena and Hiram are in the back.

Lily's hands are tight and tense on the steering wheel. She doesn't want to burn out her brakes by leaning too much on them down the hill. At the same time, it would be so easy to slip, let her automobile go off the side and down a ravine.

She and Sadie and Marvena all yelp as the automobile shoots out onto the road and almost onto the bridge across the way, a spray of rocks flying up and bouncing off the grate and front hood and even a few on the windshield. Thankfully, the windshield's not cracked.

It takes driving a few miles of easy country roads for Lily's heart to settle, her breath to calm. She understands why the man across the road doesn't like the pickup truck flying down the hill, nearly missing his property.

After another mile, it hits Lily: the rocks on the windshield had sounded as much like gunshots as the distant rat-a-tats from the park's shooting range, the reason Hiram had given for being spooked and rushing at Chalmer on the stage yesterday.

But the rocks hadn't startled Hiram at all.

He'd remained perfectly calm.

CHAPTER 14

✺

BEULAH

Thursday, July 5, 1928
12:55 p.m.

Crowds of hollyhocks, abounding with pink and red blooms and growing on the west side of the porch at Lily's farmhouse, nod over the side rails in a lulling breeze, as if whispering gossip brought by the butterflies prancing above them. Beulah pinches off wilted blooms and tries to focus on the buzzing chorus of bees and cicadas.

But she can't stop glancing over to the lane, ever watchful for Lily's automobile.

Beulah pulls the handkerchief out of her dress pocket, wipes the trickles of sweat from the back of her neck. She pauses, eyes the remaining lush blooms. She'd planned on picking a simple, cheery bouquet, a notion that suddenly feels silly. Even the two glasses of lemonade on the side table by the porch swing, by now warm, seem silly. She's acting as if Lily is making a social call to her own home, as if these touches—the bouquet, the lemonade—would somehow ease breaking the news about Esmé. Her existence, and now her disappearance.

Tires grind onto the lane. Beulah turns, sees Lily's automobile. She tucks away her handkerchief and wills herself to come around to the porch, up the steps, turn. Beulah keeps her eyes on her daughter as Lily emerges from her automobile, determined to face her squarely, with the facts. Lily will just have to—

And then Beulah notes the weariness in Lily's every step, the stoop to her shoulders, Sadie trotting along tiredly beside Lily. Before driving Beulah home, Dr. Twomey filled Beulah in on what he knows of poor Pearl Riley's death from Lily and Marvena having come to his home in the wee hours of the morning, and explained that he'd kept his office closed this morning because he was weary from being up so late.

Beulah twitches with an impulse to go to her daughter, check on her well-being, get her something to eat, nag her to rest. But then Lily looks at her directly, her eyes hard and dark, a fearsome gaze that has naught to do with weariness or Pearl.

Oh God, Beulah thinks. *She knows. Somehow, Lily knows*—and then it hits Beulah. How day before yesterday she'd left her bedroom window open to ease the heat as she worked on the quilt from Roger's old clothes. How she'd found that window closed when sweet Hildy brought her here this morning to change to go to the train station for Esmé. How she'd briefly worried whether she'd stashed away all the letters before going with Lily and Jolene over to see Marvena and Nana and Frankie on the afternoon of the third. Told herself of course she had.

Now a sickening feeling rolls over her.

Something in Lily's gaze tells Beulah that she hadn't.

"Lily," Beulah says softly. "We need to talk—"

"About Esmé Chambeau?"

Beulah takes a deep breath, trying to center herself, but the heat is choking. She manages to eke out, "Yes."

The women settle on the porch swing, and Beulah passes Lily a glass of lemonade. Lily, accepting the offer, takes a long drink, and a sense of relief washes over Beulah. She hasn't lost Lily's trust, not entirely.

Lily sets the glass down, looks directly at Beulah. "Tell me."

Beulah does not dare drop her head in shame. She simply tells Lily, as she knows she should have years before, about Esmé.

By the time Beulah finishes, Lily is staring across the yard. From out of the woods on the property across the road, a deer bounds into view. It stops, stills, looking in their direction. A hawk circles above, arcing the bright blue sky. The hawk swoops, the deer suddenly darts back into the woods, and the hawk rises again, this time with something—probably a mouse or chipmunk—in its beak. Then the hawk flies out of sight. A bee lands on Lily's arm, and she flicks it away.

Beulah takes all of this in, breathing slowly, carefully, trying not to give in to panicked gasps at the thought of what might be happening at this moment to Esmé. She sees in Lily's expression that her daughter is stiff-arming aside emotion, approaching the notion of Esmé being missing as she would any other missing child: carefully, calmly, calculating.

Sometimes Beulah gets frustrated with how cold Lily can seem.

In this moment, she is grateful.

"All right," Lily says at last. "You said Esmé Chambeau came over with a chaperone—this Madame Blanchett. There would be a record of them arriving in the United States, though not of their movements after that. The trains don't keep track of comings and goings of individual passengers—they get on with a ticket, or buy it while onboard, and what matters is that the tickets sold match the number of passengers on board. But the itinerary was supposed to be arrival in New York late on July 2, around four thirty, spending one night, then taking the first train in the morning to Columbus, arriving on July 3."

"Yes," Beulah says. "By seven fifteen p.m. Then they were to spend the nights of the third and fourth in the hotel I arranged."

"Right, so July 4 in Columbus, but leave very early on the morning of July 5 so as to arrive here on the ten-ten train." Lily sighs. "Tracking them is going to be hard. This isn't something I can have Sadie do. So let's start with the simplest possibility—could you have missed this Madame Blanchett and Esmé and they've checked into the Kinship Inn?"

"I already asked after them there," Beulah says. Good heavens, does Lily think she's an idiot? Of course she'd checked the obvious places.

149

But Lily is taking this situation with great composure, so Beulah calms her voice. "After talking to the stationmaster and the porter and walking the train, I even checked the ice-cream shop and the grocery, in case they were hungry."

In spite of everything, Lily smiles just a little. "All right—that was smart of you. Well, maybe something happened in France, something that meant Esmé . . ." She hesitates. How odd the name must sound to Lily. Beulah has had three years to get used to it—more than used to it. "That meant Esmé couldn't board the ship."

Beulah shakes her head. "No—I have a telegram from Charlotte from a few days ago that she and the priest watched Esmé board with Madame Blanchett." Tears suddenly stream down Beulah's face. Lily hesitates, then puts a comforting hand on Beulah's arm. Somehow, that just makes the tears flow. "I— I can show it to you—"

"I believe you," Lily says. "All right, then, just to be certain that nothing happened in the crossing, I'll find out who I can contact on the *Île de France.*"

"When I realized that Esmé wasn't on the train, I went to, well . . ." Beulah hesitates, gets out her handkerchief again and wipes her eyes, then her nose. Then she sighs. Why hesitate about this, after all she's held back? "Well, I went to find Dr. Twomey."

Another flicker of a smile passes over Lily's lips. Beulah blushes, chides herself for being like a silly schoolgirl. Is it that obvious to everyone that she's sweet on the doctor?

"He suggested we go to the telegraph office, send telegrams to the Columbus station and the hotels I arranged in Columbus and New York, inquiring about Esmé and Madame Blanchett. We did, but there was a telegram waiting for me. I was hoping it was from Madame Blanchett, an explanation of some sort. But it was from a Monsieur Durand. He explained Esmé had helped him with his children on the crossing, and that she gave him my name and town. He saw her and Madame Blanchett depart the ship, but he's been concerned about her."

Lily's eyebrows go up. "So, something had seemed strange about Madame Blanchett's behavior to this Monsieur Durand? I have to say

I'm impressed that Esmé herself had the intuition to pass along your information to him. And that she'd been so kind and generous with his children that he wants to look out for her." Lily pats Beulah's arm again. "She has good instincts, so that should give us some hope and comfort that whatever situation she might be in at the moment, she'll make wise choices."

Beulah swallows hard, touched by Lily already caring about this girl she's known about for only a day. Yet her heart also aches. A nine-year-old shouldn't have to make wise choices to ensure her safety. But such is the state of the world. "He said he met Esmé and her chaperone in steerage. I paid for second cabin passage."

Beula wonders if Madame Blanchett could have sold their second cabin tickets, gotten steerage for them, and pocketed the difference? Something is definitely suspicious about Madame Blanchett's behavior.

"Do you have a contact for the family Madame Blanchett was going to see in Saint Louis?" Lily's voice is clipped, as if she's interrogating a suspect. Yet Beulah is relieved to have Lily in charge of finding Esmé. They'll sort out any hard feelings later.

"Yes, I do," Beulah says.

"All right, I'll send a telegram to them, too. It's possible Madame Blanchett took Esmé there for some reason."

"I also know the hotel they were to stay at in Columbus, the Regency, near the Union Station. I found it on a street map of Columbus. I telegraphed them to make reservations for Madame Blanchett and Esmé, and wired them money from the account your father left for me."

Lily lifts her eyebrows. "I think I've underestimated your wiliness."

Beulah smiles briefly. Such is so often the case of younger people, in regard to the older generation. She'd done the same with her own mama. "We could telegraph that hotel—"

"Of course," Lily says. "But it's also about a two-hour drive from here. Asking questions in person will be more effective. I'll head there now."

Now Beulah puts a hand on Lily's arm. "Oh, thank you—thank you, Lily. I— I know how exhausted you must be, after the night you've had, and I'm so sorry about poor Pearl Riley."

Lily looks perplexed. "How did you—"

"Dr. Twomey told me."

Lily nods. "I see." Then her perplexed frown deepens. "Wait—how did you get from Marvena's over to the train station?"

"Hildy. I knew I had to tell her about Esmé. And so I did, late last night—"

Comprehension washes over Lily's expression. "Ah—that's why you wanted to spend the night at Marvena's, near Hildy's."

Beulah stares down at her hands, nods. "Yes."

"How did she take it?"

"Surprisingly well, but I think she is still sorting it out." Beulah looks up at her daughter, unsure if she should tell her Hildy's revelation. It's really Hildy's news to share, but she's held back too many secrets. "Hildy shared something else. She is unable to have children. She miscarried earlier this year. Dr. Twomey has diagnosed bleeding cysts on her ovaries."

Lily goes pale; her eyes widen with sorrow. "Oh—poor Hildy. And Tom knows?"

Beulah nods. "I think so."

"And now she's learned that Roger has a child. . . ."

"Yes, it's a lot to take in," Beulah says. "But she insisted on bringing me by here this morning, then taking me to the Kinship depot." Beulah at last picks up her own glass, has a sip of lemonade. Then she says, "She didn't wait with me, of course—"

"I can understand that," Lily says, but gently.

Beulah's eyes prickle. She's had more grace, both from Lily and Hildy, and Dr. Twomey for that matter, than she deserved. But of course, grace is never deserved or earned, only given. Beulah rubs her eyes. "I know I should have talked with you—but, but somehow, with Daniel's death, and everything you've shouldered, it never seemed the right time, and now Esmé is missing—"

"It would have been better if you'd told me about her. I would have gone to New York with you to meet the child as she came in," Lily says.

Beulah puts her hands to her face. "Oh God, I hadn't thought of that—"

Lily pats her back. "Mama, I'm sorry. That was too harsh. The important thing now is to find Esmé—and we will. But I need you to answer another question for me, and do some things for me. Can you do that?"

Beulah looks up, gazes with gratitude at her smart, strong daughter. She nods.

Lily takes a deep breath. "I told Benjamin about the letter last night, showed it to him. Right before a neighbor of Chalmer's came to fetch me. Mama, Benjamin already knew about Esmé. Chalmer had asked him for help in going through proper channels to sort out Esmé's immigration status."

Beulah gasps. "I— I didn't know, that Benjamin knew—" *Oh God. What might this do to Lily and Benjamin's relationship?* She has such high hopes for them, but if Lily feels she can't trust Benjamin over this, their budding romance will be wrecked. Lily hasn't talked about it much, but Beulah suspects Daniel kept things hidden from Lily, all in the name of protecting her, and Lily did not take well to that. And now here Beulah and Benjamin are doing the same to Lily, over Esmé.

"I believe you, Mama. But if Chalmer told Benjamin, might he have told anyone else?"

"I don't think so. . . ."

"Mama, it's possible something's gone awry that we don't know about, something that will make perfect sense once we have Esmé safely with us. But I think you should be prepared—it could be that someone else knows about Esmé. That she was, well, kidnapped. Anyone who knows her relationship to us would also know that she would be highly important to us."

"Oh God. . . ."

"Mama, I need you to be strong. If you get any kind of telegram from the Columbus station, or the hotels, or a note from anyone, you must send a telegram to me right away at the hotel in Columbus."

"I will. Of course I will."

"And I need you to do two things for me."

Beulah nods. "Anything."

"I need you to tell the children about Esmé."

Beulah stares at Lily.

"Mama, I'm hoping I will come home with Esmé. The children need to be prepared."

Beulah thinks of Jolene, just a few mornings ago seeking reassurance that her mama would still have room in her heart for her even if she had—what was it? Thirty-two more children. And Beulah had reassured Jolene that love is endless and has room for everyone. Now she'll need to reassure her again.

"I will," Beulah says. "I can do that."

"And I need for you and Nana to go to Suda Owens's place. That was going to be my next step. I need to know when Pearl came to get her baby. If Suda spotted Hiram."

Beulah listens, stunned but quiet, as Lily fills her in on Hiram's confession and arrest for the murder of Pearl Riley.

"I can do that, as well—"

She stops, as another automobile pulls down the lane. Both she and Lily watch as Hildy exits her vehicle and comes to the porch. Her jaw is set, her expression resolute.

"Dr. Twomey came to check on me," Hildy says, focusing on Beulah, "since you told him you'd filled me in about Esmé."

Beulah reels back, a bit surprised. She's not sure how she feels about Dr. Twomey doing so. But Hildy's irreproachable gaze has already shifted to Lily.

"And he told me about Esmé being missing," Hildy adds. "And Marvena came by and told me about Pearl. You must be exhausted, but I know that won't stop you from searching for Esmé. However you're planning to handle this, Lily, I want to be—I will be—part of finding her. Roger would want that. I want that."

For a long moment, all three women are silent. The air is heavy with heat, the scent of hollyhocks, the buzz of bees and cicadas.

Finally, Lily simply nods. She stands up. "I need to go to Columbus."

"I'll drive," Hildy says. "You can rest on the way."

Unlikely that Lily will do so, Beulah thinks, but she is relieved that Hildy will be driving. Beulah eases out of the porch swing, stands. "Well then. I'd best make sandwiches for you to take on the road."

So many questions remain, for all of them, but they must push them aside, shunt any emotions. The focus now is on tracking down Esmé.

CHAPTER 15

LILY

Thursday, July 5, 1928
6:30 p.m.

The lobby of the Regency Hotel, just four blocks down from the Columbus Union Station, was the exact opposite of what the name implied: cramped, dingy, and infused with a mildewy smell made worse
by the heat. Across from the shabby scratched walnut front desk, the
lounge area consisted of two wing chairs, a love seat, and a red Oriental
rug that, Lily supposes, must once have been festooned with wreathing
flowers and vines but that is now a worn-down blur, stains and spots
more prominent than pattern.

Now Lily keeps a wary eye on the hotel manager on the other side
of the front desk, as he peers over the top of his wire-framed glasses
at the photo of Esmé and Madame Blanchett, his nose nearly touching
it. He snuffles and Lily is tempted to snatch back the photo before his
nose drips on it, but he is holding it tautly and she worries she'll tear
the photo.

Earlier, while Lily quickly packed an overnight bag, including items
for Hildy to borrow so they could get on the road and not have to loop
back to Hildy's house, Mama had written out what was supposed to

have been Esmé's itinerary. Then Mama had handed over the photo of her niece.

With Hildy driving her own automobile, they'd left the house, Mama waving anxiously from the front porch. Lily and Hildy had stopped in Kinship long enough for Lily to go into her office to unload from her tote bag the work shirt and wrench that Hiram had identified as his. As she'd turned to lock her office door, her poster of Lady Liberty in the harbor catches her gaze. Had Esmé gotten to see the statue? Tears had sprung to Lily's eyes at the unbearable thought of something dreadful happening to any child, but in this moment to this particular child. Roger's daughter.

By the time she was back to Hildy's automobile, Hildy was already impatiently waiting for her, having achieved her task of sending telegrams to Madame Blanchett's Saint Louis kin as well as new telegrams to the stationmaster in Columbus and the hotels in both New York and Columbus.

Then they'd hit the road, and Lily had been determined to talk with Hildy—if she was willing—about how she is doing, both with her diagnosis and the news of Esmé. But Hildy's lips were tightly clenched, as were her hands on the steering wheel, and she'd stared with glaring intensity at the unspooling ribbon of road before them. Soon Lily's eyes drifted shut, and then the next thing she knew, Hildy was gently shaking her arm to wake her up.

And now the hotel manager is squinting at the photo of Lily's niece. *Her niece.*

This feels as foreign to Lily as the name Esmé. And yet it also feels right.

A fierce desire rises to find and protect the girl, not just because they are blood kin but also because Esmé is a little girl. A girl her own daughter's age. Her daughter and son's cousin. Her mind reels, spun by the sudden gripping, illogical notion that if anything happens to this photo of Esmé, she will be doomed to never find Esmé. And she can't let that happen.

Lily and Hildy have already shown the photo to the station manager on duty at the Union Station and a few other employees, but they did not remember either the girl or her chaperone. Lily and Hildy had arrived too late to talk with employees who would have been on duty when Esmé's train arrived from New York, and would have to try again tomorrow morning.

Now Hildy clears her throat, as close to indignant harrumphing as she ever gets. "Well? Have you seen either of them?"

The scrawny man looks up at the women over the top of his wire glasses, from one to another, as if he is enjoying this, dragging it out, torturing them.

Lily wants to grab him by the lapels, shake him, and she might—if it weren't for the photo she wants to protect. Finally, he sets it down, turns it to face Lily and Hildy, and taps the image of Madame Blanchett. "Got both your and your mother's telegrams. Haven't had time to reply. But yes, I saw her. Came in late the night of July 3. But not her." He taps Esmé.

As her heart drops, Lily pulls the photo closer. "The woman came in without the girl?"

He nods.

"You're sure?"

He gives a cawing laugh, showing yellow teeth. "Not gonna forget her anytime soon. Woman alone. Prepaid room." He waggles his eyebrows suggestively, a leering glint to his eyes. "Usually come in with fellas, or a fella follows soon after. Not this time, though. And no children. So I'd have remembered that."

"So all that stands out to you is that she was alone?"

He half-laughs, half-snorts. "No. She was snobby. Putting on airs, talking with a weird accent. And there were all these feathers in her hat."

Lily glances at the photo. Madame Blanchett is wearing a hat, but not one with feathers.

"The feathers stood out to you?" Hildy asks, incredulous.

He nods. "They were big, too big for a hat. Like from, I don't know, an ostrich. Nearly poked my eye out. And a bright teal color. Musta gotten it from that hat shop in the terminal."

Lily's eyebrows go up.

"What?" he asks defensively. "Every now and then I get my lunch at the sandwich counter in the terminal. And there's a hat shop across from it. I've thought about getting a fancy one for my missus, but they're pricey."

He pauses, as if unsure to share the next tidbit. Lily gives him an encouraging smile.

"But I complimented her hat—in spite of the feathers. She kept adjusting it, drawing attention. Figured she could use the boost. She said something odd—she deserved it after her difficult trip. A treat for herself."

Lily considers. Mama had said she'd bought passage in second cabin but received a telegram from a fellow passenger on the crossing that said he'd met Esmé in steerage. If Madame Blanchett is so greedy that she'd switch the tickets, then use some of the proceeds for a hat, what else might she do?

Lily considers the itinerary Mama had laid out for her: Esmé and Blanchett were to arrive in Columbus on the third, spend all day on the fourth, leave first thing on the fifth. "But she spent two nights—the third and the fourth—here?"

The man nods. Hope clutches Lily's heart. Maybe the man just hadn't noticed Esmé. She could have ducked in, sat quietly on one of the lobby sofas while Madame Blanchett checked them in. He could have been distracted by Blanchett's damned hat. Maybe even yet, Mama has found out that there was a mix-up, that Blanchett and Esmé have been somewhere in Kinship after all, and any minute a telegraph delivery boy will dash in with word of the good news—

Hildy must have the same thought. She asks, "You are sure a young girl wasn't with her? This girl?"

"I told you—I'm sure. There wasn't a girl with her when she came in, nor when she left this afternoon."

Now Lily's heart drops. "This afternoon?" The local from Columbus to Kinship would have left early this morning. It's the only one that runs to their town. There's no hope that they'd simply overslept, took a later train, and are just now arriving in Kinship.

He nods, turns, pulls a card from a drawer, turns back to the counter. He stares at the card for a long minute. "Yep. I noted right here, she checked out of room sixty-seven at three-oh-five p.m.—"

Hildy snatches the card from him.

"Hey!" He reaches for it, but Hildy takes a step back.

After a moment, she looks up at Lily. "It's noted here that Beulah McArthur wired the money ahead for the room, for Madame Giselle Blanchett, and Esmé Chambeau." Her voice trembles a little as she adds, "So there's no doubt. Esmé should have been here."

Their eyes clutch, sharing the question—had Esmé ever made it here from New York?

Lily gently takes the card from Hildy and returns it to the hotel manager. "So, did Madame Blanchett just stay in her room? She must have left for meals?"

"Yes, at the terminal. She complained each time about the terrible food, as if I could do anything about it. And she said she couldn't wait to leave this city—not that she saw any of it, other than the sandwich shop and the hat shop at the terminal." He sounds genuinely offended on behalf of Ohio's capital city.

"Did she say where she was going?" Lily asks.

He thinks for a moment, then nods. "Yes. Back to New York City. Didn't make any sense to me—why'd she come here, from New York, if she was going to turn around and go back to New York?"

Lily takes a deep breath, forces herself to consider this new information as objectively as possible. He's right—why come here at all, then? Why come without Esmé?

Hildy asks, "Have you let out the room she stayed in? If she just checked out a little after three this afternoon?"

"No, it's empty."

"Has it been cleaned yet?"

He waits a beat. "Yes." He turns slightly red. So, no.

"Great," Hildy says. "We'd like to rent it."

Lily looks at her friend, surprised, but then Hildy's clever purpose dawns on her: they can inspect the room. And they have to stay somewhere—not only because they are too tired to drive back but also because they'll want to talk to people at the Union Station the next day.

Lily and Hildy finish their search of the hotel room, tucked in a corner of the third floor, reserved for unaccompanied women. The floor is blessedly quiet, though God help them if a fire were to break out. The fire escape, Lily had noted when she'd opened the one grimy window to let in a steamy smudge of breeze from the alley, is missing between the second and third floor.

Which negates the possibility that Esmé had come in with Blanchett after all and then run away. Of course, if Blanchett were an honorable chaperone and that had happened, wouldn't she have sent a telegram to Mama?

They have thoroughly searched under the narrow bed, in the dresser and nightstand, under the divan—hoping to find something Blanchett, or even Esmé, might have left behind: a note, a letter, a ticket, diary, anything about where she might have gone.

But there is nothing.

All they have found is dust, bug carcasses, and mice droppings. At least the hotel is outfitted with built-in gaslights, and Lily turns the light near the divan up to a flicker. She hopes it's enough to keep critters scurried back into the shadows.

Lily double-checks the door lock, puts her gun on the side table, and eyes the worn divan, upholstered in a similar red, blurry pattern to the lobby carpet. On one end, tufting pokes through and two buttons are missing. The other end has an uncomfortable-looking dip.

Lily opts for the dipped-in side. Her rump rests uncomfortably on the divan. She pulls her hat down over her eyes, to shade them from the fancy gaslight she's left on to chase off bugs.

Several beats of silence pass. Finally, Hildy says, "I'm not sure about the cleanliness of that bed. Maybe we'd be better off sleeping in the automobile."

Lily considers: two women, sleeping in an automobile, parked by a run-down hotel or by the terminal. "I'll take my chances with the bugs."

"You're going to get a crick in your neck," Hildy says—grouchy, though a tinge of amusement nudges in. Lily gives a small smile. Ah—there's her friend. Even in the grimness of the situation, it's a comfort to hear a hint of the good cheer that usually bubbles in Hildy's voice.

"This is the most divine divan," Lily says, allowing herself a moment of humor, too.

The floorboards squeak as Hildy crosses the room, and the divan creaks as Hildy sits down on the untufted end.

For a moment, exhaustion washes over Lily in numbing waves, pulling her consciousness down to fuzzy gray oblivion. But then her delicious drifting toward sleep crashes into sharp questions. *Why would Madame Blanchett come here, without Esmé, only to return to New York? Has Mama heard something from Blanchett's Saint Louis relatives that will help make sense of all of this?* Surely tomorrow morning someone at the terminal will tell them something that would help them find Esmé. If not . . . Lily can't bear to think about not being able to find her brother's daughter.

Lines from a Shakespeare sonnet whisper from the back of her memory, and she mutters them out loud. "'Weary with toil, I haste me to my bed, / The dear repose for limbs with travel tired; / But then begins a journey in my head / To work my mind, when body's work's expired . . .'"

"Roger recited that," Hildy says quietly.

Lily sits bolt upright, and her hat tumbles to the floor. Hildy's right. That was one of the sonnets he memorized and recited as part of the senior show, all those years before in high school. "Oh God, Hildy, I'm sorry. If I'd have known, but I didn't, I want you to know I didn't, and Mama should have told us, or if not me, at least told you—"

"It's not Mama McArthur's fault."

Lily is touched that after all these years, after all that's transpired, Hildy still uses the honorific that Mama would have wanted Hildy to use for her if Hildy and Roger had wed. "I know that—" Lily starts.

"I mean, even if she'd told us, ahead of time, it wouldn't have changed the outcome—"

"She still should have told us."

"Maybe. Probably. Yes. But you can't—well, you shouldn't expect people to be perfect. Or to act in ways that fit what you *think* is perfect."

"I expect people to act honorably. Not perfectly—"

"You sure about that?"

Lily is taken aback as if slapped. Stiffly, she says, "Are you blaming me, that Mama didn't tell me about Roger because I expect perfection? Then why didn't she tell you—"

Hildy sighs. Lily feels the divan shift under their weight as Hildy tries to get comfortable. "Maybe she feared I couldn't handle it."

"You're strong. Mama knows better'n that."

Silence, as the truth stirs between them. Over the past few years, Hildy has come into her own—as a teacher, as a daughter distancing herself from the meanness of her own mother, finding happiness with Tom. But before that, after Roger's death, Hildy had been so soft, so quiet. Maybe Mama hadn't wanted to hurt Hildy. And of late, maybe Mama hadn't wanted to intrude on Hildy's newfound strength and joy.

"Lily," Hildy says firmly, "I know Roger well enough to know that if he had lived, he'd have done right by Esmé's mother. And if he hadn't met her, and made it back, well, maybe we would have married. Maybe we would have been happy enough. I don't think we'd have had the kind of marriage you and Daniel had. So maybe we would have gone our separate ways. Maybe he would have gone on to college like he talked about, become a lawyer in a big city."

Lily's eyebrows go up. He'd brought that up to her when they were younger—but not after he started dating Hildy. She'd assumed he'd put that aside for Hildy.

"He told me that he wanted that once," Hildy says. "I— I started crying. Knowing that that would mean I'd be all alone. I loved Roger, but I'm not sure I loved him in the way needed to sustain a life spent together. I know that now, with Tom. I'm ashamed I cried, but I couldn't seem to help it at the time—"

Lily puts her hand on Hildy's arm. "It's all right, Hildy. No need for perfection, right?"

She's touched by this admission, though, both about Roger and about Hildy's reaction.

Hildy pats Lily's hand. "I'm glad Roger found comfort—found love—in the middle of such a horrid war."

Lily nods. Then she says, "Benjamin found out. From Chalmer. He knew before I did, and didn't say anything."

"You can't blame him for that, Lily. He knew it was your mama's place to tell you first."

"Have—have you told Tom about Esmé?"

"Yes," Hildy says.

Lily waits.

Finally, Hildy says, "He understands that of course I'll want to be close to Esmé, just like I am to all of your family, Lily." Hildy tears up, stares down. "Tom—Tom has been so understanding about a lot of things. . . ."

And then, softly crying, Hildy tells Lily that she's learned she's unable to have children. Lily doesn't let on that Mama has already told her. She simply listens.

After that, they sit quietly, as the sounds of the city—stray voices, the occasional automobile—filter in through the window on unsavory breezy gusts.

Finally, Hildy breaks the spell of the lulling city sounds. "We have to find Esmé." Her voice is unwavering, even on Esmé's name.

Lily starts to say *"we will,"* but the words catch in her throat. She simply nods.

CHAPTER 16

BEULAH

Thursday, July 5, 1928
6:30 p.m.

Partway up the steep lane to Marvena's house, Beulah swerves to avoid hitting a chipmunk and careens Lily's Model T off to the side in a rut. When she goes to reverse, the front passenger's side tire spins and the automobile is stuck.

"Dammit." Beulah smacks her hands against the steering wheel, accidentally setting off the horn, which in turn makes her jump.

Well, there's nothing she can do about the stuck automobile now.

A few minutes later, she's already gasping on her trek, pulling in bugs and heat, her eyes stinging with sweat dripping into them from her brow. She stops, leans against a tree, takes a deep breath, and waits for her heart to stop pounding. She'd started out too fast, anxious to get to Marvena's, but she shakes her head at herself. Not as spry as she once was.

Beulah starts up the hill again, a little more slowly—she'd be no good to anyone keeled over with a heart attack—and lets the sights and smells of the leafy green forest soothe her. Early-evening light catching the perfect weaving of a spider's web—strong and fragile. The fussy scent of moss. The twittering of birdcall and the chittering of cicadas in waves of crescendos.

Yet piercing the loveliness of the summer evening is the sneaky concern that somehow Esmé's disappearance—or at least absence from the train—and poor Pearl's murder are connected.

As she hikes on, Beulah's mind wanders back to the drive over. She had gazed briefly at the Widowmaker hill where her husband, Caleb, and other men had died and been buried under the cave-in of 1924. What, she wonders now, would Caleb make of her, learning the truth about their son and then holding it back from their daughter? Would he understand—or be angry at her? And likewise, would he be hurt at her feelings for Dr. Twomey?

Even as tears rise, she smiles. She knows he'd be sympathetic on all fronts. That had been Caleb's way—and Roger's. Ever patient and kind.

She's out of breath again. Beulah pauses, gives herself a moment, wipes tears and sweat from her eyes. Caleb would also tell her to focus. Trust Lily.

Esmé will be found. Esmé will be fine. For now, what she must do is fulfill her promises to Lily. *Talk to the children. Question Suda.*

Beulah repeats these thoughts to herself, over and over, like lines of a prayer.

At last, Marvena and Jurgis's snug cabin comes into view as Beulah emerges into the clearing. The children are playing a game of tag in the front yard—all but Alistair, who works summers with Tom and Jurgis in the coal mine—and Nana and Marvena sit on the front porch, stringing green beans.

As Beulah ascends the porch steps, Nana says, "Is everything all right? I reckoned you'd be at home with, well with—" She stutters to a stop, casts a scant glance toward Marvena.

"Lily's filled me in," Marvena says.

There is no judgment in Marvena's tone or gaze. Relieved by that, and suddenly weary from her trek, Beulah leans against the porch rail, and Marvena hands her a fan, a cardboard fan with a flat wooden handle from the funeral home in Kinship. Beulah fans herself, thinks of poor Pearl there at the funeral home.

"Well, I managed to get Lily's automobile stuck halfway up here in a ditch," Beulah says.

Marvena chuckles. "Like mother, like daughter."

Beulah gives her a sharp look. "Esmé didn't arrive at the Kinship train station," Beulah says.

Nana gasps, and Marvena's expression turns to alarm. Beulah fills them in, as quickly as she can, about Esmé, Lily's theories, and how Lily and Hildy have set off for Columbus. And about the need to visit Suda, see what she can learn about Pearl retrieving the baby on the night of July 4.

Then Beulah says, "But first, I have to talk to the children, tell them about Esmé."

"It's time Frankie stops running around anyway," Marvena says. "She can come inside with us to get these beans on the stovetop—"

"No, she can hear it, too. If"—Beulah stops, clears her throat—"*when* Lily finds Esmé, she'll become part of Frankie's life, too."

Nana nods, stands up stiffly. "Let's get supper made. Jurgis will be home soon. Then Beulah and I can head over to Suda's—"

"No, I'll take Beulah. Need to get Lily's automobile out of its rut, or she'll have both our hides," Marvena says. "And then we'll go on to Suda's."

The children—Jolene and Frankie, Caleb Jr. and Micah—sit in various spots on the porch, sweaty and restless but nevertheless regarding Beulah respectfully.

"Jolene," Beulah starts, "do you remember me telling you about your Uncle Roger? When you asked me about the quilt I was making?"

Jolene nods somberly.

"Roger—that's my big brother," Caleb Jr. says. He sounds prideful and gives Jolene and Micah a pointed look. "Older even than my sister, *Lily.*" He puts emphasis on Lily's name. He just loves to point out how

Lily is his sister—as if that makes her his equal, even if he is almost twenty-three years younger than her.

"Yes, Uncle Caleb," Jolene says, mocking, rolling her eyes.

Frankie giggles.

"Well, I am your uncle." Indignation tinges Caleb's young voice, and he straightens up as if he can somehow make himself taller.

"And the youngest. And a twit." Micah elbows him, as if being a few months older gives him authority. Caleb returns the jab, and Micah pokes him back. "And our mama can still tan your hide if you act up, ain't that right, Mamaw?" He looks at Beulah for backup.

"Children! I'll tan all your hides if you don't settle down, right now."

The children quiet for a moment, and Frankie's chin quivers and her eyes well up. Beulah sighs. *That child. Always so tender—maybe too tender for a harsh old world.* But then Beulah thinks of how often she's cried over Esmé the past few days. Maybe she herself isn't as tough as she'd like.

"Roger has a daughter. From his time in France. . . ." Beulah pauses, unsure how much to detail. Mention the mother or the grandmother? She opts for keeping this simple. Well, simple as possible, leastways. "His daughter's name is Esmé. She is nine—"

Jolene looks at Frankie. "Same age as us."

Micah sighs. "Another bossy girl."

In spite of the seriousness of the situation, Beulah has to smile. Poor Micah. The youngest of the five, though only a few months younger than Caleb Jr., and so the furthest down the pecking order.

Caleb's face scrunches with the seriousness he usually reserves for working out his mathematical times table. "So that makes this Esmé a cousin to these two"—he jerks his thumb in Jolene and Micah's direction—"and yet another niece for me." He sighs as if this is a heavy burden he must bear, wrangling all these kin.

Woeful shadows flicker over Frankie's little face. "Oh. I wish I had a cousin. Or a niece."

Beulah takes in Frankie's expression, considers how the little girl had had an older half sister who had passed a few years ago.

Jolene gives Frankie a light jostle. "Well, silly, you have us. And we have you."

Beulah's heart warms, at how in Jolene's eyes and heart it's easy and natural to make room for another child.

"So Mama is gone to fetch Esmé?" Jolene asks. The name, so unusual for these parts, comes easily to Jolene.

Beulah nods. "That's right."

"Well then," Jolene says, "where will Esmé sleep? My room?"

Beulah smiles. "Is that all right with you?"

Jolene thinks a moment. "Well, yes."

"Good. There's a cot up in the attic. When we're back at the house, we'll all get it down."

Caleb Jr. says, "I can get it down myself."

But Micah looks crestfallen. "We're gonna have to share everything with her?"

Jolene elbows him. "Don't be a brat. Mamaw says there's enough room in our hearts for everyone."

Micah rolls his lip in a pout. "What does Mama say, though?"

Jolene looks stumped at that. But Caleb Jr. says, in a high-pitched mimicry of his much older sister's voice, "Esmé, get outside and help pick those beans. Sweep that porch."

Defensiveness rises in Beulah's heart for her daughter, who works harder than these children realize, and yet she is also relieved as they laugh at Caleb Jr.'s spot-on imitation. If they can see the humor in the situation, they'll adjust quickly enough to Esmé.

"Well, I reckon it's all right then if she joins us," Micah says. He looks at Frankie. "What do you think?"

"I hope she likes me," Frankie says nervously.

"Why would she like you?" Caleb Jr. says, giving Frankie a little punch in the arm, but he's grinning, and Frankie grins back.

Then she gives him a quick punch back and hollers, "Tag, you're it." She leaps off the porch and runs, with Micah right behind, and Caleb Jr., always a little slower than the others, follows after them.

But Jolene, who'd usually join right in, looks up at Beulah. "Mamaw, that quilt you're making from Uncle Roger's clothes. It's for her. For Esmé, isn't it?"

Oh. Is Jolene harboring a bit of jealousy after all? "Well, yes, it is, but I'm going to make you a quilt someday, honey, don't you worry—"

Jolene shakes her head. "That's not it, Mamaw. It's just—why didn't you tell us about her sooner? You had to know for a while, if you've been working on the quilt for a bit."

Beulah sighs. *The girl is so much like her mama. Ever curious about what sparks in people's hearts.* "I don't know. It just seemed, well, like there was never a right time to share the news. And I— I wanted to be sure that it would be the right time to tell everyone."

Jolene considers the answer, then says, "Mamaw, do you have a picture of Esmé?"

"I do, but just one, and your mama has it with her. Why do you ask, honey?"

Jolene shrugs. "Just wondering." Then she runs off to join the other children, leaving Beulah on the porch.

After a long moment, Beulah rises, goes inside to help Marvena and Nana with supper.

A few hours later, as twilight falls over the mountain, Prudence Owens runs around from the side of the cabin toward Beulah and Marvena.

"Oh! Hi, hi, hi!" Prudence cries. She throws her arms around Beulah. "Where are the girls? I'm weeding the garden, and it'd go so much easier with Frankie singing."

Suda Owens suddenly comes out of the cabin, the frail porch creaking even under her scant weight. She's holding a shotgun. Lowers it when she sees Beulah and Marvena.

"Get back to work, Prudence," she snaps. The girl looks crestfallen but obeys her mother and troops off the porch. Suda looks at Beulah and Marvena. "Prudence ran off this morning on her own to go back to the park. Good thing she thought to come back—Otto would have tanned her hide if he had to go find her."

Beulah wonders what has spooked Suda. She's not one for greeting visitors with a firearm.

"I'm sorry for your troubles. We're not going to stay long," Beulah says. "We just want to chat a bit with you—alone if that's possible?"

"Otto ain't here. He's set off to deliver some more rockers, got the other girls with him. Just me and Junior and Prudence." Suda gives Marvena a skeptical look. "You here 'stead of Nana—this ain't a social call?"

"Well, my mother-in-law sent along this tea," Marvena says, stepping up on the porch. "So we can keep it social. But we got a few questions."

Suda looks to Beulah, who nods. "Best off chatting with us," Beulah says.

Suda sinks wearily down on the rickety rocker. "All right then. Let's get it over with, 'fore Otto returns. He's still mad about yesterday. Junior's napping, thank the Lord. So make yourselves at home." She waves at the porch in general, then sets aside her shotgun.

Marvena puts the gallon jar of tea—sassafras—on a table and leans against the porch rail. Beulah helps herself to the other rocker. As she comes closer to eye level with Suda, she notes a shadow—*oh, a bruise*—on Suda's upper right cheek.

"When I heard people coming up to the house, I thought it might be the man from last night. Otto told me to watch out for him." She stops, clamps her mouth shut as if she's said too much. "But you don't need to know my troubles. Why're you up here? Surely not just to deliver tea—though tell your mother-in-law I say thankee."

Marvena nods. "I will. And we did want to check on you—Nana's been worried about you. But this man from last night. Was he causing trouble?"

"He was asking about, well, about my business. Hollering, scaring our girls. The babies. Trying to force his way in our house." Suda sniffles. "Thank the Good Lord, Otto was coming back up from his woodshop, saw him trying to push past me in the door. Otto ran him off, said he'd kill him if he ever saw hide or hair of him again."

"Did the man hurt you, Suda?" Beulah asks gently.

Suda looks down but neither nods nor shakes her head.

"Otto and me, we got into an argument after the man left. He said I don't bring in enough wet nursin' for this kinda trouble. That he's tired of folks looking down on us. That he makes aplenty for all of us. But what I got paid helped us—and I know I'll keep having babies, and it'll just be harder for us if I don't wet-nurse, too. So I hollered at him—since he couldn't get on at the lumber mill, whyn't he work in the mines then, 'stead of scrabbling tobacco bottoms and making furniture?"

Beulah glances at Marvena. From the concerned look on her face, Marvena has seen the bruise, too. Beulah's and Marvena's eyes meet—should they ask Suda about it? Yes—but even if Suda owns up to Otto hitting her, she's not likely to press charges. How would she make ends meet with five children—and without him?

"Suda, do you know who the man was, that came up here?" Marvena asks.

"Don't know his name," Suda says. "But I'd recognize him. I suspect anyone would who was at the park yesterday. He was that fella who ran up on the stage, waving his gun at Mr. Fitzpatrick."

Beulah rears back in her rocker, hand flying to her heart. *Oh. Hiram.* "Did the man say why he was here?"

Suda nods. "It was the oddest thing. Said he wanted *his* baby."

"At the park yesterday, I saw you talking with a young woman. Pearl Riley."

Beulah waits. Suda doesn't say anything.

"Is that the baby's mother?"

"I don't talk about the women I help. I shouldn't have told that much about the man, except I wanted you to know why I was spooked enough to come to the door with a gun, and I reckoned with you here"—she looks at Marvena, then goes on—"mayhap you were looking for the man in the area, mayhap he's gotten into more shenanigans, and you'd heard from someone he'd been up this way."

"Pearl has died," Marvena says. "She was found in the pond by Chalmer Fitzpatrick's. She'd been murdered."

Beulah gives Marvena an admonishing look for her bluntness, starts to say something gentler to Suda, but the struck look on Suda's face stops her. Sometimes it's best to give people time and space to react. Most folks don't like to let silence go unanswered, and quiet drapes heavily on the porch.

"I— Is the baby all right?"

Beulah waits a beat, lets the worry on Suda's face fester and foment. She feels cruel doing this—and wonders how Lily can be strong enough to do this as part of her job.

Finally, Beulah says, "Yes. Pearl left her on the Fitzpatrick doorstep. The baby is fine—being looked after by Sophia and Chalmer. Pearl must have run away, and then was murdered after that."

Suda shakes her head, moans. "Oh no, oh, that man, that man—"

"What time did the man—Hiram—come here?" Marvena asks.

"Somewhere round ten, I think. It was shortly after Pearl came. I was surprised she came last night; she wasn't supposed to come for her baby for another week—" Suda stops, bringing her hand quickly to her mouth.

"So Pearl was the mother?" Marvena presses.

Suda doesn't say anything.

"Oh, come on now, Suda," Marvena snaps. "Pearl is dead. Hiram has confessed to killing her out of jealousy over her affair with Chalmer. We just need to know the timing of her coming here, if his story fits with what you know."

Suda trembles, and Beulah pats her arm reassuringly. "It's all right, honey. Just tell us what you know."

After a long moment, Suda sighs. "All right then. At first, Pearl claimed to be the baby's mother, and she told me that Chalmer is the father. She seemed right proud of that fact—which I found odd, given that Chalmer is a married man and all. But Pearl and I, well, we got a little close. She's the one told me that Chalmer was looking to hire some more workers at his lumber mill, so that's why I passed that on to Otto." She shakes her head. "I wish Otto would have gone to the mill and applied proper like, 'stead of waylaying Mr. Fitzpatrick at the park—"

"Wait, you said Pearl *claimed* to be the baby's mother? She's . . . not?" Marvena asks.

"No—the real mother is Sophia."

Beulah is shocked. "But . . . if the mother is Sophia . . . then why wouldn't she just have had the baby—" *Oh. Hiram is the father.*

"All I know is Pearl told me that Sophia thought she wasn't able to have babies," Suda says. "But then she had an affair—I reckon with the man who was here last night—got pregnant, realized it was Chalmer who was infertile. She and Pearl went away to take care of a failing aunt of Sophia's, down in Virginia—'cept the aunt had already passed away. Sophia had the baby, and they came back here, and Sophia hired Pearl to bring the baby here. Then Pearl was to take the baby over, and leave her at their house, make it look like she was leaving her baby at the father's doorstep."

"Well, don't that beat all I've ever heard," Marvena says. "You're telling us that Sophia had an affair with Hiram, about the same time that Chalmer had an affair with Pearl—and Sophia hired Chalmer's mistress to pretend to have the baby she'd actually had with Hiram?"

Suda turns this over in her mind. "Well, yes."

Beulah calculates: "So Sophia gets to keep her child, raise her child with Chalmer's help—never mind their loveless marriage. That way, Chalmer is none the wiser that the child isn't his and that his wife also had an affair with his cousin. And Pearl gets enough money to leave, maybe start over, but—" She thinks again of Pearl following Chalmer out of his study yesterday. "But she must have rekindled her feelings for him after coming back."

"Did Hiram—the man who came here yesterday—think the baby was Sophia's? Or Pearl's?" Marvena asks.

Suda shakes her head. "I don't rightly know the answer to that. He wasn't here long."

"He says he killed Pearl out of jealousy—" Marvena starts.

"But he said he was here for *his* baby last night, you're sure of that?" Beulah asks.

Suda nods.

"Well, he did try to court Pearl at one time," Marvena says. "Maybe they got closer than she let on."

"And you're sure it's the same man who rushed onstage at Chalmer's yesterday?" Beulah asks.

"Now how am I gonna forget the face of a man who did that?" Suda sounds fairly insulted at the notion. She sighs. "All I know is Pearl told me Chalmer had broken off with her months ago, and Pearl was angry and hurt. Sophia used this as a way to hire Pearl—revenge on Chalmer, that he'd have to help take care of this baby, and meanwhile, Sophia paid Pearl a lot of money. Pearl was going to go away, start over somewhere. It was all so exciting and romantic, and oh—"

Beulah sees by the rapt look on Suda's face that she'd gotten quite caught up in all of this. Marvena harrumphs at the foolishness of it, though.

Suda doesn't seem to hear Marvena's grunt. "Can you imagine— going somewhere, far away, beyond these hills?" Suda asks. Her throat makes a strangling sound. "Sometimes, I'm like to think they're closing in on me. Or swallowing me. Anyway, Pearl and I, we became friends and she told me all of this." Her chin quivers. "But-but now—Pearl is dead." Suda drops her head and cries softly. "I reckon . . . I reckon sometimes it's impossible to leave and start over."

At this, Marvena finally softens. She reaches over, pats Suda's shoulder. "Listen, if you ever need help, if Otto—"

Suda looks up, her gaze sharp and hard. "Otto is a good man. A good daddy. He'll get on at the lumber mill, and we'll be fine soon enough. You'll see."

CHAPTER 17

LILY

Friday, July 6, 1928
6:30 a.m.

The porter studies the photo of Esmé and Madame Blanchett.

Lily and Hildy sit in the station manager's office, eagerly scanning the porter's face for any hint of what he is thinking, any flicker of recognition.

They had arrived just after dawn this morning at the Columbus Union Station. But they've scarcely taken in the marvel of construction—the soaring atrium, polished floors, arcade of shops, gleaming wooden benches, bustling crowds hurrying to the trains or to the new parking lot, recently added for automobiles.

As quickly as they could, Lily and Hildy had found the station manager, who'd received Lily's telegram and listened patiently enough as she more fully explained the situation. Then they learned that the in-station porter who would have been on duty and assigned to Esmé and Madame Blanchett's train when it arrived on the evening of July 3 would be in soon. The station manager also confirmed there had been no trains going to Kinship or New York on July 4, and the train returning to New York had left yesterday, just hours before Lily and Hildy arrived to query the hotel manager.

That explains why Mama had arranged for Esmé and her chaperone to come to Kinship on the fifth. And why Madame Blanchett had remained in Columbus, waiting for a train back to New York. Oh, how Lily wished, as she studied the schedule, that Mama had just told her about Esmé sooner. They could have, as she'd said, gone to New York to collect Esmé, or even Columbus.

The station manager suggested they have breakfast at the sandwich shop, but Lily and Hildy hadn't wanted to miss meeting the porter before he went on duty and so insisted on waiting nervously in the station manager's cramped office. If it weren't for Lily showing her sheriff's badge—which he regarded with skepticism—they'd have no doubt been ushered away.

He'd looked relieved when he spotted the porter and now sits behind his desk, grumpily frowning at paperwork, his frequent sighs indicating he will be glad to see them leave.

The porter looks up and hands the photo back to Lily. The expression on his face, as if a dark shadow is passing overhead, strikes fear within her. She looks at Hildy, sees similar fear in her expression.

"I recognize the girl," the porter says. "She was throwing a fit, being pulled off the train, hollering up a storm. In some foreign language or another."

"By this woman?" She points to Madame Blanchett in the photo.

"No." But then he frowns, tilts his head, considering. "Maybe I did see a woman get off? It's hard to say. She, well, she looks like many women. Except—yes. She was back yesterday afternoon, wearing a hat with a big plume of blue feathers."

"But the girl—you said she was being pulled off. But not by this woman?" Lily interjects.

"No, no, by a man. A small man, split the difference between the two of you in height. And plenty strong; as hard as the girl squirmed, he didn't let go of the girl's arm. Wearing overalls, long sleeves. Big brimmed, floppy hat. A farmer, I'd a guessed."

"And you didn't intervene?" Hildy is outraged. "See why the girl was crying out?"

"Well, like I said, she was speaking in some foreign language," the porter says defensively. "And no, of course I didn't intervene. Reckoned it was her father—well, maybe a brother. Hard to say." He shrugs. "Not my place to step in. No one did. She was probably hollering for a sweet or something."

Lily and Hildy exchange glances. Tears spring to Lily's eyes at the crushed look on Hildy's face.

After a moment, the porter looks at the station manager. "I need to get back to work."

"Go on. Thanks." As the porter leaves, the station manager says to Lily, "All right, do you have what you need?"

Lily gives a crisp nod and takes Hildy's elbow. They rush out to the atrium. For a long moment, the people coming and going swirl around them and the sounds around them—loudspeaker announcements, people chattering—are an overwhelming cacophony. People stare as the two women cling to each other.

"Oh God, Lily, if Esmé was pulled off by some random man— God only knows what—"

Lily shakes her head. "I don't think it was random. If it was random, Madame Blanchett wouldn't have so coolly left, stayed at the hotel, then come back to the train yesterday. She'd have reported it. I think Esmé's been kidnapped, and Blanchett was in on the plot. And who would be asked to pay ransom other than Mama?"

Hildy takes a deep breath. "What about Chalmer Fitzpatrick? He was helping Mama McArthur with the details of getting Esmé here. Someone could have found out, arranged the kidnapping, and with the business he runs and the new park he is not exactly hiding that he has plenty of money, more than Mama McArthur."

For a long moment, Lily lets the gray noise of the terminal wash over her. She closes her eyes, leans into her friend.

Roger, Roger . . .

Hiram's visage, his plaintive bleating of her brother's name, fill Lily's mind.

Could he have known about Roger's daughter? Would he have

kidnapped Esmé to get money, hoping, in his confused way, to impress his mother—or Pearl? Tell Pearl he had money to take her and the baby, start over?

I won't let you hurt her! . . .

On the other hand, he'd rushed the stage to attack Chalmer. And Hiram has never said who he meant by *her.*

Could he have meant Esmé?

Lily swallows hard.

Could the very person who'd been helping Mama bring Esmé here have, for some reason, arranged to kidnap the child?

Four hours later, as Hildy turns off Kinship Road to pull down the lane to Lily's house, Lily exhales slowly. Her shoulders, clenched up by her ears, ease at just seeing her home with its soft rolling lawn, hollyhocks nodding by the side of the house, crisp white welcoming porch with the blue porch swing, so caringly handcrafted by Otto Owens.

They'd rolled down their windows for the drive back from Columbus, hot gritty air rendering their necks and faces sticky and smudged, but the breeze had been better than baking in the oven heat of Hildy's Model T, and Hildy's speed—she'd pushed them to go right to the automobile's top speed of 45 miles per hour—had made the gushing wind so loud that they couldn't really converse, which was probably just as well. All they had at this point was theories about Esmé's fate after she'd been pulled off that train in Columbus by a small man.

Hiram.

Theories and questions churned in Lily's mind all the way home. It would have been tight, but after work Hiram could have had time to get to Columbus on the night of July 3. Or he could have left early—would Chalmer have even known?—and had plenty of time to get there.

Then he could have stowed away Esmé—but where? Somewhere on Ida's property? In a hunting blind?

Of course, to mastermind all of this, Hiram would have had to know about Esmé. It's possible Chalmer had told him; he'd told Benjamin about Mama's plans and Esmé. But Chalmer had needed Benjamin's help. Why tell Hiram? Bragging to his cousin about the power he holds in the world—versus Hiram's meeker place in it?

Well, Lily has plenty of questions for both Chalmer and Hiram. The first question is who she will talk to first. And the conundrum, which has her temple throbbing and stomach curling with a sick headache, is if Hiram did kidnap Esmé, Hiram is now in jail on suspicion of murdering Pearl. What leverage does Lily have to get Hiram to tell her what happened to Esmé—his memories of Roger? It only makes her stomach turn more to think of using her brother's memory in this way, but if it means saving his daughter—her niece—she will.

For now, in this precious moment, Lily savors the relief of her home coming into view.

In the next moment, though, relief retreats, and her shoulders again rise toward her ears.

Parked by the side of the house, in her automobile's usual spot, is another, newer Model T. Mama must have parked her sheriff's automobile behind the house. And as Hildy slows for her descent down the lane, Lily hears the rise of children's voices from the garden in back of her house. Relief—*ah, they sound happy enough, though Mama's no doubt put them to work hoeing around the cornstalks, and picking yet another bounty of green beans, and pulling fat green tobacco worms off tomatoes. So the children must be fine, and perhaps the newer Model T just means someone's come to call—*

But then the door opens, and Mama and Marvena and Dr. Twomey rush out to the front porch. There's no need to see their facial expressions up close to know—from the rigid stances, from how Mama leans into Dr. Twomey and he puts his arm to her back, from how Marvena tilts forward, shading her eyes against the bright afternoon sun, yet still hurrying them on with her piercing gaze—that they're not just eager for news about Esmé.

Either something is wrong or they have yet more shocking news.

Yet Esmé is Mama's first concern as Lily and Hildy climb the porch steps.

"Did you—" Mama starts, glancing behind them, as if Esmé might pop out of Hildy's Model T, as if they might have been playing some cruel game of hide-and-seek with the child.

Lily gives just the slightest shake of her head, and Mama cries, "Oh!"

Dr. Twomey guides her to the blue porch swing, helps her sit down.

Lily goes and sits by her mama. "I'm sorry."

Mama's eyes are watering, questioning. "I was so hopeful. I did get a telegram from the New York hotel. They confirmed that Madame Blanchett and Esmé did spend the night there. Did you find out anything at all in Columbus—"

She stops. Mother and daughter exchange a look, and in that exchange is the hurtful truth: more pain awaits.

"Yes," Lily says. "Hildy and I found witnesses that say Madame Blanchett purposefully abandoned Esmé—and a man grabbed her and pulled her away."

"Oh!" Mama gasps as if in great physical pain, clutches her hands to her heart.

"Sheriff Ross!" Dr. Twomey admonishes.

Lily ignores him—*why is he here?*—and says, "I'm sorry, Mama; I should have put that smoother, easier—"

Mama shakes her head. "There's no good way to deliver bad news. What happens now?"

Lily takes a deep breath. How can she say what she must without striking an accusatory tone? Well, as Mama just said, there's no easy way to share bad news. "You worked with Chalmer Fitzpatrick to get Esmé here. Are you sure you only talked with Chalmer about Esmé?"

Mama nods.

"Well, my guess is that Chalmer must have let it slip—or someone overheard or saw notes he might have made," Lily says. "Or he told someone, without letting you know, just as he told Benjamin. I think he either told Hiram, or Hiram overheard, and Hiram figured out how to get Madame Blanchett's help to kidnap Esmé, and planned to send the ransom request to Chalmer— Mama, what?"

"Oh, Lily. There's been another development. That's why Walter is here."

It takes Lily a moment to realize that by "Walter" Mama means Dr. Twomey. When had Mama switched from calling him Dr. Twomey? Sometime in the past day.

Lily looks over at him. "Well?"

Dr. Twomey starts; then together he, Mama, and Marvena unspool the events of the night before.

Lily turns the new revelations over in her mind: Hiram had visited the Owens cabin on the night of July 4, sometime after 10:00 p.m., shortly after Pearl had retrieved the infant Suda had been wet-nursing, demanding *his* baby.

A baby Pearl had not given birth to, after all.

A baby who is, by Suda's testimony, Sophia's child.

And, at least theoretically, Hiram's.

Lily looks again at Dr. Twomey—she's certainly not ready to call him Walter—still unsure why he's here.

He clears his throat. "Your mother thought to come to me first thing this morning, given the revelations from Suda, and ask if there was any way to check Miss Riley to confirm whether or not she'd recently been pregnant." He looks down. "I should have thought to do that when you first brought her in."

Lily's heart softens at the doctor's humility. *Maybe this Walter isn't so bad.* "And I should have thought to ask. Mama was wiser than either of us. Were you able to learn anything, upon reexamination?"

Dr. Twomey nods. "I can't say for certain. Every woman recovers differently from childbirth. But my educated opinion is that no, Pearl Riley did not recently—or most likely ever—give birth."

"And you're still sure Pearl was most likely dead before she was in the water?"

"Most likely," he says. "There was enough bruising around her neck, and red and purple splotches in her eyes to indicate that she may have been choked to death."

Lily takes a deep breath, exhales long and slow. She's so weary. Never mind that it's a stifling hot morning in July, she feels as frozen as an icicle in the dead of winter over the choice she must make. Does she first go . . .

Mama comes to Lily, places her hands firmly on Lily's shoulders. "Lily, look at me. You don't have to do everything alone. Trust us. Let us help you. I can go talk to Hiram—"

"With all due respect, Mama McArthur, I think that might be too emotional for you," Hildy says.

"Well then," Mama persists, "Chalmer and Sophia—"

"But the children—" Lily protests. "You need to watch them, if I'm going to—"

"Nana's here," Mama says.

"She can watch 'em—give me a welcome break," Marvena says. But she has a twinkle in her eye. "And Dr. Twomey can drive us over."

"I'd be glad to," he says. "It might be helpful for me to be there to explain about Miss Riley most likely not having been pregnant recently. Assuming of course . . ."—he pauses to cast a deferential look Lily's way—"that you want to let them know that you've learned that the baby's parents are likely Sophia and Hiram."

"Yes, yes, of course they need to know," Lily says. "We need to find out about that situation. It could well be pertinent to learning all the facts behind Pearl's murder." Her unease with taking Hiram's confession at face value continues to deepen.

"I'll bring it up carefully—" Mama starts.

"Or just ask," Marvena says flatly. She chuckles at Mama's admonishing look. "All righty, maybe I should go with Lily into Kinship, if Hildy'd rather go with Mama McArthur and the doc. Course, we'd need to borry your T, Hildy—"

"No, I'll drive Lily over to Kinship to talk to Hiram," Hildy says. "I want to be there to talk with him, if that's all right. We were friends long ago, and I'm still connected with Roger in his mind, so . . ." She lets the sentence, and all it implies, drift along without spelling it out.

Lily's eyes tear from both gratitude and weariness. Then a question flashes across her mind. "Wait—why can't I drive? Where's my automobile? . . ."

Mama flushes, drops her hands, looks down.

Marvena chuckles. "Seems like daughter takes after mama, including aiming for the edge of the road."

"Hey now—" Lily starts, at the same time Mama exclaims, "I didn't wanna hit a chipmunk."

"Well, we were able to get from the Owens place last night, back to mine, but the automobile started pulling funny—that's your Mama's term—so we packed up Nana and the little ones and came down here to drop them off, then we got the automobile into town," Marvena says all in one breath, "and then your mama had the good instinct to check in with Dr. Twomey, who examined poor Pearl, and he brought us back here—"

Lily casts a curious look at Dr. Twomey, who blurts, "I went home right after and then came back this morning with the telegram from New York—Beulah, your mama, Mrs. McArthur, asked me to check—and then to wait for you with Beulah, I mean Mrs. McArthur. . . ."

A long silence builds on the buzz and heat of the morning.

And then, in spite of all the grimness of the past few days, and of the fears of what's to come, everyone on the porch bursts out laughing at Dr. Twomey's awkwardness—even the good doctor himself.

When the laughter settles down after a few waves Lily pulls her mama close in a hug. "You've done good work, Mama," she whispers. "And we're gonna find our Esmé."

A half hour later, Lily sits at the small desk in her bedroom, hands to her head.

She's washed up, changed her clothes, then sat down, pulled out her notebook, and written out notes from the past few days, trying to make sure she captures timelines and facts before going to question Hiram.

In her tote bag she'd rediscovered the letter that had been in the pocket of the work shirt that Hiram said was his. The shirt and the wrench are carefully stowed away at her office; if Hiram goes on trial, they will be important evidence. But the letter must have fallen free, and in her haste to track down Esmé she hadn't noticed the letter at the bottom.

It's on her desk now, and she's just reread the two simple pages:

> *Dearest Pearl,*
> *I love you and think of you all the time.*
> *There must be a way we can be together.*
> *Please, can we just meet and figure out a way?*
> [Then the second page:]
> *You are ever in my heart and soul.*
> *I think of you with only fondness, and will abide by your*
> *wishes.*
>
> > *Yours,*
> > *Hiram*

The handwriting is the same on both pages, and the paper matches.

Yet, with this fresh read-through, Lily notes the letter starts a third or so of the way down the first page, with more space between the lines and on either side of the script. The writing on the second starts and ends closer to the edges, with tighter spacing between the lines.

The whole letter could have fit on one piece of paper.

Lily lifts her head, shakes it, willing herself to pull her focus from what is surely minutiae, to go interrogate Hiram. Yet she looks again at the letter. Something about it, beyond the feeling of staring at an intimate portrayal of a desperate, needy love, troubles her. She looks at the two pages, side by side. Flips them over.

There, on the back of the first page, she sees a shadow of one of the letters—then another. Maybe her eyes are tricking her because she is tired?

Lily blinks, squeezes her eyes, stares again. No, it's definitely there— the echo of an *e*, of an *h*. Just a few of the letters have been traced, it seems, or at least only a few have been traced hard enough to leave an impression from the lead pencil of the original on the back of the page.

But why would Hiram have traced his own letter? Maybe he'd dropped something on the original and so he'd copied it over? But why trace?

"Mama!"

Lily startles at the sound of Jolene crying her name. She turns in her chair, as Jolene runs into Lily's bedroom and throws her arms around Lily, squeezing her waist as if she's been terrified while Lily was gone.

Oh. Lily embraces her daughter. "Are you all right?"

Jolene nods, but a snuffling sound cues Lily that Jolene is fighting back tears.

Lily smooths Jolene's hair, tilts her daughter's face up so she can look in her eyes. "Was one of the boys rotten again?"

Lily had intended her question to inspire a giggle, but instead Jolene anxiously widens her eyes. "Mama, did you find the missing girl? Esmé? The girl that's Uncle Roger's daughter?"

"So your mamaw did tell you about her?"

"Yes, she told all of us. She said she'd kept Esmé a secret, that she'd been wrong to not tell you and everyone a long time ago," Jolene says.

Lily pinches her lips together. Now Mama is erring on the side of blurting out too much for tender young ears.

But Jolene's expression turns thoughtful. "Mama, a few days ago Mamaw showed me the quilt she's been making from Uncle Roger's clothes. Have you seen it?"

Lily nods.

"It's for Esmé." Jolene leans forward. "When Mamaw was telling me about the quilt, she also said in a family is where you should feel the safest. How there's always love, like the sky, endless." She looks up at Lily, her face open with sincerity. "So if you're upset, 'cause you're worried, I know Mamaw has enough love for everyone—"

Lily kneels down by her daughter. How much to reveal to her? Lily so wants to protect her, but she also knows that Jolene's keen imagination will lead her to fill in and make up stories. "We haven't found Esmé—yet. But we're not going to give up. And I know Mamaw has plenty of love for all of us, and room in her heart for more. I'm just upset that she didn't tell me—us—about the child sooner."

Jolene considers. "So when you do find her, will she live with us, then?"

Lily's heart clenches—what if she doesn't find Esmé? And if she does, will Esmé move in with them? Or will Mama want to move back out to a house in town, take Caleb Jr. and Esmé? Or what if something beyond intrigued interest develops between Mama and Dr. Twomey and she moves into his little house in town? Or he gets bored in Bronwyn County and they all move away? Lily's heart clenches again at this. As mad as she's been at Mama, she doesn't want that.

"I don't know what your mamaw will want, but it would be fine with me if Esmé lives here with all of us."

"Good!"

Jolene throws her arms around Lily again, and Lily savors embracing her sweet daughter. She closes her eyes, breathes in the scent of Jolene's hair, feels the warmth and strength of her hug. *Oh God*. What would she do if she ever lost this child, or Micah?

And yet Mama had lost Roger. And now Esmé is gone and Lily is unsure where to start looking. The tasks before her are overwhelming.

Someone clears his throat at the door. Benjamin, she finds herself hoping. But why would he be here?

But then Lily does open her eyes, and it is Benjamin.

Jolene wrinkles her nose when she sees him. She looks back at Lily. "Can I go back downstairs?" She looks serious, just like Mama. "There's still a whole row of corn to hoe."

Lily plants a kiss on her daughter's forehead and says, "Go on, then."

Jolene dashes past Benjamin, cutting him a quick, harsh look.

Benjamin chuckles. "You know, she's a lot like you."

Lily frowns as she listens to Jolene's quick footfalls down the steps. And then she takes Benjamin's meaning—and, even in the midst of these thorny problems, also laughs. She *has* been pretty cold toward Dr. Twomey.

Maybe it's just human nature to fear losing some of the focus and fondness of a loved one by having to share it. Maybe such fear isn't that far off from Hiram's desperate need.

As Lily's laugh fades, Benjamin, too, looks serious. "Word travels fast—I've heard about the tragedy at Chalmer's. And I heard that you were away last night."

Benjamin displays no recrimination or expectation that she should have filled him in, only concern. "I came down from Rossville on my lunch break to see if I can help in any way, and Mrs. McArthur filled me in on, well, everything. I'm wondering, would you want me to put together a notice to run in the newspaper about Esmé? And I can put together a search team for Esmé and start looking as soon as you tell us where to focus."

His pointed gaze and his silent repose as he awaits her response tell her, just as Mama's hug had moments ago, *You're in charge. But that doesn't mean you have to be alone.*

Lily glances away, blinks hard as her eyes sting. Then she looks back at Benjamin and nods crisply.

CHAPTER 18

✢

BEULAH

Friday, July 6, 1928
5:30 p.m.

Chalmer's face is chalky white with shock following Beulah's revelation about Esmé. He gapes at Beulah and then looks desperately to Walter Twomey and Marvena, as if hoping they'll contradict her.

But Walter and Marvena, seated on the sofa opposite the armchairs that Beulah and Chalmer occupy in the parlor, remain silent.

A sudden joyful whoop from outside makes them all jump a little and look to the window. Though they can't see the fishing pond from the parlor, it's likely that the sound came from there. Already, though news has spread of the discovery of Pearl's body in the pond late on July 4, people are back to fishing from the dock. As Walter pulled up the lane, Beulah had noted a group of older boys heading down the short path to the pond, fishing poles at hand. She'd had mixed feelings at the sight. Life does go on, yes, but so soon after poor Pearl . . . Well, in any case, the park is sparsely visited today. They'd only seen a few cars parked at the turnoff to the park and spotted the boys going fishing. Beulah expects it will fill up tomorrow.

At last, Chalmer looks back at Beulah. "I—no—we haven't received any notes or messages, here or at the lumber mill, about Esmé. Unless Sophia received one today. I just got home from the mill. But Esmé, she should have arrived on July 5—"

"I know that. But she did not," Beulah says impatiently. Yes, Chalmer has had a huge shock, but Beulah's anxiety over Esmé is worsened by the news that Chalmer has not received a ransom demand. Why would a kidnapper wait—assuming Lily is right and there is a kidnapper. Has Esmé escaped?

Or—and at this, Beulah shudders—what if Esmé is already dead?

She shakes the thought away. It can't be true. She prays it is not.

"Dammit, I told you, Chalmer, that pond so close to the house is going to raise a ruckus. I heard the whooping all the way upstairs. . . ." Sophia's voice trails off as she comes into the parlor. She stops in the doorway. She's holding the baby, feeding her evaporated milk from a glass baby bottle. The baby takes the last slurp, and Sophia puts the bottle down next to a vase on a side table by the arched entryway. She then tosses a clean cloth diaper over her shoulder and turns the baby so her face is to Sophia's shoulder. Sophia pats the baby's back to burp her.

So natural. And so odd—seeing Sophia at ease in this maternal role. She's always struck Beulah as too fussy.

"Well," Sophia says, "I see we have guests. I'd offer to get you all something to drink, on this hot day, but as you can see, my hands are full. Of course, we don't have poor Pearl with us anymore, and Chalmer fired Dorit yesterday."

"Why'd you go and do that?" Marvena blurts out.

"Her brother killed Pearl—" Chalmer starts.

"That ain't been proved," Marvena says, "and anyhow, how'd you know about him—"

"There was an article in yesterday's *Daily Courier*," Walter says. "Word got around, and Hiram gave a brief interview."

"Lord a' mercy," Marvena says. "Lily'll have a conniption fit over that. But anyway, you fired Dorit?"

Chalmer stiffens. "I didn't think it would be right to keep on a close member of an alleged murderer's family—"

"*Your* family," Sophia says, with a half snort of a laugh.

"I said close family—" Chalmer swiftly turns to Sophia, anger reddening his face.

"Close enough, and now without Dorit to tend to your mamaw, I'm burdened with checking on MayBelle until we get new help—"

"Have you checked on her yet today?"

"No, I have my hands full."

Chalmer sighs. "This is why Mamaw needs to move in here—"

"That's not going to happen," Sophia says, so harshly that the baby begins to fuss. She jiggles her in her arms a little, to calm her. "She can go to the Widows' Home, which is where she belongs—"

"No, Sophia." Chalmer's voice rapidly ratchets higher. "You'll leave to take care of an aunt you barely remember, but when it comes to my grandmother . . . anyway, we have been over this, and—"

"Enough," Beulah snaps.

Everyone jumps, looking startled. Except Walter, who gives her a slight but appreciative smile.

Beulah looks at Marvena. "Please go check on MayBelle."

"She lives in a cabin, just up the lane, where she is perfectly happy—" Sophia starts, then silences under Chalmer's withering glare.

Marvena stands, looks at Beulah. "Yes, ma'am," she says.

As Marvena leaves, Sophia takes the spot next to Dr. Twomey. Beulah studies her for a moment. Yes, she looks quite taken with the baby—her baby. Seeing them together, Beulah believes that yes, Sophia is the child's mother. Not from any resemblance—it's too soon for that. But from the way Sophia gazes at the child. Though Beulah can believe that eventually some women—though she doubts it of Sophia—might accept their husband's child by another woman, doing so would take more than two days. No, Sophia is already deeply bonded with the baby. And in spite of the circumstances, it's moving.

Beulah looks over at Chalmer, who barely notices his wife. He still looks shocked and distraught over Esmé.

"We are here," Beulah says firmly, "because my granddaughter Esmé is missing. She is Roger's daughter, born in France, but coming here now."

Sophia looks up, startled. "What? Roger had a daughter—and she's now missing? That's terrible, but why are you here—"

"It's none of your concern, Sophia," Chalmer says. "I helped Beulah arrange the paperwork, and so now she's asking me about it, so please, just go upstairs—"

"No." Beulah cuts off Chalmer. "It's possible she's seen or heard something that might help us." She regards Sophia. "We believe my granddaughter has been kidnapped. I asked if Chalmer has received any ransom notes or messages. Have you received anything like that?"

"Of course not. This is all new to me—but wait. I did overhear Chalmer talking with, why, I think he's your daughter's beau? Benjamin Russo? About the paperwork, the bureaucracy, about bringing someone over?" Sophia looks at her husband. "Was this in regard to Mrs. McArthur's granddaughter?"

Chalmer nods, wearily rubbing his hands against his cheeks.

Sophia regards Beulah, her eyebrows lifting as if something is occurring to her in the moment. "If I overheard, then Hiram might have, too." She asks Chalmer, "Wasn't Hiram in the house a few months ago? Tracking mud all over the place? Upstairs? Seems to me you hollered at him for that—"

Chalmer gives her a cutting yet confused look. "He was repairing part of the ceiling in the sewing room," he explains. "There was a roof leak—"

"Well, I hope he did a good job fixing it," Sophia says. "The room will become the baby's nursery—"

"Sophia, this isn't the time—"

Beulah clears her throat.

Chalmer looks at her. "Yes. Hiram could possibly have seen the work I was doing, the paperwork." He shakes his head. Puts his hands to his head. "My God. But I can't imagine he would do anything so violent as kidnap a girl . . . or, honestly, be smart enough to pull that off—"

Sophia gives a short laugh. "True enough. He wasn't smart enough to accept that poor Pearl didn't have eyes for *him*." She puts emphasis on *him,* not subtly, and gives Chalmer a cold look while cocking an eyebrow.

Chalmer suddenly turns bright red.

The baby girl finally burps. Then sighs and puts her head to Sophia's shoulder. Sophia keeps patting the baby, lovingly enough, but Beulah still feels sorrow for the child, who will grow up in this cold, difficult household.

"Well, anyway," Beulah says, "did you witness any tussles between Hiram and Pearl? Him following or haranguing her?"

"No, no, Pearl wasn't here—that often," Chalmer says. His redness deepens. "I mean, she was here earlier last fall. She was—is friends with Sophia through the Woman's Club. And Sophia mentioned that Pearl had expressed concern about having an income, suggested we hire her to help with Mamaw. Which worked out well, at first . . ." He trails off, the ruddiness of his face deepening.

"Yes, we all know how that worked out, dear," Sophia says, giving the baby's head a pat. "Anyway, we let Pearl go, after, well, you know. And hired in Dorit."

"But you stayed friends with Pearl," Walter speaks up.

Sophia looks at him, taken aback by his comment. "Well—yes. I forgave her. Forgave my husband. Forgiveness is what we're called upon to do, especially as women, isn't that right, Mrs. McArthur?"

"I don't know about *especially,* but yes. It is the Lord's way," Beulah agrees. Though in her experience—just as in bonding with a child sired by your husband with another woman—it takes a bit more than moments.

"Good-enough friends that she went with you to help you with your aunt?" Walter asks.

Beulah takes a long, calming breath. *Ah.* This is the second hard part of the conversation. She's glad to let Walter take over the next bit of questioning. Walter. That's how she now thinks of Dr. Twomey, since he told her this morning to just call him by his first name. And asked if he could call her by hers. She'd said *yes.* They'd fallen into first-name status instantly. Easily. Some things do only take a moment to feel right. Natural.

Sophia frowns as she answers. "Yes. I needed the help. Of course, I didn't know then that she was pregnant—turned out, she was nearly seven months along, but not showing, at least not in her older dresses. She had the baby while we were in Virginia."

Beulah notes that Sophia is wearing an older style as well—not the drop-waisted slimmer style she'd opted before for Woman's Club luncheons last year.

Sophia shakes her head. "I knew, of course, whose it was. And she told me she was going to give the child up for adoption, sell her house, leave Kinship—"

"Mrs. Fitzpatrick," Walter says firmly. "Pearl has not recently been pregnant."

The room goes stiff, still. Outside, the boys are no longer whooping over fish caught at the pond. The daytime insects and birds have lulled; it's too early yet for crickets and katydids and hoot owls to fill the silence. Beulah shifts in her seat, uncomfortably sticky and hot in the room, even though the draperies are partially drawn. But the soft grayness of the room is not enough to dissolve either heat or tension.

Sophia's face has gone pale, frozen. Chalmer, as shocked as he was to hear about Esmé, now looks even more alarmed. A mix of confusion, surprise, and rising anger plays over his expression. "What— What are you saying?—" he starts, softly.

"I reexamined Miss Riley," Walter says. "Based on testimony Beulah received yesterday from Mrs. Suda Owens, the wet nurse who had been tending to the baby—" He gestures to the child in Sophia's arms. "It is my conclusion, as a doctor, that there are no indications that Miss Riley had given birth recently—"

"But this baby is a month old," Sophia protests, her voice crackling and straining. "And women's bodies—"

"Recover, yes, and sometimes quickly. But there were no stretch marks on her abdomen. Or on her breasts, which even if her own milk had dried up because she turned the child over to the wet nurse might well be there from the initial expression of milk," Walter explains.

He says these things so practically, Beulah thinks, things that are not often openly discussed between women, what's more in mixed company. And the coolness and evenness with which he says them makes her admire him even more.

"And there is no indication in her private area of stretching or healed tears that might indicate recently giving birth," Walter adds.

Sophia shifts uncomfortably.

"I can't say she's never given birth," Walter goes on, "but—"

"But that's . . . that's impossible. Pearl didn't tell me about the baby on the morning of July 4, but she said she wanted money, or she'd let everyone know about our affair, and besides, Sophia and I tried for years to have a baby, and that never happened, and, and—" Chalmer looks at Beulah. "You saw her. She came out of my study"—he gestures wildly to the space behind him—"while you were waiting here with Frankie, before the dedication. . . ."

"I did," Beulah says. "I saw her. But as Walter indicated, Marvena and I went up to talk with Suda Owens, the wet nurse, yesterday. Lily had to go in search of Esmé, and she sent us, to find out if Suda could pinpoint when Pearl came for the baby on the night of July 4, if she could provide any information about that last night of Pearl's life—"

"Wait—how did you know to go to Suda Owens?" Sophia asks. Walter stares at her.

"Nana Sacovech—that's Marvena's mother-in-law—and I are good friends. Nana is a healer. She wanted to check on Suda just because she knew the woman is overburdened, worn down with her own brood and new baby, plus wet-nursing this little one," Beulah says. "So I'd seen this baby before. . . ." She pauses, then adds gently, "The strawberry birthmark is distinctive."

Sophia holds the now-sleeping baby a little more closely. Protectively.

Beulah leans forward. She knows what she is about to say is going to hit

Chalmer hard. It is unfair, of course, but Chalmer—most everyone—would expect Sophia to forgive him and move on. Raise the child as her own, especially since she supposedly couldn't have children. But Sophia having an affair, having a baby with a man who is not her husband . . . that is going to be much harder, if not impossible, for Chalmer to forgive. Beulah swallows hard, her throat suddenly tight and dry, and not just from the oppressive heat of a late-July afternoon. What she is about to say is going to echo through the Fitzpatricks' lives for years to come. But she must do it.

"Sophia," Beulah says softly, "Suda told us the child is yours. And that Hiram came to their cabin on the night of July 4, demanding his child. He was distraught that Pearl had already taken her. But if he knew the child was yours and his, why would he follow her, kill her, after she left your child with you—"

"This baby isn't his," Sophia cries out. "Or, or, mine. Hiram must be lying. He's crazy; you saw how he rushed at my husband on the stage—"

"Yes!" Chalmer snaps. "He was shouting, 'I won't let you hurt her!' I thought he meant Pearl—who I wouldn't hurt—that she had complained to him about me. But he meant this baby." He looks at his wife. "Didn't he, Sophia?"

"I have no idea what he meant," Sophia says. "I thought it was silly of you to hire him in the first place, and besides, like you said, we tried for years to have a child, and I couldn't—"

"Or your husband is infertile," Walter says. "It's not always because of something gone awry with the woman's anatomy that a child can't be conceived."

Beulah glances at him, thankful for the way he'd phrased that. That he hadn't said *something wrong with the woman*, as it was so often put. That she has no doubts he'd been this gentle, likely even more so, with dear Hildy in how he'd shared the hard truth with her.

Chalmer clenches his fists. "Oh my God. Sophia."

She stands, abruptly. "Very well. Yes, this baby is mine. But not Hiram's. And no, I won't say who the father is. And yes, I asked Pearl to go with me to Virginia, told her I'd give her plenty of money to go away if she'd help me with this ruse. Yes, we went to my aunt's house, though it was empty. A cousin let us stay there, no questions asked, because he's having a hard time getting it sold. My aunt died months ago."

"How could you do this, Sophia?" Chalmer cries. "How could I not know?"

Sophia looks at Chalmer. "Oh, Chalmer, you haven't touched me in months. And it's not like you've disclosed all your lovers to me over the years. Though I've found—and kept—plenty of evidence. Silly love notes. Ladies' handkerchiefs that aren't mine. So don't think you can get away with divorcing me, turning me out in the cold, with no support." She laughs, bitterly. "Though I know you well enough—you value your reputation too much to let this get out."

Chalmer collapses back in his chair as if she'd just punched him.

Sophia turns her fearsome gaze on Beulah and Walter. "And if either of you or Sheriff Lily think you can embarrass us with this information, or blackmail us, well, Chalmer won't let that happen. He can pull enough strings with other business owners to ruin Lily as sheriff—"

"Oh, for pity's sakes, that's not our motivation, Sophia! We're here because Hiram has confessed to killing Pearl," Beulah snaps. "He says he told her he would take care of her and the child, even leave with her. Of course, he would need money for this. And as I said when we first arrived, my granddaughter is missing. A man matching Hiram's description was seen pulling her . . ." Beulah pauses, swallows hard as her eyes sting; Walter gives her a sympathetic but encouraging look: *Go on. You're strong. Say what you must.* "Pulling her off of the train in Columbus. Lily is interrogating him now, to find out if he kidnapped her for ransom. Of course, he could have claimed the baby was Pearl's to cover for you. Even kill her, if he thought she was going to betray the truth about the baby to Chalmer. Could have planned on getting enough money through ransom for, for my granddaughter in order to impress you, try to lure you away." Beulah's voice has risen on a wave of emotion. She's nearly shouting as she concludes, "That's why, propriety be damned, we had to come here, tell the truth, in case you know anything, if either of you—" She glances at Chalmer. Tears course down his cheeks. Over the revelation about the baby he'll now help raise? About his wife's infidelity? About Esmé, who, after all, is the daughter of a man he'd served with and who he'd helped bring over from France? Or maybe over all of it. "If either of you know anything that could help us know if Hiram kidnapped Esmé, or if anyone else might have overheard our plans." Beulah pauses. Oh God. This is her fault. Hers. Why hadn't she talked to Lily to begin with? "Or if you might have an inkling where Hiram might have taken Esmé, for God's sake, Sophia, if Hiram ever mentioned a hidden-away cave or hunting shack or, or . . . She's just a little girl. . . ."

Chalmer puts a hand on Beulah's arm. "Mrs. McArthur. I'm so sorry. If I knew anything that could help you, I'd tell you. If I . . ."—he pauses to give his wife a sharp look—"if *either* of us think of anything, we'll tell you and Sheriff Lily right away."

Sophia stands. "I'm sorry for your troubles, Mrs. McArthur. But whatever Chalmer's cousin meant by his comments at Suda Owens's place, I barely knew him. I told my husband there would only be trouble if he hired his ratty cousins, especially given the family history. Yes, this is my child, but again, Hiram is not the father"—she slides a taunting look at her husband—"and I'm certainly not going to say which of his lumber mill employees is. He, too, has a family to consider. I hope Lily gets information out of Hiram that helps you find your granddaughter safe and sound. But meanwhile, we have plenty to deal with here." Her gaze tightens and glints. She's dismissing Beulah and Walter from her parlor.

"Oh God, I'm so embarrassed at how I broke down," Beulah says. She and Walter are standing by his Model T, waiting for Marvena. Beulah takes a deep breath of the steaming late-afternoon air, trying to steady herself.

Walter frowns at her. "Broke down? Beulah, if I may, you were strong. Asking the right questions. I can see where Lily gets her toughness."

"Maybe some of it, but mostly it's from her father, I reckon—" She starts crying, thinking about Esmé, and her nose runs, and she quickly digs out her handkerchief and blows her nose, a great honking sound, which is even more embarrassment and leads to her crying harder.

Suddenly Walter pulls her to him in an embrace. "Well," he says gently. "I'm sure she got plenty of fine qualities from her father, but I don't reckon most of them are from him, and I reckon he'd agree with me."

In spite of everything, Beulah giggles at the awkward way Walter says the word "reckon," not imitating, but trying to fit in. And in the next moment she lets herself fully collapse in his embrace and gives in to her tears. He holds her close, but not too tightly.

A few minutes later, a tentative throat clearing breaks the moment. Beulah and Walter pull apart. Marvena stands before them, regarding them gently from under her floppy-brimmed hat. "MayBelle's cabin is a far enough piece up yonder—took me a while to get there and back. Anyway, I sat a spell with MayBelle. Made her up a supper plate. She doesn't remember anything more about the night poor Pearl was found. I'm not sure she even remembers telling Lily about her visions of a young woman in the pond." Marvena shakes her head. "She needs to live here, at the big house with Chalmer. Or at the Widows' Home, if Sophia really is dead set against her being here. She's right worried about the baby, though. Focused on that. It's all she wanted to talk about. I told her the baby'll be fine." Marvena casts a doubtful glance at the house. "Won't she?"

"I hope so," Walter says. "I didn't do an examination, but the baby seems fine. I'll come back and check in a day or so."

Marvena cuts a glance over to Beulah, worried. "I reckon you didn't learn anything to help us find Esmé?"

Beulah shakes her head. "No. Though Sophia did fess up that the baby is really hers, and that Pearl was in on a ruse with her to make Chalmer think it was his and Pearl's."

Marvena looks askance. "Don't that beat all I've ever heard tell. How'd Chalmer take it?"

"Calmer than I'd have expected," Walter says. "I think he's in shock. Sophia says that Hiram is not the father, and she won't say who is. Just that it is someone who works at the lumber mill—taunting Chalmer."

Marvena gives a long whistle, shakes her head.

"So we haven't learned anything, have we, to help us find Esmé," Beulah says plaintively.

"Don't know about that, Mama McArthur," Marvena says. "We got some small pieces of information. We'll take 'em to Lily. You know our Lily. By the time she puts all the pieces together, she'll see a pattern. Figure it out. Just like one of your quilts."

CHAPTER 19

LILY

Friday, July 6, 1928
5:30 p.m.

Warden Hunter starts to follow Lily and Hildy into the holding cells area of the jail. Lily gives him a quick smile—something between irritation and amusement. He does this every time she enters the jail. "We'll be fine, Warden," Lily says. "We just need to see Hiram Fitzpatrick."

The warden regards her with genuine concern. "You sure?"

Lily gives a crisp nod. She's proud of the new jail, an addition to the courthouse as part of its renovations. She'd had to petition for the jail to be included in the expansion, shortly after her reelection two years before, angering at least one of the county commissioners and frustrating another. The board of commissioners oversee the sheriff's office, so she'd tried to tread lightly. Well, at least diplomatically. Fortunately, all three commissioners finally agreed to a unanimous public vote—always the preferred look for the public and newspaper reports—to divert funding toward a jail with eight cells with two cots each and decent bedding, a separate booking area, and wardens. She's glad about these updates, even though they mean she is still light in the deputy area. But the new jail is more humane than the crowded conditions she'd done her best to deal with when the jail was one small building behind the sheriff's house, with just four cells, and on especially rough weekends many prisoners in cells meant to hold two. As when she was jail matron, the cells are fully cleaned between uses and the prisoners are fed three square meals a day and can have water any time they ask.

Still, getting her way meant putting up with the overly solicitous concerns of this particular warden, and not a few snide comments from the most resistant commissioner when the cells weren't full up.

Now Lily says, "I'm sure. Besides, I have one of my deputies with me."

Warden Hunter gives Hildy a doubtful look, and in return Hildy just smiles beatifically, which makes Lily chuckle to herself. She knows Hildy is just as annoyed under the surface as Lily is. But the warden unlocks the door to the jail cell—not that, really, he has any choice but to obey Lily—and says, "I'll be just out here, if you need anything."

"It's been a long day. How about a couple of chairs?" Hildy asks. She means for sitting outside the cell.

Lily regards her friend, who does look weary. "Just one will do." She holds out her hand to Warden Hunter. "Please give me the keys. I want to go into Hiram's cell, talk with him there," Lily says.

At that, both Hildy and the warden look at her askance. But Lily is not afraid of Hiram. She sighs. "He's not going to hurt us. And I don't want the others to overhear what I have to ask."

Plus being close to him, in the cell, might just be enough to intimidate him, get him to tell her what she needs to know. If all goes well, he'll tell her where Esmé is and as a bonus, when she shares that she knows the baby's mother is really Sophia, he'll share whatever he's been holding back about Pearl's death. Lily just can't believe he'd kill another human.

Or maybe, she thinks as she enters the jail, she just doesn't want to believe Hiram is capable of murder. But then most people don't know what they're capable of until they're pressed too far.

"Hey, Sheriff Lily!"

"Hey, Jimbo," Lily replies. Jimbo, in one of the cells closest to the main door, is a regular whom Lily has to haul in for carousing after getting into hooch, especially after a payday.

"Miss your cookin', Sheriff Lily," Jimbo says. Lily was jail matron when her husband Daniel was sheriff. "We never get pie."

"I'll put in a word," Lily says.

Warden Hunter rolls his eyes as he gives Lily the key ring, which she pockets. He shrugs as he ducks out to grab a chair. "Not sure he's going to tell you anything you want to know. He ain't said two words since you brought him in, not on my watch, and not according to any of the other wardens."

Lily and Hildy stride back to Hiram's cell, one of the two cells with narrow, high windows. Lily had picked that cell for him for the scant breeze that sifts through when the window is tilted open at an angle—barely big enough for a cat to wiggle through, what's more a human, but at least air circulates throughout the jail, a relief on this hot, muggy evening. He's the only occupant of the cell, and though it is early in the evening, he is curled up on the bottom cot, back to the bars of the cell. His shoes are off, neatly side by side by the bed. His supper—ham sandwich, potato salad, apple, glass of milk—sits untouched on the floor just on the other side of the cell door. Lily had pushed hard for bigger cells and better accommodations in the jail.

Lily opens the cell door. Hiram doesn't respond to the sound of the door grating open. By the time she repockets the key ring, Warden Hunter is back with the chair, which he places to one side in the cell. Lily frowns at Warden Hunter, asking, "Has he been eating since I brought him in?"

"Barely. He hardly even touches water."

"Hey, I'll take his if he don't want it," Jimbo hollers.

As he picks up Hiram's untouched tray, Warden Hunter calls back, "Shut up, Jimbo." But good-naturedly. The warden hovers in the doorway.

"We'll be fine," Lily says firmly.

The warden steps out.

Lily waves at the chair. "Hildy, please sit—"

"I sat all morning, driving—"

"Yeah, and I napped, and you look like you're about to keel over where you're standing," Lily snaps. Hiram stirs, as Hildy sighs and sits down after all.

Lily gives Hiram a nudge. "Hiram. Wake up. It's Lily."

He grunts.

Hildy scoots forward. The grating of the chair legs on the floor doesn't stir him further, but then Hildy speaks. "Hey, Hiram," she says. Her voice, as always, is firm but gentle. "Lily tells me you're in a peck of trouble. Thought maybe we could talk with you. Sort a few things out."

At that, Hiram groans a little but sits up, swings his body around, puts his feet to the floor. His gaze skips over Lily, but he stares at Hildy, his eyes widening. Lily briefly smiles at Hildy. Well, no wonder Hildy has a reputation for being a good schoolmarm—sparing the rod, yet not spoiling the children.

"You—you came to see me?" Hiram asks, incredulously.

Hildy nods. "I did."

"Wh-why?"

"Oh, Hiram," Hildy says. "I remember you as such a kind, gentle soul when we were in school together." Nothing in her expression gives a hint that she might also well remember that he was a mite too obsessive in pursuing her, until Roger intervened. "And Roger, he thought so highly of you."

Hiram stares up at the tilted window, as if at some spot miles and miles away. Or, Lily thinks, maybe years distant in the past.

"Hiram?" Hildy's voice, sweet and angelic. "Hiram, would you please look at me?"

Hiram turns and gazes at her.

"Lily, we . . . have some questions for you—"

"I done told Sheriff Lily," Hiram says flatly. "I wanted to take care of Pearl and, and our baby. But she didn't want nothing to do with me. I lost my temper, got too rough with her . . ." He chokes up, suddenly unable to continue.

Lily's fists clench. She just wants to shake him. What really happened? Who is he protecting and why? "Hiram, Mama and Marvena have talked to—"

Hildy gives a stern little shake of her head at Lily, who hushes—partially because as soft as Hildy looks, Lily suddenly doesn't want to disappoint her. But mostly because she knows what Hildy is thinking and that Hildy is right: now is not the time to confront Hiram about the revelation that Sophia is, at least according to Suda, the mother of the baby. Not Pearl.

Pearl isn't coming back, and Hiram, their only viable suspect, is safely under lock and key. Right now, they have to focus on seeing if he can—or will—tell them anything about Esmé.

"I understand," Hildy says to Hiram. "I've had moments when I've lost sight of keeping my wits about me."

Hiram looks surprised. "You—you have?"

"Mmm-hmmm. And I'm guessing you were saving money, too, working for Chalmer. Wanting to take Pearl away with you, make a better life for yourself. And her. And the baby."

Hiram gulps, nods.

"But that wouldn't pay so much, would it?" Hildy asks gently.

So you kidnapped Esmé! Lily wants to scream. But a deeper, calmer instinct tempers her to stay silent, let Hildy take over.

"At least not after you helped out your own mama," Hildy says. "I know what that's like—trying to help kin who aren't, well, as appreciative as they could be." She gives a wavery smile. "My mama and yours—they are alike in many ways."

Oh. Hearing Hildy's comment is like a gut punch. But she is right. Just two years ago, Lily learned on another case just how cruel Hildy's mother could be. Yet Hildy had not only survived the experience, she'd come through much stronger, as Lily now witnesses in Hildy's steady, calm approach.

"And just because someone can become a parent doesn't mean they will be good at raising up a child," Hildy says. "And sometimes, people who would be never get that chance."

Lily's eyes fill, as Hildy's voice stays even and strong, though soft.

"But you—you would be a good father, Hiram. And you wanted to give Pearl and the baby the best chance, didn't you?"

Hiram nods. "I did. But, but why are we going over this? I've confessed—"

"I know, Hiram, I know . . . ," Hildy says. She pauses for a long moment. Lily bites her tongue to keep from speaking. Hiram looks uncomfortable. Finally, Hildy gives Lily a quick glance: *Listen carefully now.* "Lily and I just came back from the train station in Columbus. We have witnesses who say that a man grabbed Esmé Chambeau—that's Roger's daughter, who Mama McArthur is bringing over from France—from the train."

The silence stretches, long and impossible, in the hot jail cell. Lily swallows back the desire to say something—or perhaps just scream.

Finally, Hiram says, "I was just so mad at Chalmer for how he treated Pearl. How he treated all of us. Figured she was only with him for his money, so if I had money, too, she'd want me. I overheard about Esmé, when he was telling another fellow."

Oh, Lily thinks. *Benjamin.*

"I— I did grab her. I told her I was family. Took her to our place. Told her to stay in the barn, that the family wasn't ready yet to meet her."

Lily's stomach turns and it's all she can do to fight back revulsion from showing on her face. But then hope rises—could he be about to say where Esmé is? Might she still be at the barn?

Hiram drops his head. "She escaped. From—from the barn. She was safe, and fine, I want you to know that, I just didn't want Dorit or Mama to know what I'd done."

"Hiram, where do you think she went off to?" Hildy asks.

He shrugs. "I don't know. But she's fine. She'll be fine."

That shrug is too much. Lily steps forward. "Hiram, did Madame Blanchett try to stop you?" She thinks she already knows the answer, but something feels off about Hiram's story. She needs details about what really happened, to shake something out that she can use to track Esmé.

Hiram looks up at Lily, startled, as if he'd forgotten she is there. "No—no—she was in on it. I— I sent her a telegram, organized the plot . . ."

Lily doesn't believe it. She can't imagine Hiram organizing a kidnapping plot. Or even Pearl. But Sophia . . . yes, she can imagine her, especially if she and Hiram are the baby's parents, organizing such a plot. She can believe Sophia would want to get money for herself so she could eventually leave Chalmer. Sophia had to know about Chalmer helping Mama, about Esmé, didn't she? If Chalmer told Benjamin, surely he'd told his own wife about Esmé—even if he and Sophia were at odds. Wouldn't he want to brag to her about his helping Mama? Recount his war heroics? Talk about Roger?

And if Sophia was involved, then maybe Esmé is somewhere at the park.

I won't let you hurt her! . . .

Hiram's words, shouted at Chalmer on the stage at the dedication on the Fourth, echo in Lily's mind.

Oh God. What if "her" was Esmé?

What if Chalmer for some reason decided to kidnap Esmé? Perhaps thinking he could get money out of Mama, or out of Esmé's other grandmother? What if Hiram—she recollects how cowed he'd acted around Chalmer on the third when she came to return MayBelle to the Fitzpatrick compound—has simply been doing his bidding all along? Maybe Chalmer, who has poured so much money into the park, had himself taken Esmé, hoping he could get money from Mama, maybe to pay off debts, maybe to pay Sophia to go away and accept a divorce. He could have rationalized the whole thing—Esmé being fine, under his watch. . . .

If she can get Hiram to tell her that, if she can confirm either Sophia's or Chalmer's involvement, then she can confront them. Search the park. Find Esmé. Desperately, she wants this to be the case. "Hiram, I need details. When did you send the telegram?"

"Uh, I don't know, 'xactly—in the spring. March—no, April. I— I sent several."

"From the Kinship telegraph office?"

"Uh—yeah. Yeah, sure."

"And when did you leave to go meet Madame Blanchett?"

Hiram looks confused. "Well, that would have been—two days ago, right? Yes, two days ago."

"On the Fourth."

"Yes, on the Fourth. The morning of the Fourth?"

"So you drove there? In your truck?"

"No—no—I took the train."

"Which train?"

"The one to Columbus."

"Oh, and what time did that train leave?" Lily knows—having studied the schedule Mama showed her—that there was no train going first thing in the morning from Kinship to Columbus.

"Wait— I drove." Tears spring to his eyes. "You can ask the fella that lives across the road down below. He's always yelling at me to drive slower."

"What time did you leave?"

"I—look, I don't remember. It's a blur." Suddenly Hiram is shouting, the tears running from his eyes, snot from his nose, and he's wringing his hands. "I— I've been so upset, 'cause, 'cause of her—"

"Her being Esmé?"

"No, 'cause of . . . Pearl."

"So you are so upset that you can't remember how you got to the train station to kidnap Esmé, but you were calm enough to go to Pearl's house, try to talk her into staying with you, follow her to Chalmer's house, watch her leave her baby on the doorstep, then grab her and choke her and bash her head with your wrench and toss her into the pond to drown—"

"Lily, please stop—" Hildy says.

But suddenly, desperately, Lily lunges forward, grabs Hiram by his shirt, yanks him to his feet, shakes him. He's like a rag doll under the force of her fury.

"Tell me. Tell me where she is. Where Esmé is!"

Hiram slowly looks up. His expression is that of a broken man, but his eyes show her he knows the answer. His pinched lips show he is not going to say.

Hiram's eyes tear up. He blinks hard. "I let— I let Esmé go. She— She'll be fine, for another night—"

"Why are you doing this? Are you helping Chalmer? Sophia?" Lily shakes him again, then screams in his face, "Tell me!" She wants to slam him against the cinder-block wall behind him, slam him until he tells her—

"Lily!" Hildy shouts as she grabs Lily's arm, tries to pull her away from Hiram. "This isn't the way; he's not going to say—"

But Lily hangs on. Through clenched teeth, she hisses, "I would do anything—*anything*—to protect my family."

Hiram stares at her. His eyes have gone cold. "So would I."

CHAPTER 20

꙰

ESMÉ

Friday, July 6, 1928
8:30 p.m.

In the shelter the man had brought her to, Esmé makes a peanut butter sandwich from the last of the provisions.

It's warm in here, but not as bad as the barn. And the place has, besides the lamp, a table and two chairs, and a real cot—there is even a pillow and a thin sheet to pull over herself—and two big jugs of water. It's outfitted with a cabinet in which there was bread, apples, peanut butter, a box of crackers, and a jar of jelly, tins of milk, a can opener. Not the best provisions, but she hasn't gone hungry.

There is no coal-oil lamp, but there is a flashlight. He'd told her to use it only when she needed to go outside to do her business.

The man has not been back since. He'd promised he would be, that he'd bring her better food than what he'd been keeping there, he said, for himself.

But he has not come back. She's starting to think he will not.

Even before she began to wonder if he would ever come back, Esmé's thought about running several times—especially when she'd heard in the distance a large group of people, sounding like the chittering at a fair. That had been two days ago. She'd wandered out then and found that there was a path that led from the place—a thin path that looked like it was barely used. She'd wandered up it, though, toward the sound, then stopped short when she saw three girls, about her age.

They looked lost and scared, but when they saw her they seemed to forget about being lost. They tried to talk to her, but Esmé wasn't sure if she should trust them or not. Then she had run after all. They'd followed, but she'd ducked into the woods and watched them as they came to the place where she'd been staying. Suddenly she felt oddly protective of it and wished for the girls to not go in.

One of them started coughing, and wheezing hard. The other two patted her back and gave her time to catch her breath. When she did, the girls left, walking slowly, the other two concerned about the coughing girl.

Esmé had receded back to her place, staying there.

Now she pulls out the letter from Papa and finally finishes reading it by the flashlight.

Kind people. Angels, like your mama and your mamaw—maybe, Esmé thinks, like those girls had been with the one who coughed so much. *So be like them, my child.*

I know you will be. And I know you will be brave. Find your own path. Take care of yourself and others. Do what you know in your heart is right.

I hope I will get to meet you, to talk with you about these things, to show them to you instead of just putting them in words. But I wanted to get this down, just because—well, this war is hell. And life is fragile. You'll understand that, too, someday.

But whatever happens, please know—I love you. Your papa, Roger McArthur.

Esmé thinks over her father's words: *Be brave. . . . Take care of yourself and others.*

Well, she's going to need more food. And maybe it is time to *make a decision.*

A decision to leave.

But just in case she wants to come back, she takes the sheet and rubs the edge of it against the metal leg of the cot. That's sufficient to make a notch, and she tears up the sheet into strips.

She gets her bag and flashlight and sets out, making her own path up a hill, in the direction of the festivities she'd heard a few days before. Every so often she ties a strip of cloth to a tree.

Soon she hears something else.

A baby crying.

And then something else—gunshots, distant, but ringing across the clear night. She recognizes the sound from hunters who came to the woods near her *mémère*'s farm.

Esmé stops, scared.

What should she do?

She waits. The baby's cries get louder, covering the sound of cricket chirps but not quite the sound of a nearby owl's hoots.

Then Esmé makes a decision.

CHAPTER 21

LILY & BEULAH

Friday, July 6, 1928
10:30 p.m.

The moonlight hits so that the light glistens on Coal Creek, the light sparkling and dancing, as the water flows past the majestic tree—really three trees, conjoined at their base, a sycamore, maple, and beech. Thick roots curl over the steep edge like grasping fingers; the trunks cord into one; thick leafy branches rustle overhead. Lily sits on the ground, her back leaned against its base, staring at the water.

She is alone.

Hildy and Lily hadn't talked on the drive from the jail to her house to retrieve Sadie or on the drive over to Hiram's family's cabin. Lily had been hoping Sadie could track Esmé—but the attempt had failed.

On the way back to Lily's farmhouse, Lily and Hildy had been silent. Lily expected Hildy to drive off as soon as Lily and Sadie bounded out of her automobile, but Hildy had gotten out, too, followed Lily into the house, pausing only to pet and praise Sadie as the dog settled down with a blubbery sigh on the front porch. Nana and the children ran to greet Hildy and Lily in the parlor, excitedly asking if she'd brought back Esmé.

That's when Lily's face flamed with shame, as the children's faces dropped with disappointment. She'd asked briefly after Mama, Marvena, and Dr. Twomey, but they weren't back yet. And then she'd walked through the house, out the back, taken care of her needs at the outhouse, and gone on down to the Kinship Tree.

She had needed to be alone. Hell, after how she'd treated Hiram—probably bungling any chance he'd tell her anything to help her find Esmé or get at the truth of the events over the past few days—she felt that she *deserved* to be alone. Even if he'd told her everything, she'd still feel shame at how she treated him.

Eventually, her stomach growled and the sky grew dark, but she stayed down by the river. After a time, through the tree line, she heard Mama's voice, heard the children, squealing, running around. From what Lily could make out, they were chasing fireflies, catching them in jars. Of course, Mama would have the children release the fireflies once it was time for bed.

Now Lily hears a rustling on the path down to the tree. She smells a familiar scent of cigarettes. Benjamin. She doesn't move, just stares out at the river.

Benjamin sits down beside her, elbows her, holds a plate with a huge slice of pie before her.

Lily's stomach growls. Apple, from one of the last jars of canned apple filling—they'll put up more this fall—and a brown sugar streusel topping. No one makes it like Mama.

Lily thinks of the untouched tray of food in Hiram's jail cell.

Benjamin elbows her again. "Come on now. You know your mother will tan my hide if I don't bring back this plate empty—and I'm not tossing the pie in the river. Plus, your stomach growls are scaring away the fireflies."

Lily can't help but grin, just a little. Maybe just one bite. She takes the plate, cuts off just a small bite, nearly swoons at the heavenly scent as she brings the fork to her mouth. She moans at the taste. All right then. Maybe another bite.

"While your mama was making up this plate, she quietly told me that on their visit to Chalmer's, Sophia admitted that she is the mother of the baby that was left at their house. But Sophia swears that Hiram is not the father—and she'll never say who is, other than it's someone who works for Chalmer at his lumber mill."

"Well, that's interesting," Lily says. Half the pie slice is gone. "And it's going to make working there extra uncomfortable for Chalmer's employees. I can't imagine he'll just be his usual self, at least for a while."

"Lily, I came by to tell you I've rounded up several men to help with the search for Esmé—when you're ready to give the order," Benjamin says.

"Don't know where to tell you to start. I reckon Hildy told you about how things went at the jail with Hiram—"

"She just said it was rough, but that he confessed to kidnapping Esmé. That you got Sadie, went out to search at the farm, and didn't get far."

"We found a letter from Roger, written to Esmé's mother, and a blue hair ribbon, fallen in the barn," Lily says. "Not enough for Sadie to get a sniff to track. Ida and Dorit put up no fuss but said they had no idea that Hiram had kidnapped Esmé, or had her in the barn. I've put in for a search warrant at Chalmer's, and plan to go first thing in the morning to search there if he doesn't resist—otherwise, I'll need to wait for the warrant, but I'm only going on a hunch because I just can't believe Hiram acted on his own."

By the time she tells Benjamin her theory about either Sophia or Chalmer conniving Hiram into helping one of them kidnap Esmé, she's also finished her pie.

"I can't imagine Chalmer doing such a thing—or Hiram, either," Benjamin says. "But if Hiram's confessed—you know, it's odd, I don't remember seeing him at Chalmer's house the day Chalmer filled me in on Esmé."

"How did that come about, anyway?"

"He left a note at my boarding room, asked me to come see him.

We weren't particularly close during our time overseas, but I thought it might have something to do with the park, so I went. I had no idea he was going to tell me about Roger, about Esmé."

"Hiram is so quiet," Lily says. "It's possible he was there and you didn't notice him."

"That's true—"

"Oh God, Benjamin. I was so awful to him," Lily blurts. She can't bring herself to look at Benjamin, but she tells him what happened at the jail. By the time she's done, tears are silently coursing down her cheeks.

Less than halfway through her confession, Benjamin pulls her to him. When she finishes talking, he says, "Lily, you're exhausted, and worried, and the past two days have been awful."

"That's no excuse—"

"But it's a reason to give yourself a little grace. Forgive yourself. And remember—you aren't alone. You don't have to shoulder the burden of finding Esmé all by yourself."

Lily hiccups. Between crying and eating too quickly, she can't help it. "People used to come to this tree all the time. The Kinship Tree. It was such a novelty then, when the town was being settled, from what my grandmother would tell me. Before the summer Chautauquas, the moving pictures at the Opera House. Or before things like the Meuse-Argonne Memorial Park." A hiccup interrupts her story. She's not sure why she's suddenly compelled to tell Benjamin all of this. Maybe because he's right—she's exhausted. But it strikes her as necessary to tell him. "When we were young, our grandparents, on my mama's side, lived next door. My grandparents were friends with the Gottschalks, who owned this farm before me. Roger and me, we'd run over, scramble up the tree, race to do so." Lily hiccups but also smiles, remembering. "I usually beat Roger here. Even though he was older, and a boy. Even when I'd give him a head start. And—now that I look back, foolishly—we'd sometimes jump into the river, when it ran high, to the deep spot over there." She points.

"He told me about it," Benjamin says. "Daniel, I mean."

Lily startles at the mention of her deceased husband, half expects

Benjamin to pull away. But if anything, he holds her a little tighter. "Told me that you met because of this tree. Because of Roger. That you jumped in, got caught under the water, and nearly drowned, but Roger pulled you out. You were injured, and he took you across the way, to see the doctor that lived there—Daniel's uncle—where Daniel himself was recovering from a boxing injury."

"I— I'm stunned he told you this story."

"He talked about you—a lot."

Lily's face flames, at the notion of her husband, oh so long ago, talking to a fellow soldier she did not yet know, a man she now wishes to be her lover. A wish not contained just in this moment, she realizes; she's been wishing for that for quite some time now. And wishes for that for the future, too.

Lily clears her throat. "Well. I'm telling you the story because of Roger. I may have beaten him in footraces and been more likely to best him on hunting and fishing trips with our dad—trips he didn't like to take—but Roger pulled me from that river just before my six-teenth birthday." Her hand quivers as she points at the spot. The mem-ory comes flooding back—the terror of the water closing over her, the panic of kicking and being stuck, her foot caught on the outer edge in a freak accident between two heavy slats of rock, being unable to break free, seeing the surface shimmering above, her body starting to convulse as she couldn't breathe. That had been nearly fourteen years before—almost half her lifetime.

But then Roger's freeing hands reached down, grasped her. Pulled her free. Her outer toe had ripped and eventually needed amputating, but he'd saved her life. Then her brother—whom she'd teased for not being as strong as her—had picked her up, carried her, nearly out of her mind with fear and pain, up to the house where she now lived, and Mr. Gottschalk had loaded her in the wagon, and Roger had gone with her down the road for medical help.

She chokes up again. "Roger would never have treated Hiram that way. And he— he would be so disappointed in me, for being unable to find a way to convince Hiram to tell me where Esmé might be—"

Benjamin turns Lily toward him. "Lily," he says. "Roger would only be proud of you. How hard you're working—how hard you always work—to set things right. And you will find her. We, all of us, will help you find her."

He leans forward, about to kiss her, and for a brief blissful moment all shutters from Lily's mind except desire for that kiss—

"The baby is missing."

Both Lily and Benjamin jump apart, seeking the source of the dire intonation.

There, just a bit up the path, silhouetted in moonlight, stands May-Belle Fitzpatrick.

A quarter hour later, MayBelle rests in an armchair in the parlor. The old woman is so tiny that the tufted green leather seat seems to be swallowing her. Her hair hangs in sweaty gray strands, so thin that bits of her scalp peek through. She sips from a glass of water that Hildy has brought her. Her hands shake as she brings the glass to her mouth.

Yes, sympathy for the old woman rises in Lily's chest, but also impatience. Since finding them at the Kinship Tree and intoning, *The baby is missing*, MayBelle has refused to say anything, even as Lily and Benjamin helped her walk back up the path. She was so unsteady that she was weaving around, and for a moment Lily thought Benjamin was going to scoop up the old woman and carry her. But in deference to her dignity, he just held one elbow, while Lily held the other, and guided her up. The children, spotting them emerging from the river with a shaky elder between them, had stopped in their tracks in chasing lightning bugs. Mama and Nana stared at the trio for a moment, then shooed the children into the house and upstairs for washing up.

Hildy and Marvena, talking quietly at the worktable in the kitchen, had fallen silent as Benjamin and Lily ushered MayBelle through to the parlor, where they settled her in the chair, then themselves on the sofa across from her. And maddeningly, through it all, though Lily had encouraged MayBelle to say more, the old woman remained silent.

Now Lily wants to demand of the older woman, *What do you mean?*—but Hildy stands in the entryway, giving Lily a gentle but firm look: *Forbearance is a virtue.*

Lily takes a deep breath. "MayBelle, are you all right? You've come such a long way."

MayBelle scowls at her. "Well, it's about damned time you ask me how I am. Come all this way to tell you the baby's missing, clear as day, and all you can do is natter at me—*What do you mean? Mrs. Fitzpatrick, tell me more!*" MayBelle imitates Lily's voice in a high-pitched lilt, and Lily notes that Hildy and Benjamin bite back smiles.

Hmph. Let them have their fun. "Mrs. Fitzpatrick, let's have the doctor look at you—"

"I don't need a damned doctor. My feet's swollen and I'm thirsty's all," MayBelle grouses. She jabs a finger at Hildy. "That one understands." MayBelle's voice softens. "Thank you for the water, honey."

"Yes, ma'am," Hildy says.

"And anyhow, the doctor went back to Kinship a bit ago," Marvena says as she appears in the doorway by Hildy. Marvena also grins. Well, of course she'd heard MayBelle's imitation. She comes into the parlor with a cup of tea, holds it out to MayBelle. "Water is good, but my mother-in-law says life is hard."

"Ain't that the truth."

"Have tea."

MayBelle takes the cup, stares in it suspiciously. "What kind?"

"Chamomile," Marvena says, as if this is the obvious choice and she is the expert in herbal tea concoctions.

MayBelle nods. "Good choice." She takes the cup, calmed enough from the water and from sitting so that it doesn't slosh, as Marvena takes the glass from her and goes to stand by Hildy. MayBelle takes a sip. "Mmmm."

Everyone in the room except MayBelle stares at Lily. They might all enjoy teasing her for her impatience, but they trust her. Given the bungles of the past few days, she's not sure why, but her friends' and Benjamin's confidence in her buoys her.

"MayBelle," Lily says more gently, "thank you for coming all this way to tell us the baby is gone. But I can be a mite slow at times."

"Ain't that the truth," MayBelle mutters again.

"I just want to be sure you mean the baby that was left at Chalmer and Sophia's?"

MayBelle nods.

Lily takes a deep breath. "Would you like to say where you think the baby's gone to? You must be mighty concerned, coming all this way?"

"Well, of course I am. Them two fighting and screaming like cougars after the same prey—I could hear them all the way to my cabin. And I kept thinking, poor little baby, in the middle of all that—that's no good." MayBelle shakes her head. "So, I went and got her."

"The baby."

"Yes, the baby. Next thing I know, she's gone." MayBelle tears up, shaking her head.

"Maybe Chalmer and Sophia took her back?" Lily suggests.

"Well now, I'd known if that happened, wouldn't I?" MayBelle takes another sip of her tea, smacks her lips. "But no. I had her with me, out on the porch swing, trying to rock her. She's a mite colicky. I left her bundled up, safe as could be. Right there on the porch swing."

Lily tamps down a shudder, lest her reaction stop the words finally flowing from MayBelle. Good Lord, didn't she think of the baby possibly rolling off the swing?

"Thought the fresh air would help her," MayBelle says. "Then I thought—she's hungry. So I went inside to heat up some tinned milk. Just took a minute." MayBelle's face falls, all pretension of toughness sliding away. "Or maybe it was longer. It took a while to light my coal-oil lamp. The stove." Her jowls tremble. "Too long. She . . . stopped crying. I grabbed my lamp, went outside, and she wasn't on the swing. She was in the arms of a young girl, who was running away."

The room goes still, quiet. Lily exchanges looks with the others. Then she returns her focus to MayBelle. "A young girl? You're sure?"

"Yes, yes, I'm sure. Wasn't tall enough to be a grown woman. I hollered after her, and she stopped, looked back at me. A young girl. She said something, but it was all nonsense."

Lily takes a slow breath, forces her breath to stay even. "Could she have been saying something in another language?"

MayBelle looks taken aback by that possibility. "I reckon so. Anyway, I followed her but lost track. Found myself out on Kinship Road, so I thought well, I'll just fetch Sheriff Lily." She lifts her eyebrows. "For all the good it did, my other warnings."

"You didn't tell Chalmer or Sophia about the girl and the baby?"

"No. I told you, they fight all the time now. No point in going to their house. I don't want the baby back with them. That's why I took the baby to begin with."

"Mrs. Fitzpatrick, how did you know to find my house?"

MayBelle looks at Lily like she is touched in the head. "Every time you brung me back to Chalmer's you pointed it out. Trying to make conversation, I reckon."

"Thank you for coming to me," Lily says. She regards Marvena and Hildy, still standing in the doorway, staring at her, wide-eyed, awaiting direction. "A young girl on the property, speaking in a foreign language. And a missing baby. I think we have cause now to launch a search, without waiting for legalities."

"Reckon Chalmer—or at least Sophia—will approve of the search since their, well, her, baby is involved," Marvena says. "Well, I'll help search. Hildy?"

Hildy remains still, quiet.

MayBelle's tremulous voice breaks the awkward and surprising lull created by Hildy's lack of response. "Am I—in trouble? I was just trying to save the baby."

"No, no, you're not in trouble, Mrs. Fitzpatrick," Benjamin says. He looks at Lily. "I'll alert the men on the search team."

"No, Benjamin, you go with Lily," Hildy says suddenly. "I'll let the men know, and the doc, too, just in case his medical help is needed. And Marvena, I can take Nana and Frankie back home. I'm sure Jurgis is worrying about everyone."

Lily studies her friend, surprised. She'd been so determined to go with her to Columbus.

Hildy directs her gaze at Lily. "But you know I'll do anything you need me to do, so if you really need me to help with the search . . ."

Lily does know that. But in her friend's carefully composed expression, she reads the truth: now that she might meet Roger's daughter, she's feeling unsteady.

Lily nods. "Your plan is a good one. We'll follow it."

BEULAH

Beulah pauses on the second-to-last step from the bottom, taking in everything that's been said in the last few moments.

Her granddaughter. MayBelle had spotted her, along with the baby.

Esmé must have been hiding on the property, heard the baby crying, and thought she was doing the right thing by taking the baby. But it's terrifying, to think of Esmé and the baby all alone, somewhere in the park or the woods beyond the park.

And yet Monsieur Durand's telegram had indicated that Esmé had been good with his children on the passage over.

Beulah steps down, turns the corner, walks into the front entry to the parlor. "And what about me?" Everyone startles, looks at her. "Jolene and the boys can go with Nana and the others." She glances at Marvena, who nods. Beulah crosses to Lily, grabs her arm. "Let me go with you. Please."

Lily shakes her head. "No, Mama, stay here with the children. It's so late, and it can be dangerous searching at night."

Beulah squares her shoulders. "I'm going with you," she says firmly.

For a long moment, mother and daughter stand facing each other, eyes locked. Lily's mouth pinches in a familiar, defiant expression, just like when she was younger and determined to argue with her mother. But Beulah will go over to the Fitzpatricks' property, even if she has to hitch up Daisy and take the mule cart over. She will be present for the search for Esmé. Roger's daughter. Her granddaughter.

Finally, Lily sighs, capitulating. "Yes, Mama."

LILY

Somewhere from afar, an owl hoots. The sound carries on this clear, nearly breezeless night.

A usually comforting sound, but something feels wrong. Lily senses it, staring up at the house. She still doesn't really believe in the sight—but lanterns blaze in the open windows, in which curtains listlessly drift.

Chalmer and Sophia should have heard them all pulling up the lane. And yet there is no movement. If the coal-oil lamps were not burning inside the windows, she'd think they were asleep, but with MayBelle having snatched the baby, Chalmer or Sophia should be wide awake, running out, demanding to know what's going on. Had they gone to MayBelle's cabin to check for the baby, to see if she knows anything?

And then it hits Lily. In the time it took MayBelle to walk all the way to her house and then for everyone to get organized enough to drive back over here, Chalmer or Sophia should have noticed the baby missing. They'd have had plenty of time to go check at MayBelle's. To themselves come find Lily.

Lily swallows hard. Turns to see Mama and MayBelle and Benjamin and Marvena all out of the automobile, waiting for her direction.

The distant owl hoots again, its cry echoing in the pressing darkness.

Yet, the sound encourages and calms Lily. A moment of gratitude for all of them—and Hildy and Nana and Dr. Twomey, and the volunteer searchers on their way—washes over her. As Benjamin had told her just an hour or so ago, she is not alone.

And though Esmé does not know it yet, she is also not alone.

"Mama," Lily says softly, beckoning her over. "I need you to walk MayBelle back up to her cabin. I don't think you'll find anything, well, out of order there, but if you do, you run, come get me." Lily pulls a flashlight out of her tote bag, hands it to Mama. "The other searchers will be here soon. I will come get you, as soon as I make sure everything is in order here." She nods in the direction of the house.

Mama hesitates just a moment, then takes the flashlight.

BEULAH

Beulah watches Lily push open the door to Chalmer's, step inside the house with Marvena and Benjamin behind her.

She moves to MayBelle. "Let's go back to your cabin."

The older woman starts to move toward the main house. "Maybe the baby is back in there."

Beulah gently grabs MayBelle's arm, steers her away from the house. "If she is, Lily will let us know."

"Hmph," MayBelle says. But she capitulates to Beulah's guidance away from the house. "That daughter of yourn—she is yours, ain't she?"

"Yes," Beulah says, as they slowly walk away from the house. "She is."

"Well, she's as stubborn as the day is long."

Beulah presses her lips together, pinching back a guilty chuckle—though it's true. Lily is stubborn. It's an attribute that makes her a good officer of the law—she won't give up until the truth is revealed. The baby found. Esmé found. An attribute that Beulah has long experienced as both admirable and frustrating. But in these past few days, she's taken comfort in it as well.

MayBelle picks up her pace as they head up the hill, tilting forward as they walk, which seems to give her momentum.

Beulah has to push herself to keep up, the beam of her flashlight pricking the darkness and bobbing on the scant footpath before them.

"The girl you saw running off with the baby," Beulah asks, her breath catching from both effort and emotion, "how did she seem? Could you tell if she was, well, all right?"

"Spry enough to snag the baby. And she sure wasn't afeared of the woods, or disappearing into them."

"I heard you say she spoke funny." Beulah thinks, *What might Esmé have shouted back to MayBelle? Something about taking care of the baby?* "Did she say something that might have sounded like . . ." Beulah hesitates, piecing together the French she's learned in corresponding with Charlotte over the years. "Like *je vais m'occuper du bébé?*"

MayBelle cuts Beulah an incredulous glance. "Not those sounds exactly—but something like that."

Beulah glances into the dark woods. She's never been particularly afraid of the night, but thinking of Esmé, somewhere out there, with a baby, suddenly seems overwhelming. Oppressive. A question swirls cruelly in her mind: *Is this how it felt to my boy, trudging through the woods of the true Meuse-Argonne?*

An owl hoots in the distance, and for the next several steps Beulah focuses on listening to those strangely comforting cries.

And then—there it is.

MayBelle's small log-and-mortar cabin, lit from within by a coal-oil lamp still burning in the window, and from above by the waning moon, glowing in a clearing in the woods.

The owl stops hooting.

"Well, come on in," MayBelle says. "You're huffing like an old mule going up the side of a mountain. Better get you settled down."

CHAPTER 22

LILY & BEULAH

Friday, July 6, 1928

11:50 p.m.

LILY

As Mama and Beulah head up the path, Lily rushes up the porch steps, Benjamin and Marvena right behind her. The front door hangs ajar. Her sense of dread rises, and she unholsters her gun as she slowly pushes the door further open.

Still inside the entryway to the house, Lily kneels, even though she already knows that Sophia is dead. Sophia's eyes are open, fixed, glassy. Blood pools from the back of her head.

Lily puts her fingers to Sophia's neck where a pulse should be and blanches at the feel of torqued bone and tendon just below her flesh. Sophia's neck is broken.

Lying in Sophia's open palm is a revolver.

"Lily."

Marvena's voice pulls Lily's attention and gaze away from Sophia, to see Marvena shakily pointing up the stairs.

Chalmer lies on the landing, facedown. One arm drapes over the top step. His legs are behind him. He looks as if he's simply fallen at the top of the steps, but blood drips from the top step to the next one down.

Oh God.

Lily runs up the stairs, stops just short of Chalmer. He's been shot in the chest, just to the left, below the shoulder.

It looks as though they'd gotten into an argument, that Sophia had grabbed Chalmer's gun—had he been threatening her? Had she run into his office to get it?—and shot him. Then fallen down the stairs, as she ran away? Fell? Broke her neck?

But—that doesn't seem right. From where Chalmer lay, he fell just a few feet back from the top step. Lily glances back down the steps, ignores Marvena and Benjamin staring up at her as she tries to keep a fuzzy gray dizziness at bay, so she can piece this together. So Sophia would have had to shoot from the bottom of the steps or, at most, from a third of the way up.

Even if she'd fallen from a third of the way up, would the tumble have been far enough, hard enough, for her to have broken her neck? That seems unlikely. But perhaps Dr. Twomey could answer that question—

A moan.

Lily looks at Chalmer.

His eyes flutter open.

"Lily." The name drags out of his lips.

"He's alive," Lily cries out. "Go get help; we need to get him to the doctor—"

Benjamin suddenly leaps over Sophia, runs up the stairs. He pulls off his shirt as he orders, "Lily, turn him, carefully to his side—Marvena, come help!"

By the time Marvena runs up and helps Lily turn Chalmer to his back, Benjamin has folded his shirt into a neat square. He compresses it on Chalmer's wound.

Lily notes Benjamin's gaze—focused, yet distant. Unemotional on the surface, yet barely containing fear for the man he is tending. And his expertness with treating Chalmer's wound—*oh. He's done this before, with other soldiers, on the battlefield.*

"Lily, Lily—" Chalmer moans.

"Shhh, we're going to get you help—" Lily says. She turns to tell Marvena to go get more help, but Marvena is already hurrying down the stairs, carefully sidestepping around poor Sophia.

"Lily—the baby. She's—gone. Sophia thought I did something; we, we, argued—then he came, screaming, aimed at her. I tried to stop—he didn't mean to shoot me—"

Chills dance over Lily's arms. She wants to know what happened, who he is talking about, but this is taking too much out of Chalmer. "Listen, we're going to get you help; then you can tell me—"

"No!" Chalmer screams as if in pain, but it is a pain far deeper than the wound in his chest. Suddenly he finds a burst of energy to shove Benjamin aside, to grab Lily by her blouse, nearly pull her on top of him.

"Roger, Roger—" Blood is coming out now between Chalmer's lips. The metallic, acrid smell fills Lily's nose. Her stomach flips and she swallows convulsively. Oh God, he's bleating her brother's name just like Hiram had. What is he trying to tell her about her beloved brother? What? "The soldier who panicked—who Roger pulled back to safety— that was me. After . . . my first wounding—I couldn't face being back in the trenches. I didn't try to save Roger. He-he-saved me and that's when he drew sniper fire. He j-j-j-jumped up to save me. To pull me down. He fell back in the trench, and Daniel was there, I got him to Daniel, and Roger told him—"

Chalmer lets go of Lily's blouse. He falls back, his head hitting the floor with a sickening thump. His eyes start to roll back.

"Nooooooo!" Lily's scream is raw, ripping from her very core. Now she grabs Chalmer, not caring that her hands grasp blood-soaked cloth, grabs him as if she is going to shake him by the lapels. She will not be denied knowing her brother's last words to her late husband, words that her husband had not, for whatever reason, shared with her. Had those words been about Roger's daughter? But no—surely Daniel would have told her. Told Mama.

Roger had to know he was dying, in his last moments, in Daniel's arms.

His last words—*ah*—they would have been to encourage Daniel to make it home.

That would have been Roger's way.

Hands grasp her arms, pull her back from Chalmer, back from the edge of the top step.

Benjamin's hands. "Lily, Lily, Lily . . ." Benjamin incanting her name over and over, softly calling her back to calmness.

Lily looks at him, abruptly silent, no longer screaming, though she is gasping. This is too much. Too much. Roger having a daughter—here, somewhere, missing. Roger dying to save this man, who'd let her, let everyone, believe Roger had died from a random sniper bullet when instead Roger had saved Chalmer, taking that sniper's bullet for him.

She stares at Benjamin, sees his lips still moving with her name, though she cannot hear his voice, can only hear a high-pitched droning growing in her ears, can feel nothing except the sticky blood on her hand, snot and tears leaking onto her face, and then numbness overtaking her body from her arms and feet, crawling up her limbs to her heart, her head.

And then Benjamin, pulling her to him, pressing her face to his chest, rocking her back and forth.

"Lily, Lily, Lily . . ."

BEULAH

Now MayBelle and Beulah sit on the front porch, side by side on a porch swing. Beulah sips the water MayBelle has given her, grateful for the refreshment but suddenly longing for the comfort of Nana's tea.

Life is hard. Have tea.

That's what Nana, her best friend, always says, and Lord if it isn't true.

Still, there's comfort in simply sitting here, on this porch swing, sturdy and comfortable and gleaming in blue milk paint—just like the one she'd bought from Otto Owens. Hadn't Suda mentioned that a few days ago, that MayBelle had bought one of Otto's porch swings? Beulah shakes her head. That's neither here nor there.

Suddenly MayBelle sighs sorrowfully. Her face deflates in soft folds of defeat. "I forgot," she says mournfully. "I forgot about the diapering. That's why the baby kept crying. Poor thing probably had diaper rash."

Beulah offers a reassuring smile. "It's all right," she says. "We all forget things from time to time. Maybe Sophia forgot, too? And that's why you heard the baby crying at the house?"

MayBelle shakes her head. "They were fighting again, Chalmer and Sophia, so loud their voices rung all the way up the hill to here. I went down to tell them to hush up, and came in the back entry. They were in the parlor—didn't even notice me. Or the baby crying upstairs. So I just went on up, got her, and left." MayBelle shakes her head. "Fighting over the most fool things, those two. All the time. Never shoulda got hitched. I told Chalmer that, right after he brought her here. That one's never gonna settle in, I said, be happy living here, after being in a big city, getting all that schooling. This place ain't for everyone—"

The tiny hairs on the back of Beulah's neck prickle as it hits her—the big house, all lit up, but silent. Lily so stealthily entering with Marvena and Benjamin and wanting her and MayBelle to get back to this cabin. "Do you remember what they were fighting about?"

"Chalmer was screaming that he thought Sophia killed that poor girl—you know, I had a vision about a girl, floating facedown in the pond. Always thought it would be that other girl, the cousin—"

"Dorit?"

"Oh yes. Yes, I think that's her name. Anyway, Chalmer was screaming this terrible thing, but Sophia was laughing like it was nothing. Said she had to, 'cause when she went out to get the baby, the girl had come back, said she'd changed her mind, was gonna take the baby unless Sophia paid her more hush money. And Sophia said that after that— Wait, what was it—"

Beulah stares at MayBelle, taking in the import of what she's just heard. "Take your time," Beulah says gently. "It'll come back to you."

A few moments of nighttime silence pass, and then MayBelle says, "Oh—yeah. The girl snatched the baby back and ran, and Sophia ran after her. And Sophia grabbed something from a tool box left by the wood bin, and caught up with the girl, and hit her, but she'd fixed it so Hiram would take the fall—"

Hiram. Oh, poor Hiram.

"—and if Chalmer told, she'd deny it. Blame it on him. On our old family feud. And everyone would believe her if she admitted Hiram is the father. And she said she was going to check on the baby. Well, I figured I'd better skedoodle out of there."

Beulah inhales sharply. *My God.* Sophia had killed Pearl.

"'Cept then I heard Chalmer following Sophia to the front stairs, and they both screamed, and I heard a man say he was sorry, he'd just come in, looking for a job, and suddenly Sophia was hollering about what all had he heard, and the man said he hadn't really heard anything, he'd just come because he'd asked before about a job, bought a lot of lumber from Chalmer's mill to make his furniture—oh." MayBelle's eyes widen with a realization. "Musta been the man who makes these—" She pats the arm of the porch swing.

"Otto Owens."

"Yes. I reckon."

"Did you hear anything else?"

MayBelle sighs, suddenly weary from this recounting. She shakes her head. "I brought the baby here, and then she started crying. Oh. Maybe it was because she was hungry. . . ."

Beulah pats MayBelle's arm. "Everything will be all right."

But MayBelle turns suddenly to Beulah. "I— I don't know. I heard a shot. Another shot. I— I wasn't sure—maybe it was the shooting range." Her eyes widen with confusion. "I told Chalmer the shooting range was a bad idea, so close to our houses, that the sound would carry . . . but that boy don't listen to anything. And then the baby was crying, and oh, I almost forgot about the sound of the shots, till you started asking me all these questions. Then when the baby went missing, and I saw that girl—I thought it was the crying that drew her out. Do you think it was the sound of shots?"

Beulah's heart races. "I— I don't know. . . ."

Tears pop into MayBelle's eyes. "Do you—do you think they're all right?"

"Mrs. McArthur."

Both women jump, turn at the low, somber male voice.

Benjamin steps forward from the darkness, and Beulah notes with some satisfaction that he is, at least, slightly out of breath. But her satisfaction disappears as she sees his distressed expression, that he's wearing only his undershirt and that—*oh*. As he steps into the circle of light from the lantern, that the shirt is smudged with blood.

LILY

Lily hovers in the entry to the bedroom for a moment. It feels like intrusion, coming in here—even though Sophia and Chalmer are both dead.

Holding up the lantern, she gazes around the room, mapping it to memory, pinning the details to the correct places in her mental picture: A four-poster bed. A pink bedcover, matching curtains flouncing in the open window. The night breeze has picked up and stirs a heavy floral fragrance.

A wardrobe. A sitting chair, in front of a dressing table topped with perfume bottles, a box of face powder, a jewelry box. A mirror over the table, with a strand of pearls hanging from one of the ornate leaves of the mirror frame.

From the rose-patterned wallpaper, Lily detects that the dressing table and mirror have been recently moved, for a shape of where they had once been against the wall remains, the rest of the wallpaper darkened over the years by smoke from lamps and by time. In front of the pale echo of where the table and mirror had once stood is a cradle, empty.

Behind Lily are two other bedrooms—one made up, from all appearances, for Chalmer. How long had the couple been sleeping apart? It's clear that they'd been drifting away from each other for years. The other bedroom has been converted into a sewing room. Likely, Sophia and Chalmer would have turned that into a nursery for the child.

But now the baby is missing. She's looked upstairs, while Marvena looks downstairs. The searchers have arrived, but their efforts are diverted to transporting Sophia's and Chalmer's bodies to Kinship, to the funeral home. She hears Benjamin and the other men carrying Chalmer down the stairs, just feet away from her. Their voices are low murmurs when they speak at all: "Careful. One step at a time."

They'd waited, respectfully, until she'd been able to calm herself in Benjamin's arms. Then she had pulled away from him quietly. She had been unable, for some reason she's too numb to yet fathom, to meet his eyes.

Someone—Marvena?—had brought her a damp cloth, and she'd cleaned Chalmer's blood as best she could from her hands. And then she had ordered everyone to wait, while she pulled out her notebook, made note of the exact positions of Chalmer's and Sophia's bodies, sketched the outline of them below her notes. It seemed important, though the images are now seared into her mind.

Now she hovers in the doorway. Someone had said they thought they'd heard a baby wailing in the distance. For a scant second, she thought she'd heard that, too, but then just heard the owl hooting again.

Maybe she only heard echoes from time spent with her own babies in the past. Even the owl's sound could be an echo from past searches and cases.

She wills her feet forward, enters the bedroom, looking for . . . what? Something, anything, that might tell her about Esmé. About what happened here.

Lily sits at the dressing table, puts the lantern alongside a small lamp. The lantern provides more light than the lamp would, so she doesn't bother lighting the lamp. She glances at her reflection in the mirror. Her eyes are already swollen, her face puffy.

Lily opens a drawer—more jewelry. Another drawer—face powder, hairbrush, comb. Another—handkerchiefs, carefully embroidered with flowers and vines. But then a flash of paper, underneath the handkerchiefs. Letters.

Lily pulls them out.

The one on top is dated just a few months ago. There is no envelope. The letter appears to have been written and left here for Sophia.

Lily begins reading. A few minutes later, she pulls Hiram's letter, found in his work shirt, implicating him in Pearl's murder—along with the wrench and his confession—out of her tote bag. She spreads out both pages next to the first page of one of the letters from the drawer.

The page from the drawer, the only one with the same style of writing as the letter from the work shirt pocket, ends abruptly, appearing to miss its second page. Lily puts it in the middle, with the first page that was in the work shirt pocket to the left and the second page, signed by Hiram, from the pocket to the right.

Sure enough, the second page is a sensible continuation of the first page she'd found in the drawer—an intimate love letter with the salutation *Dearest Sophia.*

And all the words on the first page found in the pocket, with the salutation *Dearest Pearl,* are copied from the original first page, with the exception of Pearl's name.

Lily rereads the original first page, struggles not to cringe at the raw emotion. Poor Hiram—declaring his love for Sophia. Saying he would find a way to make enough money to take care of her and their baby. Begging her to believe in him.

What had Sophia seen in the poor man? Someone, Lily thinks, to adore and worship her unquestioningly. Or perhaps they'd both always been outsiders in their own way and as such thought that they could only find comfort in each other.

But would Hiram—as Sophia had implied—really kidnap Esmé for money? On his own? Or had they planned it together?

Lily carefully stacks the pages—the original first, the copied first, and the second—and folds them together, then tucks them back in her tote bag.

She stands up, picks up the lantern, turns just as Benjamin appears in the doorway.

"Your mama has settled MayBelle for the night, hopefully," Benjamin says. "At least MayBelle was fast asleep when we left her. But Lily—according to what Mrs. McArthur learned from MayBelle, it's Sophia who killed Pearl. And it is possible that it's Otto Owens who killed both Sophia and Chalmer."

CHAPTER 23

BEULAH & LILY

Saturday, July 7, 1928

12:20 a.m.

BEULAH

Beulah grabs Lily's arm as they reach the plateau and clearing partway up to the Owens place.

"Mama, are you all right?" Lily is alarmed.

"Just need a moment," Beulah says as she sits down on a flat rock. In the beam of Lily's torch, Beulah sees Marvena, who's ridden over with them. Beulah had shared what MayBelle told her, at least twice through—interrupted, now and again, by yelps as Lily took turns too fast.

And Lily had shared, in a careful, clipped description, what she had discovered inside Chalmer's house. Beulah's stomach had turned, even at the abbreviated description. She can't help but think she'd set all this in motion—first by asking Chalmer to help her with Esmé and then by telling Chalmer the truth about Sophia being the baby's mother.

"All right, Mama," Lily says. "We can go the rest of the way, if you'll tell us—"

"No, child, it ain't that easy to find, and stop coddling me," Beulah snaps. In the mix of moonlight and flashlight, Lily's eyes spark with hurt, and Beulah immediately regrets her snappish rejoinder. As horrifying as it must have been for Lily to find Chalmer and Sophia, Beulah can tell her daughter is haunted by something more she learned or saw. Something she's holding back. Another secret.

Beulah glances at the moon, now so high in the sky that it must be near midnight. Or just past. She rubs her eyes, so dry from exhaustion and overuse that they feel gritty.

"And Suda has come to trust me. I think I can get her to talk to us, even if Otto won't. We just need to be careful of him," Beulah says.

The three continue up, not talking, their breaths and the lulling whisper of grass blade and tree leaf stirring, and the now-rare chirring of a June bug the only sounds.

Then the cabin comes in view. Coal-oil lamps blaze inside, just as they had at the Fitzpatricks'. The back of Beulah's neck prickles.

Lily motions for everyone to get behind cover of trees and brings her bullhorn to her lips. But Beulah puts her hand on top of the horn, gestures: *Let me.*

Lily hesitates but then hands it over. Beulah finds it's heavier than it looks. She holds it to her lips, says, "It's Beulah McArthur. I've come up this late because—well—something's happened and I need to talk to you."

For a moment, nothing happens, but then Otto comes out on the porch. Beulah steps forward, even as Lily grabs at her, but Beulah pulls away. Lily curses under her breath. Well, Beulah can't blame her. She's taking a mighty risk.

But what if Otto had learned something while he was there, at the Fitzpatricks' house, that might lead them to Esmé—even now, as men still searched the Meuse-Argonne park? There's nothing she wouldn't do to try to save one of her children, her grandchildren.

"Otto, my daughter's with me. And Marvena," Beulah says. She hates how shaky her voice sounds. "They're just behind me in the woods."

She keeps walking forward as she talks and soon is on the porch. She puts the bull horn on the rickety rocker.

Otto glares at her. "I know who your daughter is. What in the hell does the law want with me at this hour?"

Beulah swallows, seeing his grip on his shotgun tighten. He surely knows that if he hurts her—or shoots into the woods beyond—he won't be able to run. Not far, not long.

And running would mean abandoning his wife, his children.

He might be a hard man, even a cruel and bitter man at times, but he would not leave them. She can see that in his face. So she decides to speak plainly. "We gotta know—were you at the Fitzpatricks' house earlier tonight? Where Chalmer and Sophia live?"

He frowns. "Why you gotta know that?"

"MayBelle says you were—"

"The old hill woman? What does she know? She's always getting folks mixed up. Musta been someone else. Besides, I ain't got need to drag myself over to Chalmer's again to beg for a job." Otto tightens his expression. "I decided today, I'm signing up to work the mines. Don't need housing, and so I got a little extra scrip—we can use it for food at the store." He straightens his already-broad shoulders, trying to put pride in his stance. But Beulah sees the flash of fear.

Suda rushes out of the house onto the porch. Otto tries to push her back, but she forces her way around him. He grabs her arm, jerks her back, preventing her from running down the steps to them.

"Otto, please, just tell them what they want to know. Who cares if you went over there? Just tell them, and maybe they'll help us," Suda cries out.

Otto smacks her hard, across the face, knocking her to the porch floor. Beulah's stomach turns as Otto shouts, "Shut up, woman!"

Lily and Marvena step forward from the tree line. Their guns aren't drawn, but their hands are at the ready. "Otto, stop," Lily calls. "We just need to talk with you."

"Goddammit!" Otto lifts his hand to backhand Suda again, but she ducks under his arm, and swiftly grabs the shotgun from him. She backs down the porch steps, training the shotgun on her husband. Otto stares at his wife in shock.

"Prudence is missing!" Suda cries out. "She ran off, after her father, but she ain't come back. Did you see her there, Sheriff?" she asks without taking her eyes—or her aim—off of her husband. She, too, would do anything to protect her children. "At the Fitzpatricks'?"

Otto sinks down onto the porch, putting his head to his hands. "I done told you, Suda. I didn't see Prudence. I don't think she followed me there."

"Then where is she?" Suda wails.

Beulah's voice knots in her throat, but she manages to say, "Suda, I'm sure she's all right. She'll turn up. She ran off once before, right, and came back?"

By now, Lily and Marvena have stepped past Beulah and are standing in front of the porch. Several of the older girls stare out, wide-eyed, from the doorway. From the back of the cabin, Otto Jr. starts crying.

And suddenly so does Otto Sr. The night has become too much for him. He looks over at his wife, chokes out, "Suda, I'm sorry. I'm sorry. We'll find Prudence, but I need to talk to Sheriff Lily."

"Daddy?" a tiny voice squeaks from the doorway.

"Please, Suda, go inside, shut the door, take the children to the back of the house. Take care of Junior. I don't want them to see me like this—or hear what I have to say."

Suda stares at her husband for a long moment, night chitters and calls, the hoot of an owl, amplifying the weary tension of unspoken thoughts between them. Then Suda looks to Beulah.

Beulah nods. "Go on."

Finally, Suda walks past her husband, still holding his shotgun. She shoos the children inside, and shuts the door softly. A few moments later, they can all hear Suda warbling off-key—Beulah thinks she recognizes the strains of "What a Friend We Have in Jesus"—and soon Junior quieting.

Otto cries softly into his hands.

Lily moves toward him, but Beulah grabs her arm. "Let me," Beulah whispers.

Lily hesitates, then says, "All right. But we're keeping an eye on him." Marvena nods, puts her hand on her revolver in her waistband.

Beulah sits down next to Otto.

"Otto, I think you know why we're here. We went to the Fitzpatricks' tonight, to follow up on MayBelle's report that the baby left at their place—the baby Suda wet-nursed—is missing. Lily found Sophia and Chalmer. She was dead. Chalmer wasn't, at least not when we found him, and he didn't name you, but MayBelle told me that she heard you there. I know she's older, and maybe she could have mixed you up with someone else—but I don't think she did, did she?"

Otto at last looks up at Beulah, tears coursing down his cheeks. "Oh God. Yes—I went to Chalmer's tonight. I wanted to try, one more time, for a job. I didn't know Prudence had followed me until I got back home tonight. It's just gotten hard to keep a small tract of tobacco going, and woodworking, and Suda wet-nursing, which I know can't last forever. And, and I don't want to go in the mines. I know about what happened back in '24, how your husband died trying to get miners out."

Beulah nods, swallows hard, trying to keep her emotions at bay. "That's right."

Otto runs a shaking hand through his greasy hair. "Anyway, I thought maybe if I talked to him one more time—or even told him what I know about that baby that got left there."

To show she understands, Beulah nods—though she really wants to shake her head instead at the foolhardiness of trying to blackmail his way into a job.

"Anyhow," Otto says, "I heard Chalmer and Sophia fighting. I went in the front door—it was unlocked—and Sophia was taunting Chalmer that she'd killed Pearl. Anger overcame me. I'd only met Pearl a few times, but Suda got on right well with her, and Pearl was kind to us. And Sophia acting like it was nothing, killing her. I pulled my gun, aiming at her at the top of the stairs, thinking I'd make her come with me, confess to you. Had some fool notion that Chalmer would want my help, but Chalmer jumped in front of me. Trying, in the end, to protect her after all. And, well, he startled me, and the gun went off in my hand. Chalmer collapsed, and Sophia ran in a rage down the stairs toward me. I— I was just standing there, stunned at what I'd done. I hadn't planned to shoot him, shoot anyone; something just overcame me—"

Otto sighs wearily. "And she fell. I could see, instantly, that she was dead. So, I left my gun in her hand. I thought Chalmer was dead, I really did, or I'd have tried to help. I came home, and found out Prudence had run off after me. She'd heard me tell Suda I was going to the Fitzpatricks', and I reckon she thought I was just going to the park without her or her mama or her siblings. Oh God. What if she saw what I did? What a horrible man her father is?" He breaks down, no longer crying but unable to say more.

Suddenly Beulah stiffens at the sound of rustling from the woods behind Lily and Marvena. They hear it, too, turn, alert. Jurgis emerges from the woods.

He pants softly as he runs toward them, nearly collapsing as he stops alongside Marvena. "I didn't expect—why are you all up here?" He takes in the scene, Mama and Marvena and Lily and Otto, confusion flashing over his face.

Marvena puts an arm around her husband. "Why are you?"

"Nana and Frankie woke me up. Frankie was a tearful mess, said she'd promised Jolene not to tell, but—"

Lily cries out, "But what? What?"

"Seems Prudence came by. The girls were out on the back sleeping porch—it's such a hot night. And Prudence had followed her father to the park—not understanding, I reckon, it wouldn't be open—but then she saw a girl they met, briefly, at the park on July 4. A girl who doesn't know how to talk, according to Frankie. And Prudence spotted the girl tonight but with a baby," Jurgis says. "And the girl looked scared and ran off. Frankie said Prudence came to tell her because maybe they should go help the girl, and she didn't want to go home to ask for help." He gives Otto an apologetic look. "Jolene said she thought it was her missing cousin and the baby—and they ran off to look for her. Tried to get

Frankie to go. But Frankie was scared about her asthma kicking in if she walked that far, so they made her promise not to tell, and Jolene took off with Prudence. Frankie's conscience got the better of her when Jolene didn't come back, and so she told Nana, who woke me up, told me how to get here, with the hope that Prudence and Jolene might be here."

LILY

An hour later, Lily turns the key to lock Otto's cell. He hasn't said anything since his arrest and immediately goes to the cot, lies down, and turns his face to the wall. At least Chalmer's dying testimony—*he didn't mean to shoot me*—corroborates Otto's claim that his gun went off accidentally. Otto will likely be tried for manslaughter.

Marvena's waiting, just in the entry to the cells, but Lily catches sight of Hiram. He sits up on the edge of the cot, staring at her.

She needs to return to the search at the Meuse-Argonne park, and her heart flutters anxiously with hope that by the time she and Marvena get there, the search party will have found Jolene and Prudence and Esmé and the baby.

And then it hits her—maybe she can use the events that have transpired to get Hiram to help her.

She crosses to Hiram's cell. "We think Esmé ran off to the Meuse-Argonne Memorial Park," Lily says.

He looks down, away from her.

"And we think she has the baby. Your baby. Your and Sophia's baby."

At that, he looks up, gasps. "Why—how—"

Oh. She hasn't thought about how hard this news is going to hit him. "MayBelle came to find me, to report the baby being gone. I went to investigate and— I'm sorry. I found Sophia and Chalmer both dead."

Hiram's face freezes.

"I'm sorry, Hiram," Lily says. "I also found evidence—and we have testimony—that Sophia was really the murderer, and that she pinned it on you."

He swallows, hard. Then he says, so softly that Lily barely makes it out, "I know."

"You know she killed Pearl, let her pin it on you?"

His face remains blank and yet answers the question—yes, yes, he had.

Why? Lily wants to ask. But more than that, she wants to find her daughter. Her niece. Prudence. The baby.

"Listen to me, Hiram, it's going to go better for you if you just say that you didn't kill Pearl. That you knew Sophia did. And it will go much better for you if you tell me where you think Esmé escaped to. . . ." Lily hesitates, trying to phrase things carefully. "Or where you helped her escape to. Because I don't think she escaped on her own. I think you had second thoughts, taking her, and you let her go. Took her elsewhere—or told her how to get somewhere in the park to hide safely."

He shakes his head. "I— I can't—"

"Dammit, Hiram! Why are you still protecting Sophia? She's dead. And she was willing to let you rot in prison—or get electrocuted—for a murder you didn't commit. Even after you kidnapped a child—Roger's daughter—to try to get money to impress her. Did you really think she'd run away with you? Live with you and rear your daughter together? And now your daughter is with Roger's daughter—and mine, too, and another child—and God knows what could happen to them out there in the woods. Why won't you help me? Roger would be so disappointed in you."

Hiram cries out, hurt more by these words than by Lily's earlier physical assault.

But Lily presses on. "Yes—he'd be ashamed of you. And rightly so. Esmé doesn't know this terrain, and my daughter and Prudence are too foolhardy to know how dangerous it is. There are snakes out there. Coyotes. Bears. Places to fall and break a neck."

Hiram whimpers.

"For God's sake, if you won't help me for the sake of my daughter, for Roger's, what about for your own daughter? Who could be more important to you than that?"

Hiram looks up. His face suddenly clears. "No one. No one. Yes—I set Esmé free because I couldn't go through with it. I thought . . . I thought I'd find another way to get money to . . . to be with Sophia. I took Esmé to the old coal car I was fixing up as a trailer, a prototype. I thought we could get several, fix them up, Chalmer could rent them—well, that doesn't matter now." He clears his throat, rubs his eyes. "I can draw you a map."

Quickly, Lily gets her notepad and pencil from her tote, hands them through to him. She watches as he sketches a path, directions, and then he gives the notepad and pencil back to her.

"Thank you," she says, and turns to leave.

But Hiram's voice, rough and low and catching on itself like a long, lonesome, distant train whistle, stops her.

"Sophia said we were outsiders. That she never really fit in here, that I never did, either, after I came back from the war."

Lily turns back around. Hiram is standing now by the cell bars, grasping them. "I want her to be all right. My daughter." Hiram's face twists with sorrow. "Now that you know Sophia really killed Pearl, I can go free, right? It was Sophia's idea to kidnap Pearl. I— I want to rear our daughter. I know I can do it."

Lily's heart breaks open with pity for Hiram. "You'll still face charges for kidnapping, even if it was Sophia's idea. And so by law," she says, the words like bile as she says them, "the baby will go to her nearest kin."

He recoils as if Lily has struck him. And the wail . . . "noooooo!" . . . breaks from him so wildly that it seems to swirl around him, rather than come from him. Hiram collapses to his knees.

"No, Lily. No!" He stares up at her, his expression a wide, plaintive pleading. "It wasn't me that kidnapped Esmé. It was Dorit. Working at the Fitzpatricks', she overheard your mama and Chalmer talking about planning to bring Esmé here, and she hatched the plan. She wanted the money to finally leave here, break free from our mama. She wanted my help, said I could go, too, but I couldn't; I wouldn't. Roger, Roger—"

Lily stumbles back. Benjamin had said earlier that he didn't recall seeing Hiram at the Fitzpatricks' house, the one day he was there, learning about Esmé.

And she's struck by Hiram's bleating of her brother's name again, as before. He'd wanted to tell her, to warn her—*Roger's daughter.* If only she'd taken time to sit with him, to listen. Would he have told her? He is riven between loyalty to his mother and sister, bound by years of them lashing him with his perceived weakness, the belief that he could not survive without them, and wanting to do the right thing by the only person who'd ever truly been a friend to him. Roger. And now wanting to save his daughter from being ensnared by his mother and sister's bitterness, as he had been.

Lily moves to the cell door. *I would do anything—anything—to protect my family. . . .* For Hiram, that even included his cruel mother, his devious sister. Lily's eager to get to that railcar where the girls might be, but she owes Hiram this much. Perhaps owes Roger this much. "Hiram, I'm listening, I believe you. Please . . . tell me—"

"Dorit arranged everything with the lady that was supposed to chaperone Esmé here. She went to the Union Station, dressed in my clothes, my hat, driving my truck—she told me later she wanted the man across the lane to see her leaving, think she was me. Dorit brought Esmé to the house on the morning of the Fourth, and shackled the girl up in the barn. I— I thought I could change Dorit's mind—"

You can't hurt her; I won't let you hurt her! . . .

Hiram's words as he'd rushed the stage on the Fourth echo across Lily's mind. She thinks back: when Hiram had rushed the stage, in his field of vision had been Chalmer and Sophia but also off-stage Dorit and Pearl.

What had he meant, in his desperate cry, *I won't let you hurt her!* He wouldn't let Chalmer hurt Sophia? Or, was he afraid Chalmer would hurt the baby if he found out about her? Afraid Pearl might hurt either Sophia or the baby? Or had he feared his sister Dorit hurting Esmé?

Or, in his mind swirling with fear triggered by the sound of gunfire at the shooting range, had he been worried about all of these possibilities?

"Hiram," Lily says as gently as possible, "I can try to keep your baby from being with Dorit and your mother, see if there is a family who will take her in, but I need to go now, to find her, and Esmé. She can confirm what you've just told me. All right?"

For a moment, Hiram relaxes. He sinks back to the cot. Nods.

"Try to get some rest, Hiram," Lily says. "And Roger would understand. He'd be grateful—"

But her belated kindness is not enough, not in this moment. Hiram sits back down and lowers his head to his hands.

BEULAH

The first light of morning breaks through the canopy of trees in this low dip of the Meuse-Argonne park. Beulah walks alongside Lily, the others behind them. They're following a path, recently scythed from the main entry to the park, down into a holler.

The head of the path, though, would have been difficult to find without Hiram's help.

Again, Lily had wanted Beulah to stay safe at home while Lily followed the instructions that Hiram had finally given her on how to find the railcar.

Or at least she'd started to express such but stopped when Beulah cocked an eyebrow.

Now Beulah trudges alongside Lily, keeping up, though her bones scream with weariness.

She glances up at her daughter, sees the dogged determination on Lily's face. All Lily wanted was to protect her family, her community. And sometimes that spurred her to harshness.

It was all Beulah had wanted, too. She'd wanted to find a simple, easy way to tell Lily about Esmé, a way that wouldn't be hard. To protect Lily from feeling hurt or disappointed in her big brother. She sees now that she'd been foolish.

"There." Lily points.

A flash of metal in between the trunks and limbs of tree and brush.

Lily runs to the railcar, and Beulah follows.

The door on the back is hanging open. From inside comes the sound of girlish chatter.

Beulah finds a burst of strength and she and Lily reach the door at the same time.

Jolene, Prudence, and Esmé all sit cross-legged on the floor in a small circle, staring up at Lily and Beulah. The baby is peacefully sleeping, right next to Esmé.

"We found her," Jolene says proudly. "Best we could put together, she heard the baby crying at the cabin near the big house at the park. And so she took the baby to take care of her. And I'm trying to tell her she should come with me. Home."

CHAPTER 24

⤜⤜⤜

LILY & BEULAH

Saturday, July 7, 1928

2:50 a.m.

LILY

"Lily, why are we stopping here?" Marvena asks as Lily pulls up to the jailhouse a few hours later.

"I want to let Hiram know we found the girls and his baby," Lily says. All four are now with Mama at Dr. Twomey's. He's checking Esmé for cuts, bites, other small injuries she might have sustained in her flight from Ida's house to the railcar hideaway. "And warn him that we're going to be bringing in his sister and mother."

"Poor guy shouldn't have to be around those two," Marvena says.

Lily and Marvena hurry into the jail. The warden glances up from his desk. "Sheriff Lily?"

"Just checking on Hiram."

"It's been quiet," the warden says.

Lily lets herself in.

The sharp smell of blood hits her, as it had at Chalmer and Sophia's. A quick glance at Otto's cell—he's still curled up on his cot.

She rushes back to Hiram's cell, sees him on the floor, glassy-eyed, the inside of his forearm raw and bloody. His mattress is turned up, the blanket and pillow tossed to the other side of the cell. He's sawed his flesh against the metal slats of the bed frame.

Lily quickly unlocks the cell door, rushes in, drops to her knees beside Hiram. She hears his breath, soft and rattly.

She grabs the pillow, presses it against his arm as a compress. "We need help! Get Dr. Twomey!"

Lily and Marvena come into the clearing at the top of the hill, where sits the Fitzpatricks' cabin. The sun has burned off the last of the early morning mist. A bug buzzes by Lily's ear. Not yet mid-morning and it's already hot, and bugs are biting.

"What d'ya reckon?" Marvena whispers.

Lily scans the property. The truck sits to the side of the house. *Good*—Dorit, if she got spooked, would leave in the truck, not try to run by foot. Ida couldn't get far without Dorit driving her.

In any case, both women must be so sure that Hiram wouldn't have a change of heart about taking the full blame for Esmé's kidnapping that they're still here.

"They're here," Lily whispers back. "Be ready, lest they try to run."

"Soon as you announce you're here to arrest them, they won't run. Ida will start shooting."

Lily looks at her friend. Exhaustion lines Marvena's face. And Lily, too, is weary to her bones. "You don't think I'm foolish enough to lead with that, do you? Let me do some talkin', and then I reckon you'll know when to come out."

"We can't just start with shootin'?" Marvena asks.

After Mama had coaxed Esmé to talk with them—Mama, it seems, had learned an impressive amount of French from her years of corresponding with Esmé's maternal grandmother, and Esmé knew a lot more English than Lily would have expected—Esmé affirmed Hiram's story, as well as when and why she'd taken the baby. Finding poor Hiram as Lily had, she can surely sympathize with Marvena's desire.

But Lily proffers a scant smile. "'Fraid not. You take the side approach."

As Marvena melts back into the woods, Lily walks out into the yard, toward the cabin, still scanning, hand ready to draw her weapon if she must. "Yoo hoo," she calls. "I'm here with some news about Hiram. Sorry to say, it's bad news."

She pauses as the door opens, and Ida lumbers out, followed by Dorit. "Well, out with it," Ida says.

A shadow moves from under the porch. The shepherd. It trots over to Lily, eager and friendly. Lily takes a moment, scratches between the dog's ears. Fleas and all, someone is going to have to take care of this fella. Her hound, Sadie, could use a friend.

Lily returns her attention to the women on the porch. "Hiram's on his way to the hospital, up at the men's prison in Columbus." After Dr. Twomey had stabilized him, Marvena had fetched Jurgis and Benjamin to take him, which meant temporarily deputizing them.

Ida snorts. "You came up here to tell us that? So what'd he do, fall off his cot?"

But Dorit is tensing, about to turn and run back into the house.

Lily pulls her weapon, as Marvena comes around from behind the truck to the porch, her revolver pulled. How had she moved that fast, that stealthily? Lily gives a little shake of her head, in wonder at Marvena and as a warning to Dorit. "Don't try to run, Dorit. Hiram told us what really happened—and my niece confirmed it. I'm here to arrest you for kidnapping."

Dorit sinks to the porch, puts her hands to her face, and starts crying.

Ida gives her daughter a hateful look. "Well, now what am I supposed to do, just wait here alone, till Hiram gets back with his little injury? Why, this is more than I oughta have to bear—"

Lily's look is so sharp that Ida hushes, reels back.

"Not a little injury. Hiram tried to kill himself. Despondent over all he's lost. All the pain he's had to bear from you finally becoming too much," Lily says. Dorit gazes up, shock and fear for her brother finally overtaking her. "But you won't have to tend to him. He'll still have to serve time as an accessory for kidnapping, by virtue of not turning in Dorit. And so, Ida Fitzpatrick, will you."

BEULAH

Beulah's hands tremble as she stares at the telegram, just delivered a few minutes ago.

It's nearly noon, and the children—Jolene, Esmé, and the boys—have had their lunch. Jolene is tasked with cleaning up from lunch by herself, a light punishment for having run off in the middle of the night from Marvena's, but the only one she'll get if Beulah has anything to say about it. After all, Jolene's heart had been in the right place, tracking down Esmé and the baby, both of whom are sleeping now upstairs. The boys are playing out back. Prudence has been returned to her mama. And oh, what a hard road Suda will now have to bear.

But as Beulah studies the telegram again, she thinks how most everyone must trek a hard road—even knowing that for all of us, it comes at last to an inevitable end.

Just after lunch, she'd come out onto the porch to sit a spell when an automobile pulled down the lane. Her heart had leapt, hoping it was Lily, but it was a man delivering the telegram. Good news never came in a telegram, and indeed the deliveryman had looked somber as he trotted over to her, holding out the paper. *It's from France,* he'd said.

Beulah had dropped back into the blue porch swing, and by the time he'd pulled back out on Kinship Road, she'd read the telegram. It turned out she did have more tears to weep, after all.

Now the only sounds are the chittering of insects, the rare daytime hoot of an owl, the keening squeal of the porch swing's metal chains on eye hooks.

At last, another automobile turns down the lane—this time it is Lily. "Mama?"

At the sound of Lily's voice—strong, yet softened with concern—Beulah starts crying.

Lily rushes up the porch steps, sits down by Beulah. "Mama, what is wrong?"

Beulah hands her the paper and waits as Lily reads it; Beulah's already memorized the telegram from the priest in Sainte-Menehould, France.

Sorry to report the death of Madame Charlotte Chambeau. The parish sends sympathy to Mademoiselle Esmé.

Lily looks up from reading the news. "I'm so sorry, Mama."

Beulah wipes her tears away. *Enough,* she tells herself. She looks up at Lily. "I'm going to be sorry to tell Esmé."

Lily nods. "We will help her get through it," she says.

Damn it, if her eyes don't dampen again. But Beulah blinks back the fresh tears as she pats Lily on the forearm. Thank God, for her dear strong daughter.

From inside the house comes the sudden wail of the baby. Through her tears, Beulah can't help but laugh. "Life goes on." She starts to rise, with a weary sigh. She'll need to tend to the baby, at least until Lily gets the child placed in the orphanage.

But Lily puts her hand on Beulah's arm. "Mama, I've been thinking, on my drive back from Marvena's. Hildy said she'd do anything to help me. Maybe—maybe she could take care of the baby for a while."

Beulah gasps at the notion.

Lily's expression puckers in a worried frown. "But maybe that's cruel. To ask her, when she can't have children, though I was thinking, well, if she's taken with the baby, and she and Tom are thinking of getting married anyway, maybe . . ."

Beulah smiles. "I think it might be the kindest idea possible. I know that even if she doesn't want to take the baby, she won't see the request as cruelty. Let's go find out."

An hour later, Lily pulls up to Hildy's house. Hildy is out front, tending to the hollyhocks. Beulah turns around in the front seat and admonishes the four children crowded in the back, "Now just wait here."

Esmé's eyes go wide.

"They're both bossy," Caleb Jr. says, "but you'll get used to them."

Beulah gives him a harsh look. She's going to have to do something about his sassy mouth, but not right now—though she's satisfied with seeing him shrink back a bit.

"Esmé, please hand me the baby," Beulah says gently.

The girl clutches onto the baby a little tighter. Protective. Beulah's heart goes out to her granddaughter—such a shocking introduction to her new country, her new family, she's had. Beulah's decided to wait a few days before telling her about her Mémère's passing.

"It's all right," Jolene says. "Miss Hildy is family. La famille." She beams, proud of herself for already learning some French.

Esmé lets Beulah take the baby, and both Lily and Beulah get out of the automobile. Hildy watches as they approach, the hollyhocks forgotten.

"You said you'd do anything to help me," Lily says. "We need someone to care for this baby, until I can sort things out and"—she gestures back at her automobile—"well, we already have quite the collection of children. . . ."

Hildy's lips twitch at Lily's attempt at humor.

"You don't have to do this," Beulah says. "We just wondered—"

Hildy looks at her, and Beulah's heart quickens. Oh, how she would have loved to have had Hildy as her daughter-in-law. But Jolene is right. Hildy is, and always will be, part of their family.

Gently, Hildy takes the baby from Beulah. For a long moment, Hildy stares down into the little girl's sleeping face.

Then she looks up, smiles at Beulah and Lily. "Did you bring diapers? Tinned milk?"

Beulah nods.

"Well, good. Bring them in. And the kids, too—lest you want them frying in that hot automobile." Hildy turns, starts toward her front door, calls over her shoulder, "I have oatmeal cookies. And lemonade in the spring house."

EPILOGUE

≫≫

LILY & BEULAH

Thursday, August 2, 1928

3:20 p.m.

LILY

Down by the Kinship Tree, Lily stands on the edge of the bank, her waistband rolled up so her skirt doesn't drag on the ground and her shirtsleeves rolled up, too. She wears her working boots and a hat slouched down over her ears and brow, both too much for the August heat, but the boots keep her from slipping and the hat keeps the bugs out of her eyes.

Lily casts her line. A fool's effort. It's the wrong time of day for fish to be biting.

But this is her birthday—her thirtieth. And so she'd taken off work for the afternoon and then come down here for some time to herself before going with the family for a picnic at the Meuse-Argonne Memorial Park.

The park now went by the simpler name, since Michael Fitzpatrick—Chalmer's brother, who lives up in Columbus—inherited the land and park, sold most of the land, and then donated the park to Bronwyn

County to manage. She and Mama had asked the county commissioners to remove Roger's name from the park, not out of anything against Roger, but because they shared the feeling—and knew Roger would, too—that the park should be in memory of all veterans.

Back up at the house, there is a hubbub of activity—Mama fussing and planning far more food than necessary for an evening picnic, and insisting that Jolene and Esmé and the boys can help her get ready, and shooing Lily away to enjoy some time alone.

And so after noon dinner she'd come down here, theoretically for a little fishing. But, really, to enjoy the quiet, the sweet shimmery heat of August along the bank of Coal Creek.

Lily casts her line again, watches the hook and worm bob up and down in the cool, still spot below the jumping-off branch of the Kinship Tree.

There's another reason Lily is down here.

She's no more a believer in spirits hovering than she is in the sight. And yet ever since Esmé has joined their household, when Lily is down here she senses Roger's presence in the shimmer and flash of light and shadow of leaves in the Kinship Tree. She'll stare up into its branches, and suddenly days and memories will cluster like the leaves: all the times she'd run here with him, down from Mamaw and Papaw's house, to jump into the creek and swim, the times they'd talked about their futures, the times they'd fought. Her pride in seeing him speak at the Opera House. Her sorrow in waving good-bye at the train depot as he left for the Great War. And fourteen years ago, just before her sixteenth birthday, her relief in his strong arms pulling her from the water when she was caught below—saving her life. In many ways, giving her her life, because he'd taken her for help and she'd met Daniel as a result. All those memories, shimmering and flashing together, silvery bits of light, like the sun between the leaves of the Kinship Tree.

And on a branch of the Kinship Tree: an owl. She's seen it three times now, since Esmé came here, perched in the tree in daylight. Such a rare sighting. She's been waiting, to see it today, on her birthday.

She reels in her line. Casts. Waits. Reels. Casts.

And finally, better than a bite on her line, there's a rustling in the tree, and Lily looks up.

The owl stares at her, and she goes still, staring back.

BEULAH

Up in her bedroom, Beulah pushes back from her sewing machine. She snips the line of thread, puts the cut end through the eye of a sewing needle, and stitches the thread down in the corner of the quilt.

She stands up and spreads the quilt over top of her bed.

It is done, this quilt made from Roger's clothes.

In the very center is a star, cut from the army cap of Roger's that Esmé had brought with her all the way from France. Several days after Esmé came to live with them, Beulah broke the news that her *mémère* had passed away. Esmé had burst out crying and, for the first time, let Beulah hold her. After Esmé dried her tears, she'd disappeared for a moment to the bedroom she shares with Jolene and came back with the cap. Her *mémère*, Esmé said, wanted Beulah to have it.

At first, Beulah had been reluctant to cut up the cap. But then she'd carefully cut the thick material and made the star that forms the heart of the quilt.

Beulah senses someone in the doorway to her room and looks up. It's Esmé.

"Grandmère?"

Beulah smiles at Esme. "You can come in."

Esme proceeds cautiously. "Jolene says the boys are—" But then the quilt catches her eye, and she stops carrying whatever tale Jolene had put her up to. She points to the star in the middle of the quilt. "From Papa's cap," Esmé declares.

Beulah nods.

"Where do all the other pieces come from?" Esmé asks. She hesitates every few words. She's mastering English with impressive speed but still has much to learn.

"All from clothes your papa wore. I'll tell you the stories sometime." Beulah blinks hard, her eyes suddenly prickling. She swallows back a lump in her throat. "It's finished—and I'd like you to have it."

Esmé looks up, awe flashing in her eyes. "Really?"

"Really."

Esmé rushes to Beulah and throws her arms around her.

Beulah pats the top of Esme's head. "Well," she says gruffly, "you needed a good quilt anyway."

Esmé squeezes her hug tighter, and Beulah wraps her arms around the child. Then she says, "It's time to get a move on. I need to pack up. Is your Aunt Lily back?"

Esmé shakes her head.

Beulah sighs—that daughter of hers can spend untold amounts of time alone. She'll need to go get her . . . and then an idea hits her.

"Esmé, would you go fetch her? She's down by the Kinship Tree. Jolene can show you the old path that leads to it."

LILY

At the rustling sound, Lily turns to see Esmé, peeking from the other side of the Kinship Tree like a shy forest creature. The dog, the one they'd rescued from Ida Fitzpatrick, trots alongside her. Esmé seems particularly attached to the dog, though she hasn't named it just yet.

Adjusting to these new circumstances will take time.

"Grandmère says it's time to come back to the house."

It is. Her birthday though it may be, she needs to help Mama pack up for the picnic.

The owl hoots.

Lily stares up at it.

What do you want? Lily thinks. *Mama brought her here. We rescued her. She has a home—a roof over her head, food, clothes. The other children have accepted her to the point that all four got in trouble together the other day for trying to get Caleb Jr. to ride on the new dog's back. And Hiram, well, he'll be all right.*

Hiram had healed, physically at least, from his attempt at suicide, and is in prison pending trial as an accessory to kidnapping. But Lily will continue to check on him, and will do what she can to help him find his way after he is out. She hopes he'll move elsewhere; already, she's talked to Chalmer's brother in Columbus about helping Hiram eventually get re-settled and find a job. Dorit is in the women's prison for kidnapping, as is her mother as an accessory, and Lily has no plans to help them out. The only culprit in the wind is Madame Blanchett; her Saint Louis kin have had no word from her, and she seems to have disappeared. But though Lily is disappointed that justice is not even-handed in this case, she doubts the woman will succeed long with no community to help her.

Lily's thoughts continue: *Even MayBelle has settled in at the Widows' Home—I've been checking on her once a week. And on poor Suda. She has a hard row to hoe with Otto in prison for manslaughter. She'll find a way, though. We'll check on her and her young 'uns. And I'm at peace with Mama. Hildy and Tom are taking good care of the orphaned baby. Hildy is at peace with you. I'm at peace with you,* Lily thinks.

The owl blinks at her.

Still, she feels pinned to her spot on the bank.

A shuffling sound. Esmé and the dog have come closer. The dog turns a few times, settles down in a curl to snooze. Esmé's gaze wanders to the fishing pole, curious.

Suddenly Lily smiles. "I think everyone can wait for us for a few more moments, don't you?" She tilts her head, encouraging Esmé to come over.

Lily notes the sunlight on Esme's fair skin. The child is going to end up sunburned by day's end if they aren't careful. Lily pulls her hat from her head and plops it on Esmé, who straightens it carefully. Lily hands her the fishing pole.

"All right, you're going to reel it in, recast it . . ."

Esmé looks up at her wide-eyed, nervous. "But what if I get it tangled up?"

Lily shrugs. "It's just fishing line." She gives a teasing smile. "Just don't let the hook catch on me—or you."

Esme's eyes widen, fearful, and Lily chuckles. "I'm not going to let that happen. Just follow my instructions."

Soon the pair are caught up in the process of fishing, losing track of time and forgetting worries outside the moments that add up to fishing. Which is, after all, at least for Lily, the point of the hobby.

Then they hear a rustling in the brush behind them, and turn, and see Benjamin coming down the slope.

"Beulah sent me."

Esmé says, "We haven't caught a thing." She sounds so woeful.

"That's all right," Lily says "It's not really the right time of day for fishing—and you learned a lot."

Esmé lights up. "So we can try again?"

Lily smiles. "Of course. I'm counting on it."

Esmé starts to hand back the fishing pole, but Lily shakes her head. "Carry it up to the barn—hold the tip end, and point the butt end forward. Less likely to snag on the brush. We'll catch up with you by the barn."

Lily watches; then after the child disappears through the brush, she starts closing up her tackle box. "I think she's gonna be a natural. She must have gotten it from her mother—"

"Or her aunt." Benjamin smiles.

"Well, she sure didn't get it from Roger. . . ." She pauses. Something is different in the light and in the air.

She looks up.

Oh. The owl is gone.

And Roger.

Roger, too, is gone.

And yet Lily doesn't feel sad or disappointed. She knows he'll live on in their memories and hearts—and in Esmé. And so she feels at peace. Because Roger is, at last, also at peace.

"Are you all right?" Benjamin asks.

Lily looks up at him. "I'm fine."

He doesn't question the tears gleaming in her eyes.

BEULAH

Beulah settles down on the ground on the edge of the picnic cloth. The meal she'd cooked up—with Lily's help, who'd insisted, although the feast is for her thirtieth birthday—is now set out: fried chicken, potato salad, slaw, and a black raspberry pie.

Gratefully, Beulah looks from face to blessed face. Lily and Benjamin. Caleb Jr. and Micah. Jolene and Esmé. Marvena and Jurgis and Frankie. Nana, on a chair Jurgis had insisted on bringing for her. Oh, and Hildy and Tom and Alistair and the baby, snuggled down and napping in a basket. They are still taking care of the child.

"Quite a crew you have here, Beulah," Walter says.

Beulah looks over at him. "It's true."

For a moment, their eyes lock, and then she hears a throat clearing. It's Lily.

Lily cocks an eyebrow but smiles. *Mama, it's fine.* "Maybe you could say the blessing?"

Beulah bows her head. After all that had happened a month ago, she is not sure exactly what to say. "Thank you, Lord, for this day, and all gathered here. Bless us all. Amen."

Well, it wasn't much of a blessing, but it would do. And everyone tucks in quickly.

After a bit, the baby starts to wriggle and whine.

Tom swoops the child out, holds her overhead, cooing. Hildy fusses at him to be careful, and Alistair rolls his eyes—but then tickles the baby's tummy and smiles when she coos. A string of drool drops from the baby's mouth onto Tom's nose, which makes him laugh. Hildy whips out a handkerchief for him; then she takes the baby from Tom, nestles her in her arms, and looks up and grins at everyone. Hildy is over the moon.

Hildy and Tom exchange glances. Tom gives a little nod. Hildy clears her throat. "Tom and I have something to tell everyone. We . . . we're—"

"Hitched!" Tom grins, ear to ear.

Everyone gasps and offers congratulations.

"And since Hiram, his mother, and sister are all in prison for now, and have signed away their rights to the baby, we've put in paperwork to adopt her," Hildy explains.

"That's the best birthday gift I could get," Lily says, looking at her friend. "Hearing that."

Hildy smiles. "And I'm hoping you'll put in a good word as a character witness for me, Lily. I want to petition to still teach. Nana's said she'll watch the baby."

Marvena nods. "We'll get her down to your place each day."

Nana reaches out and pats the baby's head.

Beulah can't help but smile—well, she helps Lily, after all, so why shouldn't Nana help Hildy? Still, Beulah's not sure she'll ever entirely understand young women these days.

The baby coos.

Esmé pipes up. "Can I—can I hold her? Aunt Hildy?"

A silence falls over the group and the moment teeters, and Esmé starts to look worried, not sure of what she's said that has the adults' attention, and even that of the other children, so that everyone has fallen silent.

But then Hildy gives Esmé a big smile and says, "Of course." She transfers the baby to Esmé's arms, and the baby stares up, and Esmé stares down into her eyes.

Beulah blinks hard. These two newest additions have come to them in such a rough way. And Esmé, in being unsure of how to refer to Hildy, has stumbled on a truth deeper than formality and bloodlines. How had Lily put it? Family, kinship, is really the place where you can feel the safest, no matter what. This is what she is most thankful for, in her silent blessing.

Beulah clears her throat. "What are you going to name her?"

Hildy smiles. "Hope," she says softly. Then Hildy looks at Esmé and back to Beulah. "Hope Charlotte Beulah Whitcomb. If that's all right."

Beulah swallows, nods rapidly. "That sounds lovely to me. Esmé?"

"Oh. I— I think it is—*beau*." Esmé says.

"That means 'beautiful,'" Caleb Jr. says, in a pompous, knowing tone. Everyone laughs. He looks confused. "What?"

"It just means it's fine," Micah says, rolling his eyes.

Hildy looks to Lily—seeking approval from her as well for using Beulah's name.

And Beulah also watches Lily, wondering what her daughter will say.

Lily grins. "It means, the name is perfect."

Beulah smiles. *Ah.* Why has she ever doubted her daughter?

LILY

Later that evening, Lily and Benjamin walk away from the bowling and games area.

"I will never get the hang of it," Benjamin says. "And why are you so good at bowling?"

"I don't know—" Lily stops. It is dusk. A red-tailed hawk circles overhead. Lily stops in her tracks and stares up at it.

"Lily, are you all right?" Benjamin puts a hand on her arm, concerned.

Three years ago, on her birthday, she and Mama and the children, Marvena and Hildy, Tom and Jurgis and Nana, Alistair and Frankie had gone black raspberry picking. A hawk had soared overhead then, too, and she'd thought, *Daniel.* So much has changed in the last three years. Her family, the circle of her kinship, has grown.

The hawk disappears from view.

She blinks back tears. Earlier today, she'd said good-bye to the owl.

But that is the mystery of true kinship, even more miraculous than signs or the sight, isn't it? In true kinship, loved ones live on in our hearts. Slowly, her heart has been healing, so there is space enough for all the loved ones she carries there, space enough for new loved ones.

Lily looks back at Benjamin. At last, she nods: *Yes.* She is all right.

The sound of a band starting up a waltz lilts through the trees, through the dusk of the coming night. Up the hill, dance-floor lights powered by a gasoline generator sparkle through the forest.

Suddenly Lily turns to Benjamin to ask him a simple question—as if on impulse, but really born of the past few years spent mending her heart so she can let it open again. "Benjamin Russo, will you dance with me?"

Benjamin smiles back. "Yes, Lily Ross. I will dance with you."

They tuck their arms around each other's waists, and they walk up the hill, toward the lilting music and the twinkling lights.

AUTHOR'S NOTE

Years ago, my family and I went hiking fairly often in a local park, Possum Creek MetroPark. On one of those hikes, we came across the remnants of an amusement park built several years after the Great War (or World War I, as we now call it) for veterans and their families. By the time my husband, young daughters, and I took that hike, all that was left of the amusement park were remnants such as the metal skeletons of old railcars that served as camping shelters, part of a dance floor, part of a swimming pool.

Of course I was intrigued, and so I began researching. I read everything I could find in the archives of the *Dayton Daily News* about Argonne Forest Park, as the amusement park was called, and about the men from the area and from Ohio who served in the Great War. I located and interviewed the nephew of the man who had built the park. I learned that the park's developer began building the park in 1926, that he built it in memory of a friend who died in the battle of the Meuse-Argonne, and that at one time, the park had a clubhouse, a dance floor, a swimming pool, a baseball diamond, and a camping area. The park was popular for almost two decades. Now, of course, "amusement park" has a very different connotation.

I wrote a detailed newspaper article about the park for the *Dayton*

Daily News. (Side note, in looking up my own article—which I wrote in the 1990s—I learned that another writer discovered the park a few years back, and also wrote an article about it. As the saying goes, everything old is new again.) My article appeared several years before I would go on to be a weekly freelance columnist for the *Dayton Daily News* for twenty years.

Anyway, I always knew that the Argonne Forest Park, which continued to haunt my imagination even after I wrote that article, would appear in a novel. And so it does, or at least, my reimagining of it does, as the Meuse-Argonne Memorial Park in *The Echoes.*

As I developed the novel, I realized that I wanted to explore how past traumas can echo in people's lives for years. Lily and her family are haunted by the long-ago loss of her brother Roger in the Great War. Many survivors of that war, including Lily's husband, Daniel, from the first Kinship novel, would have suffered from PTSD. One pivotal character in particular in *The Echoes* suffers from PTSD. Of course, PTSD didn't go by that name in the 1920s. (I'm ever fascinated by how human experience and suffering is the same now as it ever was, even as our understanding and naming of those conditions develops and changes—thus Hildy's experience with what we now call endometriosis.)

As a very little child, I heard the story of how my maternal grandfather (who died several years before I was born) was "haunted" from time to time when he'd work his tobacco field; two German soldiers would appear before him, and he was sure they were the ghosts of enemy combatants he must have killed in the Great War. I'd guess that he was probably experiencing a form of PTSD. My father was a BAR gunner on the frontlines in World War II. I was born later in my parents' lives, but I still recollect as a little girl in the 1970s hearing my father cry out from nightmares. Much later, he confessed to me that these nightmares were from his time on the frontlines in France during the war. By the time he was in his late eighties, my father finally had a name for what he experienced, and he didn't shy away from using it: PTSD.

He was brave enough to call it what it was, so I'll take some inspiration from Dad and share that I have been diagnosed with PTSD. I have not served in the military, but PTSD can develop from a variety of traumatic experiences.

My interest in exploring PTSD in *The Echoes* thus comes not just from my fascination with that old park, but from family and personal experiences, and the ever-compelling variations of ways humans do—or do not—deal with trauma as it echoes through families and personal lives.

For U.S. veterans who are experiencing PTSD, help and information can be found at www.ptsd.va.gov/gethelp/crisis_help.asp.

Other resources for help:

THE VETERANS CRISIS LINE
(www.veteranscrisisline.net; 1-800-273-8255)

NATIONAL SUICIDE PREVENTION LIFELINE
(https://suicidepreventionlifeline.org; 1-800-273-8255)

The Trauma Informed organization's website also provides a list of resources for help for survivors of violence and trauma: www.traumainformed.org/hotlines-for-survivors-of-violence-and-trauma.

ACKNOWLEDGMENTS

Though I wrote *The Echoes* during the COVID-19 pandemic, and in great part while isolating, I did not write this novel alone. This is my first novel written entirely during a pandemic, and hopefully my last—well, written during a pandemic, that is. (It's definitely not my last novel.) I am thankful to have so many thank-yous to share.

Thanks go, first and foremost as always, to my husband, David: sweetie, I appreciate that full month of dinners cooked or bought, so I could finish the initial draft of *The Echoes* on schedule. And thank you for always believing in me and my creative work. Right back at you, pal: keep the whole world singing!

Thanks also go to my friends, who always cheer me on in writing and life, and in particular to my friends-who-also-write, who never fail to listen to my thoughts about the writing life (even if they've heard those thoughts a million times before): Erin, Heather, Jessica, Mariah, Marti, Katrina, Kristina. Hey, we made it through a mad, mad year *and* produced creative writing!

As I wrote *The Echoes*, I also needed to connect with readers of past Kinship mystery novels. This past year was particularly challenging, so thank you, readers and book clubs, who pivoted with me to virtual events and welcomed me into their reading lives via Zoom, FaceTime,

ACKNOWLEDGMENTS

Skype, and Facebook Live. Thank you loyal viewers and listeners to Tea with Jess, via my Facebook Author Page and now my new podcast version of the program. (Special shout-out to Jessica, for casually suggesting, hey, you could start a podcast . . .) It's been fun to connect with you, and particularly to share chats with other authors and artists with you. Now, more keenly than ever, I embrace the value of community.

Thank you, bookstores. If this past year was tough for writers, well, I can only imagine the challenges of being a bookseller! Shout-outs in particular to these independent bookstores who supported my series this past year with virtual events, offerings of autographed book stickers, and more: Aunt Agatha's Online Bookstore, The Book Loft of German Village, Mystery Lovers Bookshop, Murder by the Book, New & Olde Pages Book Shoppe, The Poisoned Pen Bookstore, and Riverstone Books.

And of course, a big thank-you to my publishing team. Elisabeth, thank you for your invaluable encouragement and helping me learn to trust my own ideas. Catherine, thank you for showing me the way to the heart of the story of *The Echoes,* and of the Kinship series. Sarah, Nettie, Joe, and Maddee, thank you for keeping me on track and focused. I'm in awe of and grateful for each of you. Big virtual hugs!